*T*HE
*B*AKER
*A*FFAIR

LOU BARBER, AUTHOR
P.O. Box 2404
Ruston, LA 71273
www.thebakeraffair.com
www.tabberer.com

THE
BAKER
AFFAIR

Lou Barber

For Col. John Long
Thank God we completed
our tour in the Vietnam War.
All the Best, *Lou Barber*
Gary Owen 12-7-2003

CREATIVE ARTS BOOK COMPANY
Berkeley • California

For information contact:
Creative Arts Book Company
833 Bancroft Way
Berkeley, California 94710

ISBN 0-88739-264-4
Library of Congress Catalog Number 99-61370

Printed in the United States of America

A ton of thanks to my beautiful wife, Ella, for all her help. Her suggestions and editing made this story much better.

Thank you, Nancie Weber,
for your help, too.
I appreciate it.

Contents:

THE
BAKER
AFFAIR

Preface

This is a fascinating story of life in a small New England town portraying the fictional characters functioning with historical people, places, and events. True-to-life examples of triumph and tragedy experienced by the family present realism and interest to the reader. A message of success being within the reach of people with the poorest beginning is depicted through hard work, reliability, and determination. Romance is cleverly woven throughout the story which holds the attention of both male and female readers.

The story reveals the shrinking in size of the world. The first generation of the Bakers, at the turn of the century, travel about in horse drawn buggies or on slow moving trains. A trip of twenty-five miles or more usually included an overnight stay in a hotel or with friends. These are the people who lived through the greatest technological advances in the history of mankind. Most of the men of this era developed a love for the automobile which they retained for life. The second generation of the family is thrilled with the thought of traveling at speeds of thirty miles per hour between towns. The third generation finds it normal to travel in excess of fifty miles per hour by automobile or at much higher speeds in an airplane for trips of long distance!

The author's great imagination, insight, and sensitivity mixed with a wide variety of his personal experiences molds a story that draws a vivid picture in the mind's eye of the reader. One has the sensation of being there feeling the happiness, anxiety, or sorrow depending on the particular event. His choice of words and strict attention to detail makes this novel worth reading by any adult age group.

—June Streeter Foster

Chapter 1

BERNARDSTON, MASSACHUSETTS, 1900

BERNARDSTON, Massachusetts, is at the junction of U.S. Highways 5 & 10 just south of the Massachusetts and Vermont border. It is a typical New England village and as pretty as a picture. Fall River flows through the town and empties into the Connecticut River a few miles south. There is an abundance of trees including white birch, maple, oak, and evergreens. The small mountains run generally north and south. Mother Nature paints unbelievably beautiful pictures here each fall using the leaves of the trees.

The winters are long and cold with snowfall reaching as much as ten feet during some winters. Before the automobile became a dominant fixture, the snow-covered roads were rolled to provide easier traveling for horse-drawn sleighs. Each conveyance had its own characteristic sound caused by bells attached to the harnesses. The stouthearted folks had no idea they were part of such a beautiful New England setting as they traveled about their picturesque towns in one-horse open sleighs. People were bundled in warm clothing with lap robes covering their legs. The breath of their horses turned to tiny ice crystals and appeared to accentuate the rhythm of their gait as they trotted along. The tinkling of the bells underscored by runners sliding on the snow and ice was wintertime music in Bernardston. To this day, many quaint towns exist in settings as beautiful; and still, most of the people who reside there are not aware of it.

Each spring, sap buckets are hung from the Sugar Maple trees, harvesting the flow of sweet sap that moves up or down the tree's veins after a freeze at night followed by a daytime thaw. Farmers collected the sap at least once each day and transported it in a horse-drawn, skid-mounted vat to their sugarhouse. The sap was cooked in large segmented containers and maple syrup was drawn off. It takes approximately thirty-two gallons of sap to make one gallon of maple syrup. The sweet aroma of the sugarhouse mixed with the musky smoke of wood fires permeates the air.

The Bernardston Grange, a farmer's organization, had fund raising dinners throughout the year with the ladies providing the home cooked food. Items on the menu coincided with the time of year they were freshly available. There were blueberry, strawberry, and sugar suppers. A sugar supper consists of maple syrup boiled down to form maple sugar candy poured on fresh fallen snow. The snow was placed in a wide deep dish and warm maple syrup was ladled onto the snow. It was then rolled up with forks and savored by old and young alike. Howard and Evelyn Grover of the River Maple Farm furnished the maple syrup.

During the winter months, Mill Pond and Silver Lake were frozen solid providing perfect skating rinks until they were covered with snow. Attempts were made by the local children to move the snow off the ice. Most often, nature won the battle and the young engaged in skiing, tobogganing, and sledding. Young adults on West Mountain during the nights of a full moon sailed down the snow covered slopes. Moonlight reflected off the snow and provided nights nearly as bright as day.

During the spring of 1901, Abbie Burrows Coy arrived in town by rail for a short stay at the New England House. She stopped at Shears Store and expressed her interest in the quaint village of Bernardston. Mrs. G. F. Shears offered to give her a tour of the town, which Mrs. Coy accepted. They visited Cushman Library, Powers Institute, and several business establishments. Mrs. Coy was thrilled at the natural beauty blended with neat, sturdy, and well kept buildings and grounds throughout the township.

She was so impressed that she offered to give a large clock to the town provided an appropriate tower was built to install it. The town fathers voted to build a tower on the town hall. By fall of that year, the clock was installed. It was a masterpiece and cost Mrs. Coy $600.00. The clock struck on the hour and half-hour. It could be heard as far as five miles depending on the weather and wind direction. Many parents gave instructions facilitated by Mrs. Coy's gift. "When the clock strikes five, I want you here at the house."

Matt Baker lived on Bald Mountain Road at the foot of Huckle Hill. He and his younger brother were up every morning before 5:00 a.m. They helped their dad do the chores that were always waiting on dairy farms. Eric started milking as soon as they got to the barn. The boys fed the cows and cleaned the gutters. Both Matt and Larry finished up by milking three cows each before it was time to eat breakfast and get ready for school. Their mom always had a big meal of eggs, home-cured bacon, fried potato, and hot biscuits ready for them. When they hitched up Spike, the horse they drove to school, both boys had a strong smell of cow-barn. They were not aware of this ever-present smell but it didn't really matter because most of the other kids had it also.

Matt was in his senior year at Powers Institute and he was the only boy in the class of twelve students. He was very much in love with Julie Parks, one of his classmates. He couldn't remember when he didn't love her. There were times when he thought that she cared for him and other times when he wasn't sure what she felt. He had managed to sit beside her on the last Halloween hayride and they held hands. He didn't quite have the nerve to put his arm around her.

Julie was skilled at driving a horse. She brought her brothers and sisters with her to school each day in a buggy that had two seats. She was from a large family and they lived about five miles away from Powers, on West Mountain. She wasn't the oldest child in her family but was the most proficient at driving their high spirited horse.

One day, Matt and Julie both came out of school at lunch time to drive to Shears' Country Store. That store carried just about everything anyone could ever want in life. Matt's dad had told him to pick up a new hoe and Julie was going after a hundred pounds of grain. Matt said, "Julie, you can ride with me if you like." With devilment in her eyes Julie answered, "No, let's see who can get there first." Spike was no racehorse, and Matt had observed Julie driving her horse at a fast pace more than once. Matt wasn't enthused but agreed. They both unhitched their horses, jumped into their buggies, and swung away from the hitching rail. Matt had two things going for him: He was closer to Library Street than Julie, and Julie's buggy was at least twice as heavy.

Matt and Julie had their buggy whips in their hands and almost simultaneously they both swatted their horses. The horses started off at fast trots with Matt in the lead. They turned on to Library Street with just a short distance to the left turn on to Church Street. Both buggies slid sideways as they made the turn. Julie immediately swatted her horse with her whip and it broke into a gallop. She was gaining easily on Matt while he applied a couple of serious swats with his whip. Both horses were galloping but it was evident that Julie was gaining. When the two were racing neck and neck, a horse and driver turned from Depot Street onto Church Street, headed in their direction. Matt and Julie both pulled back on the rains, yelling "Whoa...Whoa... Whoa."

They slowed down and Julie dropped back behind Matt. Harrison East was driving the third rig and voiced disapproval. He told Matt and Julie in no uncertain terms that Church Street was not the place to have a horse race. He said that they were old enough to know better and threatened to tell their parents. When they got to the store, Julie laughed and said, "If old man East hadn't shown up, I'd have beaten you easily." Matt grinned shyly, "It sort of looked that way to me too." Matt loaded her bag of grain and they both drove back to school at a slow trot. He thought how beautiful she looked when both horses were at a gallop, side by side, and Julie was nearly standing up in her attempt to pass him. She was grinning and her hat was blown back, held on by the tie string under her chin. He wondered if he would ever get the chance to be alone with her.

Matt had danced with her at school dances but there were always other students and teachers around. The proper way to dance required one to be about as far from one another as possible. During the summer months, he seldom went to town because there was so much work to do on the farm. They both attended the Unitarian Church on Sundays and Matt always hitched his horse next to hers if possible. A couple of times he even managed to squeeze her elbow and tell her that he missed seeing her. She giggled both times but other than that there wasn't anything he would call a real response. He hated being in Church on the Sundays that Julie didn't show up. When she was there,

he regretted it when the time passed and he was on the way home. He thought about asking his Dad to use the horse and buggy to drive the six miles to see Julie. He had opportunities nearly every day, but the words wouldn't come out.

It was a happy day when his Dad returned from a trip to town and said he wanted Matt to hitch the team to the utility wagon and drive to the Parks farm. Eric had met C.D. Parks at Shears' store and had bought a plow from him. Matt couldn't believe his good fortune and then his Dad said, "Do you want Larry to go along to help you load the plow?" Matt couldn't refuse fast enough. He had a wonderful chance to see Julie and he didn't want his brother around.

In record time, Matt was driving the team down the road. Then he thought, "Oh God, please let Julie be home." He knew that he was trotting the team more than his Dad would want, but he was anxious to get there. The last three miles of the trip were mostly uphill except for the last half mile. That was quite a steep down grade and he was a little embarrassed because the horses were wet with sweat. Mr. Parks hadn't been home long because he was unhitching his horses. He looked up and said, "Boy, I can see that you didn't waste any time and it looks like those horses need a rest. Back over to that shed and I'll help you load the plow." Once the plow was loaded, Mr. Parks told Matt he had better hitch the team under a large Maple tree nearby and let them rest a spell. Matt had the team at the tree just a few minutes when Julie came bounding out of the house. She headed in his direction with a smile on her face and said, "Let's go down by the pond." They walked down a two-rut road and soon they were out of sight of the house. Matt reached over and took Julie's hand. She seemed pleased and Matt's heart felt like it would jump out of his chest. She looked so beautiful and here they were alone, finally. He wished now that he had taken a few minutes to wash his face and comb his hair before he left the house.

Before they reached the pond, Matt stopped Julie and put his arms around her. He kissed her on the forehead. As they both looked into each other's eyes, Matt felt her body against his. Suddenly their lips were together and they were kissing. Julie pulled away and said that they should get back. She started walking at a fast pace towards the house. Matt caught up with her. "Wait a minute. I have something to tell you." Julie looked at him, with bright eyes and obvious interest. Matt hesitated and said in a whisper, "I love you."

She giggled and said, "I love you too and I was beginning to wonder if you would ever tell me."

Matt drove home on cloud nine. Claudia noticed the change in him and she guessed why it might be. "Matt, are you going to be courting Julie Parks?" He turned beet red and didn't answer. Claudia said, "There isn't anything wrong with that idea. Don't think for a minute that I haven't noticed your interest in her. When your Dad bought that plow, I told him to have you drive over to pick it up."

"Mom, you're wonderful. Yes, I do want to court Julie and she is on my mind all the time. It appears that she likes me too."

Town of Bernardston, Massachusetts - View from Fox Hill

Clock on the Town Hall, Bernardston, Massachusetts

Chapter 2

MATT BAKER / COOK ICE WORKS

For the last four years, Matt had worked for the Cook Ice Works in town when his Dad let him off. He had saved every penny and he had just over a hundred dollars in the bank. Mr. Charles O. Cook already had asked Matt to work for him when he finished high school. He still had to do chores at home to offset not working at the farm during the week. He would be at the Ice Works from eight to six each day. Matt also had to do the chores at home every Sunday except one each month. Working full time, his pay would be $18.00 a week and he was thrilled thinking about all that money.

He started working for Mr. Cook the first Monday after graduation. It was back breaking labor handling those huge chunks of ice. They were stored in a barn the floor of which was sunk into the ground. A thick layer of sawdust was under the ice and a thicker layer of sawdust covered it with a canvas tarp on top. This storage method kept ice all through the summer months with little loss. Each day, he worked with the Cook brothers to get the chunks of ice loaded onto the delivery wagons. The first two weeks, Matt rode with Mr. Cook on deliveries. This phase of the job was fun because Matt liked talking with people. Stores took large chunks of ice for their coolers. The homes had cardboard cards displayed with the number of pounds of ice families needed for their iceboxes. Kids followed the wagon and when a block was chipped, splinters of ice fell on the ground. The kids picked up the splinters, wiped them off, and sucked them. It was refreshing on hot days.

The worst part of Matt's job came with the winter ice extraction from Cook's pond. A special saw was used to cut the ice, which was tough to operate. It was difficult getting the blocks pried up and lifted onto the wagons. The weather was always cold with temperatures as low as 35 degrees below zero. When the wind blew, it was nothing less than painfully severe. The feeling that kept crowding into Matt's mind was, "I'm cold. I'm cold. I'm cold." All other thoughts were blocked out including wonderful daydreams of Julie.

It was common knowledge to everyone by the winter following graduation that Matt and Julie were dating seriously. Matt was still apprehensive because he loved Julie so much. His Dad had even let him take the Jenny Lind buggy three times during the summer on Sundays. He and Julie had gone on picnics for Old Home Day, the annual Sunday School outing and once by themselves.

Matt turned the horse down an unimproved lane a mile or so from her folks house. Less than a half mile down the road there was a clearing. It was carpeted with thick moss. They hitched the horse and spread a blanket on the moss. There was a large white birch tree nearby. Matt took out his jackknife and carved a heart in the tree. Then he carved their initials in it and the date below, Aug. 11, 1915. The picnic basket was beside them on the blanket and Matt took Julie's hand and pulled her close to him. He put his arms around her and softly kissed her neck, and then he moved his lips to hers. She responded with equal enthusiasm and they both lay back on the blanket. They kissed passionately with their bodies pressed together.

Suddenly, they heard loud voices and sat up immediately. Two of Julie's brothers walked out of the woods with rifles. They were hunting squirrels and they sat down with Matt and Julie. Her brothers said they were hungry so they shared their picnic lunch with them. The brothers wolfed down most of the food, totally unaware they were intruding. After they left, Julie said she needed to get back. She had told her mom they would be gone only for about an hour.

Matt was disappointed, they shared a long and delightful kiss, standing, pressed together, for several minutes. Finally Julie broke off the kiss, tilted her head back and whispered, "We have to go. I don't want to, but we must." She brushed her lips against his quickly and pulled away. Matt would have given anything for this moment in time to never end. He loved Julie Parks and he yearned for the day when they would be man and wife.

Between Matt's job and the cold winter weather, the two lovebirds had hardly a moment alone since the picnic. They did sit together in church. A couple of times, they stole a quick kiss in the cloakroom when they were lucky enough to be by themselves. Once, Deacon Messer had nearly caught them. Matt saw that Julie was blushing and he wondered if his face was red. The Deacon didn't seem to notice.

Streeter's Store or Bernardston Auto Exchange

River Maple Farm
Bernardston, MA

Chapter 3

MATT / MERCHANT MARINES

About a year and a half went by without much change in the modest routine of living in the country. Matt and Julie were seldom together and then only for the briefest of moments. He had been saving nearly all the money he earned at his job. For the last year he had been paid $22.00 a week because the Cooks liked the way he worked and he made the rounds to the customers by himself. Mr. Cook appreciated Matt because of his upbeat attitude and he was selling more ice than ever before.

When Matt turned 19 on August 22, 1917, the War in Europe had been going on nearly three years. He had been thinking about joining the military service for several months. The day after his birthday, he told his Dad that he had decided to join the army. Eric was not pleased with the idea and he told Matt in strong terms how he felt. Matt was determined to go but he agreed to join the Merchant Marines, which made Eric feel a little better. Matt would not be involved in the trench warfare.

When Matt told Julie, she was heart broken and she could not see any valid reason for his enlisting. She begged him not to go. Once she realized that Matt's mind could not be changed, she tried to make the best of it. Her mother told her that men do things like that.

In less than sixty days from the time Matt announced his intentions, he was home on a ten day leave before reporting aboard ship in New York. His work at Cook's Ice Works had put him in excellent physical condition and he had found basic training quite easy.

Matt and Julie were together as much as possible during the ten days. Their passion for each other seemed stronger than ever and a couple of times it nearly had gotten out of hand. Julie saved the day each time by crying which deflated Matt's enthusiasm.

Matt reported aboard the *Pride of Boston*, a cargo ship tied up at pier 89 in New York. The Boston was already loaded with supplies and scheduled to depart for France in three days, waiting for other ships to be loaded that would be in the convoy. Matt was granted a six-hour pass the second night aboard ship and went ashore with some shipmates. They headed for a bar just off Times Square.

Matt had never had alcoholic beverages before and here he was drinking beer. He tried not to show that he didn't like the taste because the other men apparently did. Frank, the one that Matt liked the best said, "Hey Matt, drink up. We are having another round." Half way through the next beer, Matt was feeling the effects. He thought that maybe the stuff wasn't so bad after all, and it was only a nickel a bottle to men in uniform. After the third beer, one of the men suggested that they all get tattoos. Matt jumped up and said, "That's a great idea." The next morning Matt had a terrible hangover, a tattoo on his inside left forearm, and he wasn't too clear as to how he got back to the ship. He vaguely remembered throwing up on the pier. He kept promising himself that he would never drink beer again. It was noon before he attempted to eat chow and another two hours before he was sure it would stay down.

He was assigned to the deck force. Frank Dorey was among the men in that group as well. They were busy cleaning, chipping paint, and painting. It didn't look to Matt like the work was necessary but Clyde Fagan, Boatswain Mate, 3rd Class, was thoroughly enthused. Matt was glad when the ship finally got under way; however, in less than an hour, he was seasick. He felt worse than he had the morning after the night of beer drinking. It took a couple of days to get his sea legs and it was back to the deck gang. He was even starting to like the food served aboard ship.

There were twenty-eight ships in the convoy plus five destroyers. Frank told Matt that they were watching for submarines and floating mines. Eleven days out of New York, Matt was working on deck when he heard a loud explosion. A ship to the left of the *Pride of Boston* had blown up. The front of the bow was gone and it started to sink. Matt could see men jumping off the ship. In less than five minutes the fan-tail of the damaged ship rose high in the air, hesitated for a few seconds then slid beneath the water. Two of the destroyers dropped behind to retrieve survivors. Approximately one third of the crew were trapped below decks and went down with the ship. Matt thought to himself that maybe his idea of joining the service wasn't so good after all. The deck hands on the *Boston* were ordered to the bow to watch for mines.

They docked in France with no further problems. The crew was not allowed off the ship because all hands had to be aboard to offload cargo. But a week went by and they had not started to offload. Another week went by, and a third. The Captain and some of the officers had left the ship for short periods, but the men were not allowed liberty. During the fourth week, the Captain announced that the War was over. A big cheer went up. He said they would be returning to the States without unloading the ship.

Matt and Frank were among those who were allowed a six-hour lib-erty that evening. Matt had mixed emotions about going. It turned out that the town was a terrible place for liberty because of so many ser-vicemen. All of the joints were packed and there wasn't even a place to sit. During the first three hours, they managed to buy two beers, which took forever to get. Matt didn't like the beer, the crowded conditions, and he was tired. He finally told Frank that he didn't feel well and returned to the ship. He stayed aboard until it departed five days later. The return trip to the States was without incident. Two days out of New York, the radio room received a message that stated: *Any individual with less than six months of active duty would be discharged upon arrival at the port of New York.* There were four other seamen along with Matt that came under that order. It was a happy day when Matt arrived home to pick up his life where he left it a few months back.

Chapter 4

BAKERS BUY GROCERY STORE

Matt's brother, Larry, graduated in 1919. Eric came home from town one day and said that Crowell's Grocery Store across from the Bernardston Inn was for sale. The owner was old and wanted to get out of the business. Eric had talked with Mr. Crowell. He was willing to sell his inventory for three hundred dollars plus an additional two hundred dollars as down payment. The balance of eighteen hundred dollars would have to be paid monthly for twenty years at three- percent interest. After several evenings of discussion, Eric convinced Matt and Larry to form a partnership, and buy the business. Eric agreed to put up Larry's share of the down payment, which he would be required to pay back at no interest. Both boys were to work for Mr. Crowell for twenty dollars a week for three months to learn the business.

Matt and Larry took to the grocery business like ducks to water. Once they were on their own, as the new owners, they implemented a new policy that increased business each month. They took orders for groceries over the new-fangled telephone and delivered them to the customers' homes for an additional five cents on each dollar purchased. Larry started the deliveries about four p.m. and he was usually back by closing time at seven. The boys joined the Independent Grocer's Association to receive better wholesale prices. They changed the name of the store to Baker Brothers' IGA. It was a proud day when the new sign went up on the storefront.

There was a small two-room apartment on the second floor above the store. Matt and Julie were married November 26, 1919, and moved into the little apartment. Business had increased to the point that both boys were needed all day. Julie took up the job of delivering groceries. They were making more money than they had ever dreamed possible, but Eric encouraged them to save for a rainy day.

The brothers had seen several horseless carriages over the last five years. They were both intrigued; however, Matt showed a greater degree of interest. He even bought a couple of books about the advent of the automobile. Matt had bought the books from two men who had three vehicles on display at the Franklin County Fair. The men said they wanted to give rides but the fair committee thought the vehicles would scare the horses, and turned down the idea.

Matt made arrangements to have one of the men drive his 1912 Marmon to Bernardston the last day of the fair. He paid a dollar for a ride to the country store and back. He was absolutely thrilled and they did scare a horse pulling a buggy. It was Harrison East and he was as mad as hell.

Several men in town had automobiles, which added more fuel to Matt's desire to own one. Ervin Barber had an Orient Buckboard and a 1907 Stanley Steamer. Willis Stratton and Edward Carson both owned Maxwells. John Chapin bought a 1908 two-cylinder Reo and Everett E. Benjamin drove his Winton. The day that Harry Chapin drove into the grocery store yard on a motorcycle, Matt couldn't get outside to see it fast enough. Chapin worked in town at the E. S. Hulbert Company, manufacturer of fine table knives. He commuted from Greenfield every day. Matt came back in the store talking with great enthusiasm about the motorcycle. Julie was in the office balancing the company checkbook. She came out and said to Matt, "You buy a motorcycle and I am all done working in this store." Matt laughed and headed back to the meat counter where he had been cutting up a side of beef. "I mean it, Matt."

Eric didn't like motor cars and he told the boys many times that they wouldn't last. He pointed out that a team of horses had more pulling power. Cars were unreliable with numerous mechanical breakdowns and flat tires. They became totally useless during the spring muddy season when the frost came out of the ground. Matt and Larry had to agree that a trip of any distance was not possible. Where would one find the gas to keep the thing running? But all of the negative talk did not discourage Matt in the least. He was sure that the first chance he had to own a motor car, he wouldn't give it a minute's hesitation. This desire gave Matt all the more reason to save as much money as possible.

By 1925, the grocery store was doing a thriving business. Julie and Matt had three little boys. Matt's opportunity to purchase his first car arrived. Israel Snow who lived on Center Street owned a 1920 Franklin, four door, open touring car. Mr. Snow had bought the car new for nearly two thousand dollars, expensive for those times. He had paid cash and could well afford it. Everyone knew that Snow played the stock market and he was very successful at it. Now there were rumors going around, though, that his luck had changed and he was in financial trouble.

Matt had not paid any attention to the rumors until Mr. Snow walked into the grocery store one Monday morning. He asked Matt if he could speak to him in private. They went into the office and Matt closed the door. Snow said, "I will get right to the point. I need $300.00 dollars today. I am offering you the Franklin for that amount and it is well worth it. It has been driven a little over 2,000 miles. I have kept it in a shed when it has not been on the road." Matt was well aware of the fine condition of the car. Every time he had seen it over the years, he couldn't resist looking it over, but had never entertained the thought of owning it.

Matt said, "Let's drive to the Franklin County Trust Company in Greenfield and get your money." Snow offered Matt the driver's seat and off they went. It was a pleasure to drive that luxurious motor car. Less than two hours from the time Snow walked into the store, Matt was back with his Franklin. He rushed up the stairs to tell Julie. When Matt told her how much he had paid for the car, she started to cry. "How could you spend all that money. I thought we were saving to build our own store. Don't I have anything to say in these matters?" Matt had anticipated taking her for a ride and here she was mad at him. He went out and jumped into the car, drove to the country store, filled the tank with gas, and drove to Northfield. He loved that car. On the way back, he had a flat tire, which did not dull his enthusiasm. He sort of enjoyed removing one of the twin side-mounted spare tires to get back on the way.

By Sunday, Julie showed no sign of hurt feelings. They all went to church in the Franklin and it was the happiest day of Matt's life. It was more than thirty minutes before he could leave the churchyard to drive home. Nearly all the men of the congregation looked at the car and talked with Matt about it. After dinner, Matt suggested to Julie that they drive to Greenfield with the boys and have an ice-cream treat. He put the top down and they all enjoyed the ride. They reached speeds as high as thirty miles per hour on the better stretches of road and not one tire went flat. That car attracted more attention.

The only other vehicle Matt had used belonged to the business. It was a Model T Ford pickup truck that was used to deliver groceries. He and Larry had taken turns using the truck on weekends. Larry had gotten married in 1922. He and his wife were living at Eric's house. They had a baby girl named Opal. Matt told Larry to use the pickup all the time now that he had the Franklin.

There was a shed attached to the back of the store. Matt fixed the roof and closed in two of the open sides. He put doors on the south opening, which made a nice stall for the Franklin. The cloth top was in good condition and he wanted to keep it out of the weather. Within a couple of weeks, he had the painted metal surfaces and all the chrome polished to a high luster. The dual side mounts had chrome covers that sparkled.

It was a joy for Matt to drive the family to Sunday functions. When there was no community activity to attend, they went to visit one of their many friends or relatives. Occasionally, it would rain on the way home and it bothered Matt to have the car get all mud streaked. He always buttoned on the side curtains, which kept most of the rain out of the car.

Church St., Bernardston, Mass.

The Cushman Mansion

New England House

Powers Institute
Church ST, Bernardston

Chapter 5

ALVIN MARTIN / MELISSA McHENRY

One Saturday night in October, 1925, just before closing time, the phone rang. It was Sarah Magoon on West Mountain Road. She wanted to place an order for delivery. Matt started to explain that all delivery orders had to be called in prior to 3:00 p.m. and they were about to close the store for the weekend. Mrs. Magoon said she was aware of the policy, but friends of theirs would be visiting the next day. They had just called. She pleaded with Matt to take the order and she offered to pay an additional dollar. He reluctantly agreed. He left the store in the Franklin at about 7:45. He left the Magoon's house a little after 8:00 p.m. and it was dark. As he was driving down the hill, just before the hairpin curve, the left front tire blew. It was a dangerous place to change a tire; however, there was a logging road off the middle of the hairpin curve. He drove slowly on the flat tire and turned onto the road. He continued about two hundred feet to a level spot. As he was about to turn the ignition off, he realized that his headlights were reflecting off the front of an automobile.

Matt grabbed his flashlight and walked to the car. As he approached, he recognized that it was a new Buick two-door sedan like Alvin Martins. Martin was a man in his late forties who owned the Bernardston Inn. Matt shined his light in the car and he could see two people crouched down on the back seat. Alvin Martin sat up and said, "What in hell do you want?"

"I'm sorry, Mr. Martin. I just turned off with a flat tire and I was checking to see if someone needed help."

"I don't need any help and I'd appreciate it if you'd get the hell out of here."

Matt immediately turned off his light and said, "I'm sorry," as he walked back to his car.

The other person in the car stayed crouched down but Matt knew that she was a female. She had red hair and it looked like she had little or no clothes on. A young couple lived in East Bernardston and the wife had red hair. They did their shopping in his store. Every time they came in, Matt couldn't resist looking at her ample bosom. Julie sputtered about her saying that the woman was trying to show the men how much she had and it was disgraceful the way she switched her hips around. Matt had to admit that she actually showed some cleavage and once he spilled a pound of beans due to the distraction.

Before Matt had finished changing the tire, he heard the door of the Buick open. Mr. Martin came up to him and said, "I hope you can forget what you saw here tonight. I would really appreciate it if you'd keep your mouth shut. In fact, I will be more than a little upset if I find out you have told anyone."

"Mr. Martin, the only thing I have seen this evening, of any count, is a flat tire. I am in the process of changing that."

Martin said with a smile, "I owe you one."

The next time the couple from East Bernardston came in the store, he tried to keep his eyes off the woman. After a few minutes, he glanced in her direction and she was watching him. She immediately grinned and winked at him. Matt snapped his head away and turned red as a beet. He got busy cutting meat behind the refrigerated display case and heard a female voice say, "Hi, Mr. Baker. My name is Melissa McHenry and that is my husband looking at the hardware. We live on Hoe Shop Road, the third house on the left, after turning off Route 10." She was standing at the end of the meat case. She was an attractive woman. She had on a tight fitting dress that showed too much at the top and he could even see her ankles. He knew that his face must be red and he answered nervously, "That's nice. That's nice."

She continued on, "We moved from New York City. We really like it here because the people are so friendly."

Matt wondered if she was referring to Alvin Martin. "That's nice."

He was nervous and he wished that she would stop talking to him.

She said, "If you are ever over our way, please stop in for a cup of coffee."

Matt thought, she must know I saw her in the car that night with Alvin Martin. How can she talk to me like it never happened and have the nerve to invite me for coffee. That's all I need to get the whole town talking. Stop at her house for coffee. He was jolted out of his thoughts when he accidentally sliced his thumb on his left hand to the bone. As Julie was putting on a bandage, she said "That woman seems to have quite an effect on you." Matt blushed and said nothing.

Chapter 6

JULIE LOUISE BAKER

Julie Louise Baker considered herself a lucky lady. She was married to a respected businessman in town, they had three beautiful little boys, and they lived in a nice two- bedroom house on Library Street. That two-room apartment over the store just wasn't large enough after the first baby was born. They could well afford the $275.00 down payment two years ago for the house. Their monthly payments were only $24.00 a month. But twenty years did seem like a long time to pay on a house.

Life hadn't always been so good for Julie. When Julie was nine years old, life was mostly hard work with no end in sight, and certainly no future. She had to work as hard as her brothers and there were few things that she could not do. She knew that her dad was proud of her ability to drive a team of horses. He never told her directly, but when anyone came to the farm, he would say, "You ought to see Julie drive the horses. She can plow as straight as any of her brothers, and she can even back a load of hay into the barn."

She attended the district school on South Street. There were six grades in the one room school, with a row for each grade. Each year, there were thirty five to forty students. Julie loved school for several reasons. Reading, writing, and arithmetic were interesting and fun. She didn't care for history much, but she always got a passing grade. She liked being with the other kids, and best of all, school got her away from the continuous hard work on the farm.

The winters were bitter cold and it seemed like Julie's house was either too hot or shivering cold. When the cooking stove in the kitchen and the chunk stove in the living room were both going, it was hot in the house no matter what the temperature was outside.

When they got up each morning, both stoves had been out for hours. The cooking stove had a water reservoir, which provided hot water for coffee or dish washing. It was not unusual to have a layer of ice form in the reservoir over night during the winter. Julie hated climbing out of bed on those cold mornings and then washing in freezing cold water. One of her jobs was getting both stoves going and filling the wood boxes. The wood was piled in rows on the south side of the house, often covered with snow, and frozen together. She had to knock the pieces apart by hitting them with an ax. She had to get most of the snow and ice off the pieces because her Mom didn't like it when the floor got wet. She wished she had the job of helping with the barn chores like her older sister, Lois. At least in the barn, it was always warm because of the body heat from the animals.

Each spring, the fields had to be plowed in preparation for planting. A new batch of stones was always turned up and they had to be removed. They hitched the horses to the stone sled, which was like a heavy-duty toboggan. Julie wondered where all those stones came from each year. They built fences along their boundary lines with the rocks. Her fingernails always filled with dirt doing this job and it was a back breaker. She hated handling those stones. Once the crops were in, the cultivating and weeding commenced for most of the summer. Canning the fruit and vegetables at the end of the summer was easy compared to the other work.

About the only fun at the Parks house was the first and third Saturdays of each month. Mr. Parks hitched up the team late in the afternoon and they all rode in the hay wagon to the country store. The kids were each given a nickel to spend as they wished. Julie liked the old fashioned chocolates and they were five for a penny.

As the years went by, Julie came to believe that she was not going to be able to continue her schooling after the sixth grade. That really bothered her. Both of her folks were of the opinion that a girl did not need more schooling. Halfway through her sixth grade, she told her mother that she wanted to graduate from high school. Her mom wasn't enthused but she told her to ask her dad. She waited until her father was in one of his better moods to spring the request on him. He said that he would have to think about it. Her older brother must have heard her ask. He came in from the next room and said, "Dad, Julie is a good student and we can handle the work like we always have in the past." She believed that Hal's comment really helped because she was allowed to start the seventh grade at Powers Institute.

Edward Epps Powers was the donor in March 1856 of ten thousand dollars to the town of Bernardston, Massachusetts, for a public school. This money provided the means to construct one of the finest school buildings in New England. The building was still in excellent condition. It was perched on a rise of ground, on the north side of Church Street, less than a quarter mile from the junction of Routes 5 and 10.

On the first day at Powers, Julie realized that her dress was not nearly as nice as the other girls' clothes. Her shoes were terrible although they were her best pair of work shoes. She really felt inferior. She wished she had not begged to continue her schooling. She said almost nothing all day. When she got home, she went to her room and cried. Her mother heard her and asked what was the matter? When she finally got the problem out in the open, she left Julie's room. She returned a few minutes later with a pair of shoes and two of her church dresses. Julie wiped her eyes and went from crying to laughing.

By the time she was a junior in high school, her Mom had modified a total of six dresses to fit her. Julie had learned to fix her hair fashionably and she was always on the honor roll. All things considered, she felt accepted in school by the teachers as well as the students. Matt Baker was the only boy in her class. It seemed like all the girls liked him. He had a good physique with blond hair and blue eyes. He was the life of the class and he could even make the teachers laugh some times. Julie liked him but she didn't think she had much of a chance competing with ten other girls. In her opinion, Gloria Stevens made a spectacle of herself in front of Matt at every opportunity. It was obvious that she had her sights set on him from the start.

In the early part of her senior year, Julie felt that Matt had more than just friendly feelings towards her. It seemed like once or twice a week, he told her she looked pretty. When they were in study hall, he seemed to be looking at her each time she looked up. He would grin and look back at his book. She even talked her folks into going to church, the summer before, so she could see Matt on Sundays. When something prevented their attendance, it seemed like ages until the next Sunday. The day Matt came out to her place to pick up the plow was a happy one for her. They both expressed their love for one another.

Their years together as man and wife had been good. At times, Julie thought Matt was too harsh with their sons but they seemed to have a great deal of respect for him. It was a trying time when Matt attempted to teach her to drive the Model T. It was a chore learning to use the gas, clutch, and brake pedals at the proper time. She found herself pulling back on the steering wheel when she wanted to stop. That was the procedure for stopping horses. Matt would yell, "brake, brake, brake!" Finally, Larry, her brother-in-law, finished teaching her and it seemed much easier.

The Honorable Henry W. Cushman's generosity during the 1860's greatly improved the town of Bernardston for the residents. He donated Cushman Hall, a large residential building, across the road from Powers Institute. The first floor provided a fine apartment for the school principal and the second floor was used for housing out-of-town students. An additional two and a half acres went with Cushman Hall for a town park and it bordered Church and South Streets. Fox Brook flowed through the park. In later years, band concerts were held during the summer.

At the one hundred-year exercises, Mr. Cushman donated the library, at the corner of Library and Church Streets, to the town. Being co-located with Powers Institute, it became a definite asset for the students and teachers. A two-story brick building, it was constructed to last many years.

The Unitarian parsonage was south of the Baker Brothers' IGA store across Fox Brook. The building was a huge mansion that had been the home of Lieutenant Governor Cushman. It was a stately structure with four large columns, a full porch, and large granite steps in front. Heat for the mansion came from the wood stove in the kitchen and a fireplace in the dining room. During the summer of 1926, a large crack had developed in the chimney of the fireplace. The estimated cost of

Top: Bernardston Inn; Bottom: Cushman Library

repairs was more than the church trustees were willing to approve. They voted to put the mansion up for sale at a modest price of $2,500.00.

Matt wanted that place and he spoke to Julie about it. She was against the idea because she knew about the broken chimney. She agreed that they could afford to buy the house, but the estimated thousand dollars for chimney repairs was too much. She pointed out that everything was primitive compared to the house they were presently occupying. Matt still wanted it and he kept Julie awake nights talking about the possibility of installing chunk stoves. She always countered with the fact that a new chimney would still be required.

Matt checked with Kohler's Stove Company in Greenfield. The company would install a furnace in the basement and put up a chimney on the north side of the house for five hundred and fifty dollars. The furnace would burn wood and provide ample heat for the first floor of the big house. Matt convinced Julie to let him make an offer of $2,200.00 for the mansion. The church trustees turned down the offer, which was a relief for Julie. Their financial situation was good and buying that monster of a house could be no end of problems.

When fall arrived, the Unitarian minister told the church trustees that it would be impossible for him and his family to spend the winter in the parsonage. The house had been uncomfortably cold. The trustees decided to sell it to Matt if his offer was still good.

Matt was thrilled at the thought of owning that mansion. He and Julie signed the papers three weeks later. In less than a month, the new furnace was installed. The heat would rise through a three-foot square register cut in the floor of the dining room. Matt purchased a winter's supply of wood from Almon Flag and he was anxious for cold weather to set in. They spent every spare minute moving their belongings and Matt was like a kid fixing this and that about the house. There were three carriage stalls attached to the west end of the mansion and at the back of the third stall was an attached out-house.

Doors were installed to enclose the first carriage stall adjoining the house. The Franklin was still in mint condition and Matt planned to keep it that way. Since they purchased a new Model-T Ford station wagon in 1925, the Franklin was driven only on Sundays when the weather was good. That stately vehicle attracted attention wherever it went and Matt enjoyed driving it to community functions.

Harold S. Shears had taken over the country store from his Dad, G. F. Shears. H. S. [everyone called him H.S.] had gained the reputation for being an innovative salesman. He called Matt a few months after his move to the Cushman mansion. "Matt, I have a matched team of driving horses that I'd like to leave in your barn for a while. I'll leave you the harnesses and buggy so that you can use the team. In fact, I want you to use the team when you find the time." Matt agreed and in less than an hour, HS drove into the store yard. The first week, Matt hitched up the team twice and went for early morning drives. The horses were well broke and it was a joy to drive them. Before the end of the second week, Matt had traded one of his cows, a mowing machine, and some cash for the team along with the buggy and harnesses. Julie was not enthused with the deal, but it wasn't long before she went with him in the buggy. She enjoyed driving those beautiful horses too.

Chapter 7

SAMUEL AND CHARLES BAKER

August 3, 1927, Samuel Grant Baker was six years old and he resembled the Parks side of the family. In those first years of Sam's life, he looked just like Grampa Parks' baby pictures. He was a fine looking boy and he would start classes in September at Green School. Matt and Julie had purchased a Kimball piano since they moved into the mansion. Sam showed an intense amount of interest in that piano. Matt had taken piano lessons when he was in school and he taught Sam to play a couple of songs using one finger. He planned to hire Carl Mesic, a piano teacher in Whately, to teach Sam properly.

Charles Duncan Baker had been born October 23, 1922 with blonde hair and blue eyes and he resembled the Baker side of the family. When Charlie was nearly three years old, he went with Matt to the blacksmith shop on River Street. While his father and the blacksmith were talking about the new whipple tree Matt needed, Charlie walked out the back door. He climbed into an old farm wagon without wheels. He sat in the seat and made believe he was driving a horse. Matt, subconsciously, knew he was out there but he didn't pay close attention after that. Fred Allen, the blacksmith, showed Matt a whipple tree that he had on hand pointing out some slight modification required to replace the broken one. It wouldn't take more than a few minutes, so Matt decided to wait. While the work was being done, Matt and Mr. Allen talked about the proposed town water system. Several springs converged together on Fox Hill. J. B. Kennedy submitted the idea of constructing a large reservoir to store the water. The water could then be piped to the homes and businesses in town. The plan was under study by the town planners.

When the whipple tree was finished, Matt went out the back door to get Charlie. He wasn't there. Matt walked around to the front of the shop and he wasn't in the Model-T. Matt went back behind the shop and called his name several times and received no answer. Then he noticed that it looked as if someone had walked through the high grass towards the river. He ran, following the path, yelling Charlie's name. He came to the steep bank of the river that dropped about twenty feet to the water. Matt started down the bank, slipped, slid to the edge, and would have gone in the water, but he managed to grab a small hemlock tree. Charlie was no where in sight.

Fall River was flowing with a swift current, at the time, due to heavy rain showers during the last week. Matt climbed up the bank in a panic, ran to the Model-T, and drove to Shears' store just a quarter mile to the north. He stopped in front of the store and yelled, "I think my little boy fell into the river! Please help me!" He immediately started out of the yard as two men climbed into the car with him. Others started for their cars to follow. Matt drove through the underpass just south of the blacksmith shop and turned left along the railroad embankment to the river. They searched along the bank to the dam. When more people showed up, Matt asked them to look below the dam. Water was flowing over the top and there was a possibility that Charlie washed over.

Many of the town people arrived and the search had been going on for more than two hours. They had searched both sides of the river, above and below the dam with no luck. Matt was back near his car, looking tormented, and talking with some of the men about getting grappling hooks to drag the river. They heard a loud yell, "Hey." It came from the direction of the road. They all looked and saw Mr. Allen walking in their direction hand in hand with Charlie. He had apparently walked up to the tramp house, gone inside, and had fallen asleep. Mr. Allen heard him crying and saw him coming down the road looking as though he had just woke up.

The tramp house was a one-room shack halfway between the blacksmith shop and Shears' store. Down-and-outers passing through town were allowed to stay one or two nights before being told to move on.

Matt was relieved, happy, and couldn't stop hugging Charlie for several minutes. Tears were running down his face as well as some of the others in the search party. Charlie kept pointing at the river, saying "Water. Water." Matt thanked the people who had been helping. He announced there would be a picnic in Cushman Park Sunday afternoon, for all who helped look for Charlie. They would celebrate the happy turn of events.

Melissa McHenry had become the talk of the town. When members of the Extension Service for Homemakers, Agricultural Club, Bernardston Community Club, Bernardston Grange No. 81, Union Mission Club, or Senior Club were at their scheduled meetings, talk always drifted to the McHenrys. Josh McHenry was in New York City on business most of the time. She gallivanted about town in a surrey, driven by their gardener and handy man Hershall Latfield. Everyone knew when Mr. McHenry was in New York. The surrey would be parked at the Inn. It got there at 11:00 a.m., when the Inn opened for lunch, and remained until late at night. It was rumored that Mrs. McHenry got along well with the owner, Alvin Martin.

Mr. Martin hired Melissa to sing in the lounge with the piano player. Included with the job was a room on the fourth floor. When her husband was in New York, she stayed at the Inn. Some of the local men, who stopped there, told their wives about her. They said that she wore tight dresses, high-heeled shoes, silk stockings, and her legs were visible up to her knees. She sang popular songs and had a lovely voice. She danced the Charleston with zest and at times, it looked like her upper torso might fall out of her dress. They never mentioned that most of them were hopeful that it would.

The piano player, Don Pitman, from Louisiana, was as fine a musician as there was in New England. He played a Baldwin seven-foot grand piano and his repertoire seemed to be unlimited. He played classical, jazz, and swing with equal ease and he did not use sheet music. Don was blessed with the God-given gift of playing by ear. He could be playing in the best lounges in Boston, New York, or Baton Rouge, but he loved the New England countryside and the winter sports.

The Inn had clientele from as far away as Springfield, Mass., and Troy, New York. They always called and reserved rooms for the night.

The lounge was supposed to close at one a.m., but when business was good Alvin told Melissa to keep the show going. The restaurant served dinner until nine p.m. and the meals were excellent. The menu included lobster, fried clams, scrod, cod, steaks, and prime rib.

Melissa sang or danced for about twenty minutes and then mingled with the crowd. Her overall appearance could only be described as sensational. The women called her voluptuous.

She was able to sense the attitude of the females at a table. If they appeared hostile, she just nodded. At other tables, she joined the group and everyone seemed to enjoy her company. After a few minutes, she was back on the stage doing another routine. Generally, she was a hit and the Inn's business grew at a steady rate with nearly half the crowd coming from long distances and reserving rooms at the Inn.

One Saturday night about 7:30, a chauffeur driven limousine, with New York license plates, pulled into the parking lot of the Inn. Four men dressed in expensive suits, overcoats, and homburg hats got out of the vehicle. They did not have reservations to stay at the Inn and they refused to check their coats. All four men were stocky, but one was very tall and he must have weighed 250 pounds. He told the hostess that they wanted a stage-side table. She told them that none were available and the big man asked for the manager. She went to the office and got Mr. Martin. He was about to tell them that all tables were full when the big man offered him a twenty-dollar bill. Martin said, "Just a minute, gentlemen, we will have a table in a moment." In a few minutes, the front tables had been re-arranged and the four men were seated at a table in front of the stage.

It was about fifteen minutes before Melissa appeared on stage to do another show. She started to sing *Daisy*, one of the popular songs of the era and focused on the four men. Her voice broke and she turned to walk behind the curtain. The big man that had done all the talking got up and started after her. Al Martin was watching from the bar and he sensed that something was wrong. He nearly ran to the back stage area behind the curtain.

He arrived just in time to see the man slap Melissa across the face with a force that knocked her against the wall. Al made a diving lunge at the man and tackled him. They both went down on the floor. The man, from New York, put both his hands behind Alvin's head and slammed his knee into his face. Al felt his nose break just before he passed out. The man got up and kicked him twice in the stomach.

Melissa headed for the stairs and ran up to her room on the fourth floor. She locked the door and turned off the light. She was trembling and whimpering with fright. Her cheek hurt where the man had struck her. The other three men came back behind the curtain. The tall one, who was in charge, told one of them to bring one of the cocktail waitresses to him. When they returned, the big man said, "Lady . . . if you don't want your face ruined, tell me the room number of your singer, NOW." She started to cry and said, "402." The four men headed for the stairs. When they got to room 402, one of them stepped across the hall, then lunged against the door. The door casing broke and the door flew open. They turned on the light and Melissa was cringing in the corner by the bed. She was sobbing and mumbling, "Please don't hurt me." Two of the men grabbed her by the arms and held her up. The big man walked up and punched her in the face with a fierce impact. Almost immediately, blood started to ooze out of her eyes and ears. He then went to the window and opened it. The two men threw her out the window like a rag doll.

It all happened in less than ten minutes, from the time Melissa started singing, and the four men were gone. It was close to a half-hour when the town constable, H.S. Shears arrived and another hour before the State Police arrived. Alvin Martin was taken to the Franklin County Hospital in critical condition. Melissa's neck and back had been broken. She had died on impact from the fall.

The next day reporters were everywhere trying to find someone who had witnessed the tragic event. The waitress who gave the man Melissa's room number was sick to her stomach with crying spells. Nothing like this had ever happened in Franklin County. Julie said that she was sorry for "that woman" but she knew that someone like her was not good for the town. Alvin Martin's condition was still not stable and he might not come out of it. He had a severe concussion, a ruptured spleen, and a collapsed lung.

John Cutler, the *Greenfield Gazette* reporter, had a lengthy article in the paper the following day. He speculated that the McHenry's were connected to New York mobsters in some way and they apparently made a mistake. He further stated that a *New York Times* reporter had called the Gazette and asked for details of the event. Cutler asked the man how he found out about the incident and he said that an anonymous person called their paper. It appeared that the person responsible wanted the people in New York to know about it.

Josh McHenry never returned to Bernardston and no one had his New York address. Many of the ladies in town felt that he had his wife killed for running around with Alvin Martin. The men didn't believe it because they couldn't see why the man would want the story in the New York papers. They agreed with John Cutler's theory. Several weeks went by before that Saturday night faded from being the favorite topic of conversation. Alvin Martin remained in intensive care for nine days then died from complications.

The Inn remained closed since the incident. The local men who had frequented the establishment missed being able to stop for drinks and a good meal. They also had enjoyed the entertainment provided by Melissa. Many of the wives who waited for their men to come home evenings were glad the Inn was not open for business.

Chapter 8

BERNARDSTON INN IS FOR SALE

Moses Aldrich, President of the Franklin Savings Bank, called Matt and asked him to stop at the bank on his next trip to Greenfield. After Matt hung up the phone, he couldn't imagine why Mr. Aldrich wanted to talk with him. He did all his banking with the Franklin County Trust. He called Mr. Aldrich back and asked him what reason he had for seeing him. Aldrich said that he would not discuss it on the phone, but he would appreciate seeing Matt in his office.

Matt's curiosity was up and as soon as he could, he drove to Greenfield to see Aldrich. He had to wait more than twenty minutes before he was free. He invited Matt into his office and closed the door. He said, "I think you will understand in a few minutes why I couldn't talk. Those switchboard operators seem to enjoy listening to others talking on the phone." He then explained to Matt that his bank held a large mortgage on the Bernardston Inn. After the New England house burned in 1906, Franklin Savings financed the construction of the Inn for a Horace Mott. In 1922, Alvin Martin bought Mott's equity and assumed the loan. The Inn was closed after Martin died and no payments had been made for nearly three months.

Aldrich asked Matt if he would consider managing the Inn and get it back to a paying proposition. The bank had to wait a year to foreclose in circumstances where payments were not made due to a death. It was to give relatives of the deceased time to come forward and salvage the loan. He further explained that he and his board of directors were aware of his success in the grocery store. The idea seemed perfect to them with Matt living across the road from the Inn. Matt sat there, speechless.

Mr. Aldrich continued. They were willing to pay Matt a weekly salary of $100.00 and in nine months, he would be offered the opportunity to assume the mortgage. Surely by then everyone would know whether or not Matt Baker was a hotel manager. Matt was still beyond words. Mr. Aldrich finished up with this statement, "Don't try to give me an answer now. Go home, discuss it with your wife, and both of you think it over. Come back a week from today and give me your decision. Remember one thing, we would not be making this offer if we didn't think you could do it."

"Thanks" and he walked out.

When Matt explained to Julie the offer made by Mr. Aldrich, she was immediately against it. She wanted to know how he could possibly manage the hotel when he already had too much to do. She also pointed out that church people shouldn't be in that sort of business.

Later in the day, Matt and Larry discussed the idea at great length. After repeating the entire story to Larry, Matt was surprised at his response.

He said, "That is a wonderful opportunity. It sounds like the bank will let you have it for what is owed."

The two of them discussed numerous possible options during a three-hour period. They knew that the piano player, Don Pitman, was still in the area. He had taken a job with the Nichols Brothers in Greenfield. Nichols was a manufacturing company producing high quality taps and dies. Don was only playing the piano for special events so Matt and Larry felt he would return to the Inn.

By the end of the three hours both brothers were quite optimistic. If the deal worked out, they agreed to make it a joint venture. Larry would continue to manage the store and, of course, they would have to hire more help. When Matt spoke to Julie again, she sensed his enthusiasm and said, "You are actually considering the offer from the bank, aren't you?" He started to relate some of the options that he and Larry had discussed. Julie burst into tears and said, "Don't, I don't want to hear about it. That is not something we should be doing." She turned and headed for the bedroom and slammed the door. Matt left for the store, disheartened.

Matt did not bring up the subject to Julie for the next two

days. Every time he and Larry were together, they both talked with more enthusiasm. They had decided they would make the Inn a place with class. Families from all walks of life would feel at home there if they could afford the prices. Only the best food would be served and they would try to get the Bernardston Inn added to the "Big Band" circuit. The closest town that hired a known band was Northampton. If their plans worked, it would put Bernardston on the map.

On Saturday, Matt had only two days left before he was supposed to give Mr. Aldrich his decision. The brothers had convinced themselves that they should give it a try, but Matt was concerned about Julie's feelings. He walked to the house for lunch. As he was eating oyster stew with Nabisco crackers, Julie said, "Matt."

"Yes."

"I can tell that you boys have talked yourselves into taking on the bank's offer."

"How do you know that?"

"Every time I walk into the store, both of you stop talking together and get busy doing something. If you are sure that you want to try it, go ahead but remember that I am against it."

"Julie, you are beautiful, wonderful, and a great partner. I want you to know that I appreciate all the work you do. You are the best cook and housekeeper a man could ever hope for." They stood up and hugged each other. "I love you, Julie."

"I love you too." Tears were rolling down her cheeks. She said, "I like things stable and secure."

"I know you do, honey, but I have nearly nine months to decide before it is permanent. In the meantime, I draw down a big weekly salary!"

It took nearly six weeks before the Inn was open for business. Don Pitman and his Baldwin grand piano were moved into the dining hall. He played for the lunch and dinner crowds, six days a week. On Sundays, brunch was available for individuals staying at the Inn and the lounge was closed all day. Matt doubled the parking space. He hired Lester Lanin's orchestra on Friday and Saturday nights the first month they were open. Full-page ads were placed in newspapers in

Brattleboro, Vermont; Keene, New Hampshire; Greenfield and Springfield, Massachusetts. A new sign was hung at the southwest corner of the building.

Bernardston Inn

Finest Dining in New England

By the summer of 1936, Matt had installed water pipes and electric lights in his home as well as at the Inn. Everyone talked about the depression. Baker Brothers' IGA and the Bernardston Inn; however, did well compared to failed businesses listed in the paper. Matt and Larry's businesses had always made enough to meet all expenses including their payroll. The Bakers extended credit to several families in town that could not pay for their groceries. In some cases, they received fruits, vegetables, or a portion of butchered live stock as payment. People in town who owed them money were merely down on their luck due to the depression. Occasionally, a couple skipped town owing their hotel bill.

The hard times provided Matt with the opportunity to purchase additional classic automobiles at bargain prices. He now owned a 1924 Packard four-door touring car and a 1914 Overland. Both cars were in mint condition and he still owned the Franklin. He had traded the matched team of driving horses to Louis Parks, Julie's youngest brother, for the Packard. Louis won several blue ribbons at the Franklin County Fair in team driving competition the year he got the team. A wealthy horse rancher from Great Barrington bought the horses from Louis. The price was more than twice the considered worth. He left the fair with a fat wallet and his characteristic big grin.

Matt had hired some of the unemployed house builders in town to build a two-story apartment house, a five-stall garage, and a cow barn over a five-year period. Those men were happy to work for two dollars a day. They agreed to work for Matt at that price with no other work available. As money was available, Matt purchased building materials. He got a bargain price on lumber because he ordered it from Almon Flag when his business was slow. The lumber was stored under canvas tarps until needed. Almon also delivered saw dust for a dollar a load. It made good bedding for the half dozen cows Matt kept.

Sam Baker was fifteen years old and he had been taking piano lessons from Carl Mesic for more than three years. Mr. Mesic recommended that Matt send Sam to the Boston Conservatory of Music. Sam showed a natural talent for the piano and he enjoyed being at the Inn when Don Pitman was playing. They got along fine and Don showed Sam some of the special techniques that he had developed over the years. Like Don, he could also play by ear. He used sheet music to learn a new song and then he could play it by ear. It wasn't long before the two of them were dueting on Don's grand piano. The customers dining at the time enjoyed their virtuosity.

Charles Baker was fourteen years old. He was a good student and he loved winter sports. He was attending Deerfield Academy in South Deerfield and he gave the upper classmen a run for their money in skiing and skating competition. He had mastered the ski jump in Brattleboro, Vermont, and placed second or third in speed skating. He mentioned to Matt that a coach from Dartmouth College was at Deerfield looking for potential students for scholarships. The man had talked to Charlie for about a half-hour and he wrote his name in a small notebook. He encouraged Charlie to keep his academic grades at a "B" level or higher through high school. The man said, "We can't offer a scholarship in sports unless a student has good grades."

Lester Mathew Baker was thirteen years old. He was a fair student and he loved anything mechanical. He had a knack for keeping all Matt's vehicles in good running condition. No one knew just when he acquired the ability but his reputation got around. Hardly a week went by that one or more of the car owners in town didn't come looking for Lester.

Hershall Latfield had been living in the McHenry house on Hoe Shop Road since the tragic death of Melissa. He kept pretty much to himself. When a strange vehicle was in town with New York license plates, everyone knew that it belonged to someone visiting Latfield. It was one of those things that town folk acknowledged, but they didn't dwell on it.

Matt was a little surprised to see Latfield walk into the Inn one day during a Saturday afternoon. Matt was coming out of his office and it was obvious that Latfield wanted to see him. They shook hands and he said, "Mr. Baker, I have heard that you have a son that is a good automobile mechanic."

"That is true. He seems to come by it naturally." Latfield owned two vehicles. One was a 1932 Packard coupe with a soft-top and rumble seat. It was a beautiful motor car. The other was a 1935 Ford station wagon and still looked like new even though it was more than a year old.

"Would it be possible for me to take your son to my house? The Packard won't start."

"Certainly. Les is in the basement peeling potatoes." When Les realized that he would be going with Latfield to work on the Packard, he jumped up and took off his apron with enthusiasm. In just a few minutes, Les found the problem with the Packard. The fuel line to the carburetor was stopped up. Les took it off, blew it out, and had the car running in no time.

Latfield invited Les into the house for a glass of iced tea. While he was there, the phone rang. Les couldn't help hearing Latfield's side of the conversation. His first words were, "Hey, how many times do I have to tell you that my name is Hershall Latfield." Then he talked for several minutes and it was clear to Les that Latfield and the person knew each other. It seemed strange that the other person didn't know Latfield's name. Les got a ride back to the Inn in the Packard. Latfield thanked him and handed him a five-dollar bill. Les was thrilled.

When Les walked into the Inn, his dad was talking to John Cutler, the Gazette reporter. Les told them both how easy it was to get the Packard started and that he received five dollars from Mr. Latfield. He would have been happy with a dollar. Then he said, "Something kind of funny happened while I was there." He explained about the telephone conversation. Matt and John looked at each other and John said, "That is peculiar. I've never given it any thought, but I assumed that the house on Hoe Shop Road had belonged to the McHenrys. Maybe I'll drop in at the courthouse and see whose name is on the deed. It is none of my business, but it is interesting."

John Cutler called Matt the next day. He said, "That house is and has always been in Latfield's name. All this time I thought the McHenrys employed him. He also owns most of the acreage around him and there is not a mortgage on any of it."

Les Baker attended Greenfield high school his freshman through senior years. They had a trade school offering cabinet making and automotive maintenance. Les, naturally, enrolled in the automotive department. At the end of those four years, there wasn't anything that he could not do when it came to automotive maintenance. This included doing a complete professional paint job. He enjoyed every minute of those four years, primarily due to his instructor, Mr. Packard. He was excellent at his teaching profession and maintained a good relationship with his students as well. Most of the auto mechanics in surrounding towns had been students under Packard. In all the time Les attended, he missed two days of school. It was caused by the blizzard in January 1940. More than four feet of snow fell during a ten-hour time span and it brought traffic to a stand still. Strong winds made snowdrifts ten feet high in places.

After he repaired the plugged gas line for Latfield, Les did more and more work there on Hoe Shop Road. He took care of the maintenance on both of Latfield's cars and mowed the lawn once a week in the summer. Once Les had his driver's license, he drove Matt's doodlebug over and plowed out Latfield's yard after each snowstorm. The part time work became so frequent that he seldom received less than $25.00 a week. That wasn't much under what people were paid for full time work in those days.

A special relationship developed between the two. Les had a great deal of respect for Mr. Latfield and he became fond of Les. The summer after Les got his driver's license, Latfield hired him to chauffeur the Packard on three short vacation trips. He was paid five dollars a day plus expenses. Les loved driving that car so much that he would have done it for nothing.

Latfield had a Heli-crafter radio that intrigued Les. It had four control knobs for tuning in stations. Most of the time it was tuned to WHAI in Greenfield. At night when the "F" layer in the ionosphere developed, the range of the received signals was limitless. The transmitted radio signals bounced back and forth between the "F" layer and earth and literally walked around the earth in this manner. It was a chore adjusting those tuning knobs, but it did work by following the instruction manual. One night, Les tuned to a station in Berlin, Germany. They heard Hitler making a speech. Neither could understand German but there was no doubting the voice. Their favorite station with news and excellent music was KMOX in St. Louis, Missouri.

The night of December 7, 1941, Les and Mr. Latfield listened to the war news on KMOX until three a.m. Les had just passed his sixteenth birthday. He said that as soon as he was old enough, he would join the service. Just before Les left to go home, Mr. Latfield said, "Les, would you do me a favor? Please don't join up before you graduate from high school." Les hesitated for several seconds then said, "Okay. I'll join as soon as I graduate." Latfield went to bed hoping that the war would be over by then.

About six months after WW II started, Les drove Mr. Latfield to New York City in the Ford station wagon. Les was on his own most of the time during the three days they were in the city. Latfield had given him a fifty-dollar bill when they arrived and said, "Les, have a good time and stay out of trouble." He spent his time going to movies, seeing the sites, and eating great food. He went to Radio City Music Hall, the Statue of Liberty, Coney Island, and even a Broadway show. One night he went to a basement bar called Birdland just off Times Square. The Earl Garner Orchestra was there and he enjoyed their music. He drank a couple of beers and no one even asked to see his I.D. He had never seen a prettier girl than the waitress. He got up enough nerve to ask her for a date after his second beer. She said that he was real sweet but that she was dating the club manager.

When they got back to Hoe Shop road, Latfield gave Les the Heli-crafter radio. He had bought a new Philco radio in New York that could be tuned with only one tuning knob. It was called a superhetrodyne receiver and it was a great improvement over the old four knob radios.

Les had never seen anything as beautiful as that floor model radio. It stood three feet high and had a lighted tuning dial that looked like a car speedometer. He was thrilled to get the old radio. It was placed on a nightstand beside his bed and he fell asleep most nights with it on.

Chapter 9

LESTER BAKER JOINS THE US NAVY

*I*n June 1942, Les joined the U. S. Navy. Julia Newsom, his girl friend, accompanied him to the Greenfield railroad station along with his brother Charles. He had asked his folks not to be there because he was afraid he might break down. He rode the train to the Naval Training Station at Great Lakes, Illinois.

There were five other recruits on the train with him on the trip west. They had a lot of fun laughing and joking around. When a pretty girl was on the train, they talked with her. Some of the fellows managed to get names and addresses and promised to write. When they arrived at their destination, a seaman first met them from the training base. He got them into two columns and told them to follow him. There were nearly forty men assembled when they arrived. At several stops en route, more recruits joined the group on the train. It all seemed a lark until they sat down at the reception center building. A second class petty officer started talking to them as if they were scum. If a recruit had the audacity to ask a question, the petty officer made him look ridiculous. One recruit made the mistake of asking him what his problem was. The petty officer flew into a rage. The result was the recruit holding a sign in front of the room that said, "I am Stupid." They spent three days at the reception center receiving hair cuts, uniforms, shots, physical exams, taking tests, and filling out a ton of papers.

Eight weeks later, Les graduated from basic training with orders to report aboard the U.S.S. *Resolute*, a PCS (patrol craft small) stationed at Long Beach, California. Leave was not authorized due to the country being at war. It took two full days on the train to make the trip. There were other sailors on the train headed for Long Beach. One sailor was

First Class Petty Officer Clarence Phillips returning to the *Resolute* after attending a school on the new Sonar system that had been installed aboard ship. They talked and Phillips realized that Les was an experienced automotive mechanic.

When they both reported aboard, Phillips introduced Les to the ship's operations officer, Lt.(jg) Walters. He suggested to Mr. Walters that Les be assigned to the engine room gang. His boss in charge of the engine room was 2nd Class Petty Officer Myron Swicegood. Les, did not like Swicegood. He was a "smart ass" type person and had an attitude that no one knew as much as he did. Les sensed that Swicegood did not like him either. In less than two days, Swicegood assigned him to six months of compartment cleaning. This entailed that all sleeping quarters be kept spotlessly clean. Les spent each day scrubbing the painted areas with sand soap and polishing all the brass fittings. It was a job that never ended and Swicegood continuously found fault. Les felt an ever-growing hatred for the man; however, he never showed his feelings or complained.

The U.S.S. *Resolute* stayed tied to the dock at Long Beach for five weeks, taking on supplies for a cruise to Hawaii. Scuttlebutt had it that they would be joining the invasion forces after that. The boat was equipped with a three-inch gun, four 20mm guns, depth charges, and two torpedo launching tubes. The PCS was powered by two 1,000 horsepower diesel engines. Normal cruise speed was 22 knots with a top speed of twenty-eight knots. Les spent most of his free time reading a book on the diesel engines. He had gone on liberty a few times, but did not enjoy it. There were so many sailors in town that everything he wanted to do was a hassle. He went to a couple of movies and both times there were loud-mouthed sailors, obviously drunk, making it impossible to enjoy the show. A couple of his shipmates invited him to go to town. After going to three bars and finding sailors falling over each other, Les bid his friends goodbye and returned to the *Resolute*.

The day they were scheduled to depart, one of the engines would not start. After more than two hours, Swicegood came looking for Les. Within twenty minutes, Les found the engine timing was off. In a few more minutes, he discovered that the timing chain had slipped. He adjusted the chain and tightened up the linkage. He touched the start button and the engine purred into life. He didn't know it, but Mr. Walters had told Swicegood to give Les a shot at fixing the engine. The *Resolute* departed for Hawaii. Four hours out of Long Beach, Les was told to report to Lieutenant Skahill, the ship's Captain. He was a little surprised to see Swicegood was there too. Skahill said, "Gentlemen, we are at war. It appears that Seaman Baker is the most qualified person aboard to maintain our engines. We must have them operating. Baker, you are now a First Class Petty Officer and Swicegood is your assistant." Les Baker was promoted four grades on the spot. Swicegood looked less than pleased with the situation.

Les felt he needed to have a talk with Swicegood. He asked him to go back on the fantail where they could talk in private. He said, "Swicegood, the tables have been turned. You now work for me and this is what I expect. You do your duty as the job demands and give proper respect to me as your boss as I did you and we will get along fine." Swicegood smirked and walked off.

The rest of the trip to Hawaii was uneventful. Swicegood was always on the edge of going on report for his attitude, but it didn't happen. The *Resolute* tied up at Barber Point and half the ship's company was granted liberty. Oahu was beautiful in the extreme; however, war time status resulted in every bar and restaurant being crowded with service men. Les and two of his shipmates bought facemasks and snorkels. They enjoyed swimming off the beach and seeing the myriad of fish, other sea life, and coral growth in glorious colors. This respite from sea duty lasted eight days. They departed Hawaii as part of a screening force in support of a nineteen-ship convoy made up of cargo vessels and fuel tankers. The weather was beautiful, without a cloud in the sky. Les had learned a lot about the engines and they were functioning well. He fine-tuned the timing on both and their top speed was now just over thirty knots.

Lt. Skahill was pleased with the command change he had made. He had not liked Swicegood's attitude and he had no confidence in his ability. Les was a natural leader and he assumed his new duties with ease. Although he was only nineteen, he appeared more mature than some of the crew who were in their mid twenties. The engine compartment had never looked so good.

Skahill had a policy of teaching his senior enlisted men to con the ship. He knew anything could happen in combat and the more men capable of commanding the *Resolute*, the better. He also gave classes to these men in navigation to include taking star fixes to verify their location. Les showed such a sincere interest that Lt. Skahill taught him the fundamentals of chasing submarines and the proper method of shooting a torpedo at surface ships. He reached the point of conning the ship for as long as two hours at a time without one criticism from the skipper.

On October 19, 1943, a rendezvous was made with an invasion task force. The objective was Tarawa although the senior commanders were the only ones who knew it. The war ships consisted of three battleships, five cruisers, five escort carriers, twenty-four destroyers, one LSD with Sherman tanks, and sixteen transports carrying 18,600 Marines of the 2nd Marine Division. Tarawa was the heaviest defended atoll in the Pacific and the Japanese believed that it could not be taken by any invasion force.

It took a full day of maneuvering before the two convoys were merged into one unit. Viewing the total group of ships from above, the *Resolute* had a screening position at the 10:00 o'clock point. A convoy moves as fast as its slowest vessel which in this case was 11 knots. It seemed dreadfully slow to Les. Two destroyers bracketed the *Resolute*. The *Ringgold* was one thousand yards ahead and slightly right. The *Dashiel* was behind by the same distance and slightly left. The screening ships were assigned sectors in degrees to search for submarines with their sonar. These sectors overlapped so that, theoretically, no submarine could penetrate the convoy undetected.

Mid-morning, October 25th, the *Dashiel* reported submarine contact off its port beam at 5,000 yards. The *Dashiel* changed course towards the contact and went to full power. The skipper sent a signal-light message to the *Resolute* with instructions to follow. They were to stay behind 2,000 yards and be prepared to drop depth charges or engage the enemy if the submarine surfaced. Lt. Skahill went to full power and followed at the assigned distance.

The Japanese commander realized that he had been discovered when sonar kept pinging on his position. He wanted to fire torpedoes at the convoy before taking evasive action to avoid the destroyers. He was giving ranges and bearings to the nearest escort carrier. His personnel at the attack plotter were recording the information to determine the azimuth required for the torpedo to strike the ship. The submarine commander was experienced and a true professional at his trade and was cool. Finally, he ordered, "Fire one…fire two…fire three….fire four…CRASH DIVE…CRASH DIVE…"

The *Dashiel* had been closing the range to the submarine. When the last torpedo left its tube, the destroyer's skipper could see the submarine's periscope. He gave a course change to the helmsman directly towards the periscope. They were less than a hundred feet away when it went under water. In a few seconds, the crew on the destroyer felt the impact when the ship's keel hit the conning tower of the submarine. Aboard ship, it felt like brakes had been applied due to scraping across the top of the submarine. Suddenly they were clear of the sub and the skipper called for a damage report.

The conning tower of the submarine had been nearly torn off and water was pouring in. The Japanese commander ordered, "Surface…Surface." Lt. Skahill, aboard the *Resolute* didn't know the submarine had been rammed. Suddenly he saw the sub coming to the surface to the right rear of the *Dashiel*. He shouted over the intercom, "Prepare to fire the port torpedo tube!" He gave a heading to steer directly towards the submarine. The Japanese sailors were attempting to get their deck guns firing. At two hundred yards, Skahill gave the order to commence firing the three-inch gun and the 20mm's. Almost simultaneously, the Japanese returned fire. A round from their deck gun landed off to starboard about two hundred feet.

At a distance of 300 feet, Lt. Skahill ordered, "Right ten degrees rudder. Fire the torpedo." Once the torpedo was clear of the tube, he ordered, "Right full ruder. Prepare to fire the starboard torpedo." As they turned broadside to the submarine, machine gun bullets were raking the *Resolute*. Two seamen on the fantail by the depth charge racks went down. A moment later, the submarine exploded just forward of the deck gun. The Japanese sailors there were blown into the water and the fantail of the sub started to rise. The torpedo had struck a disastrous blow to the submarine and in minutes it was sinking to the bottom.

The Japanese sailors blown off the deck were killed. One sailor on the fantail of the *Resolute* was killed and another was seriously wounded. Lt. Skahill had been hit in the hand but it was only a flesh wound.

Three of the enemy torpedoes had hit their mark and an escort carrier was burning out of control. All of the planes had time to take off and they were directed onto the other carriers. Once the survivors had been picked up, the task force commander ordered the damaged carrier sunk. He also sent his congratulations to the skippers of *Dashiel* and *Resolute* for sinking the submarine.

Les was pleased that he withstood his first time in combat without panicking. In fact, the ordeal had not bothered him in the least. He felt no fear and he enjoyed the excitement of the encounter with that enemy submarine. He was impressed with the skipper's proficiency of command in a combat situation. Every command was clear and concise.

Swicegood was in the engine compartment with him and he had a look of stark terror all during the ordeal. Les thought he might have been hit and said, "Are you all right?" Swicegood just stared at him as he held on to a stanchion for dear life. The reason for both Les and Swicegood to be assigned to the engine room was for backup in case one got wounded or killed. Les could see that Swicegood would not be able to take over if he was needed.

Chapter 10

USS RESOLUTE SHOOTS DOWN A P-38

L t. Skahill was pleased with the performance of his crew, which resulted in the sinking of the enemy submarine. The morale had improved noticeably with the exception of Swicegood. He was the only one who did not talk with enthusiasm about the event. In fact, he looked depressed and had lost his smart-ass expression.

Les considered talking with the skipper about Swicegood's performance during the event. He decided against it for two reasons. Swicegood might be okay when they got into combat again and Seaman First Class Hartwell, was a member of the engine room gang and capable of handling the engines. He was a lookout on the bridge during General Quarters and he could be moved to the engine room if necessary.

On October 28th, the *Resolute* received a signal-light message from the U.S.S. *Maryland*, convoy flagship. The text of the message was: *Detach from convoy. Proceed directly to unnamed island twenty-two miles northwest of Majuro Island. U.S. planes returning from bombing Japanese bases in the Gilbert Islands report sighting SOS signals flashed by mirror. Proceed with caution. May be a trick.* Within minutes, Lt. Skahill gave the order, "All ahead standard. Make turns for 25 knots. Maintain present heading." As soon as the *Resolute* was a mile in front of the convoy, the skipper said, "Come right to two-eight-five degrees."

The weather was beautiful and traveling at more than twice the convoy speed provided a cooling effect. It had been about four hours since they were out of sight of the convoy when the starboard lookout reported, "Aircraft...five o'clock...high." The skipper locked onto the single plane with his binoculars. He said, "It looks like a P-38." Seconds later, he said, "It *is* a P-38." They watched as the plane continued in a westerly direction. When it was off the starboard beam, it made a left turn and started to descend. It continued in this manner until it had reversed direction passing down the port side of the *Resolute* about a half-mile away. The ship's crew waved and cheered. The plane straightened out in an easterly direction but continued to descend. It was nearly a mile to the port rear quarter when it turned left again and lined up directly behind *Resolute* about a hundred feet in the air.

All the men on deck waved at the plane. When the P-38 was about a quarter mile to the rear, red flashes could be seen at the center of each engine. The skipper yelled, "He's shooting at us!" Each engine of a P-38 had a twenty-millimeter cannon mounted to fire through the center of the propeller shaft. Before the skipper could say another word, he was hit in the chest and knocked to the deck. Lt. Walters had started up from below decks when he heard all the commotion. He saw the skipper go down and he immediately sounded the general quarters alarm. Everyone was at their assigned locations before the P-38 lined up at the rear again. Walters gave the order, "Be prepared to return fire." Only the 20mm guns could be directed to fire to the rear. The three inch deck gun could only be fired from beam to beam across the front. The pilot must have known that because he made a steep left turn directly over the ship on his first pass. When the P-38 started firing at the *Resolute* again, Walters shouted, "Commence firing...commence firing." Bullets from the plane strafed the ship. Two men at one of the gun mounts were hit and Walters went down. He had been shot above the right knee.

The helmsman took a round against his steel helmet. The bullet hit the right side and glanced off but the impact knocked him down. As he fell, he turned the steering to full left rudder. The ship commenced a sharp left turn just as the P-38 was directly overhead. The pilot made a left turn again and in moments the three-inch gun crew had him in their sights. They fired three rounds in rapid succession and the third one made a direct hit. The P-38 blew up in a ball of fire.

Lt. Skahill and one 20mm gunner were killed. Mr. Walters had a severe leg wound and another 20mm gunner had been knocked unconscious with a shrapnel wound on his back. It was not serious. The two who died were buried at sea. Walters was confined to his bunk. After everything settled down, Walters called the two senior petty officers to his quarters, Phillips and Les. He informed them, "The *Resolute* will continue on the assigned mission. You two will take turns conning the ship. Baker, I want you to write a detailed description of the P-38 incident into the ship's log. Be sure to include the fact that I gave the order to return fire. When it is complete, bring the log to me and I will sign it." Les said, "Aye, aye, sir."

When Les brought the ship's log to Mr. Walters, he read it and said, "Very good," as he signed his name. He commenced to write a paragraph of his own into the log. *"Due to the loss of Lt. Skahill and the disabling wound of Lt.(jg) Walters, I hereby promote 1st Class Petty Officers Clarence Phillips and Lester Baker to the rank of Chief Petty Officer with a date of rank, October 28, 1943"* and he signed it again.

Les said, "Thank you, sir."

"Let Phillips see this log and I offer my congratulations."

"Aye, aye, sir."

Chief Lester Baker then said, "I have a bit of good news to report, Sir."

"What is it, Chief?"

Les smiled and continued, "Sir, during the incident of sinking the submarine, I was concerned about Swicegood's performance. He seemed gripped with fear and he couldn't perform his duty. Today he was completely in control and I believe we can depend on him. He seems to have lost his poor attitude as well."

"I am glad to hear that. I was concerned about him too."

As Les departed, he thought, here I am, not quite twenty years old and I am a Chief Petty Officer in the United States Navy. Who would believe it?

The change in Petty Officer Swicegood was remarkable. When he pulled his shift on the engines, he kept the entire area shipshape. He showed no animosity towards the new chief. The day after they were attacked by the P-38, Swicegood said to Les, "Thanks for not reporting my yellow streak during the sub attack. I don't think it will happen again."

"I don't think it will either. Let's see if we can get through this war alive."

Two days later their island destination came into view. Walters was

still hurting too much to leave his bunk. He told the two chiefs to circle the island a half-mile off shore and to be ready to return fire if fired
upon. They had the American flag flying and they were half way
around on the second trip when a bright flash reflected from the beach.
Chief Phillips could read code and he copied down:
a..m..e..r..i..c..a..n.....g..i. It could still be a trap. He flashed a signal
back. "Home town of the Red Sox?" Flashed back: b..o..s..t..o..n. He
flashed: "Home town of the Yankees?" Flashed back: n..e..w..y..o..r..k.
He flashed: LSMFT [lucky strike means fine tobacco]. Flashed back:
c..i..g..a..r..e..t..t..e..s

"That's it. They're Americans."

They rescued two naval aviators off the island. They were pilot,
Lt.(jg) Harry Ford and gunner, Petty Officer 1st Class Patrick Paulson.
Their plane, a U.S. Navy Avenger had been hit in the fuel tank on a
bombing mission. They had bailed out when they ran out of fuel and
landed just off shore. They had existed ten days on a diet of coconuts.
The two men had been tail-end Charlie on a bombing mission to the
Gilbert Islands. Lt. Ford tried to radio his dilemma to the flight leader
but he didn't get an answer. He figured later that he had been on intercom rather than transmit so no one heard him except the machine gunner in his own plane. They were most grateful to the crew of the
Resolute.

The time Lt. Skahill spent teaching Les navigation paid off. He fixed
their position with star sights and determined a course towards the projected position of the convoy when they would arrive in four days,
November 10th. He was conning the ship six hours on and six hours
off with Phillips. He was pleased that Swicegood and Hartwell were
doing a fine job with the engines so he did not have to be concerned
with them. The damage done by the P-38 had been repaired and he
wondered why the pilot didn't recognize them as friendly? He hoped
that the convoy had not changed course.

The *Resolute* rejoined the convoy in its original screening position.
Mr. Walters sent an encrypted radio message to the *U.S.S. Maryland*
reporting their success, the incident with the P-38, and a casualty
report. He was surprised when a message came back congratulating
them, not only for picking up the aviators but for shooting down the

P-38. The enemy had captured that plane. It had been joining up with American aircraft returning from bombing missions. Whenever a damaged plane fell behind, the enemy pilot shot it down.

On November 19th, the *Resolute* received another message from the *Maryland*. It confirmed the planned invasion of Tarawa Atoll the next morning. The *Resolute* was assigned plane-guard duty for the escort carriers during the invasion. This entailed steaming in close proximity to the carriers to retrieve downed American pilots. Just before dark, the escort carriers departed the main convoy to assume their assigned locations for the invasion.

Les felt excitement building up as he conned *Resolute* to accompany the carriers. He wondered what his folks would think of him conning a ship during an invasion. It seemed like ages since he left Bernardston. In the last letter he received from his mom, she said his dad had bought a 1939 Ford four door convertible with low mileage in good condition. She said he was out under the big maple tree polishing it while she was writing her letter. Les grinned to himself; he knew how enthused his dad got with a newly purchased car.

On that day before the invasion, Matt and Julie were busier than ever. He started his days doing the barn chores with Paul's help. After that, he helped Larry in the grocery store between daily management duties at the Inn. Julie kept up their large house, worked in the garden, bottled the milk from their cows, and managed three apartments. They had turned the upstairs front rooms of the mansion into a small apartment and there were two apartments in the two-story house they had built. The only meal Julie cooked at home was breakfast. They ate lunch and dinner at the Inn. When the chef was off, Julie filled in there, too.

They were both very tired at the end of each day, Monday through Saturday. Matt had insisted that they reserve each Sunday for themselves and that was usually the case. They left Paul with the chores and the two of them left early in one of their vintage cars for a day to themselves. Sometimes they packed a picnic lunch and other times they stopped at a country restaurant.

Matt and Julie both liked the scenic drive on Route 9 over Hog Back Mountain to Bennington. One Sunday during the winter, they had to spend the night in a ski lodge due to a heavy snowstorm. It had been fine weather when they left but clouded over and started snowing in Bennington. When they got on the mountain heading home, the snow was coming down so heavy they could only see a few feet in front of the car. It was mid-afternoon the next day before they got home.

Other times they visited friends or relatives at a nearby town. The men played horseshoes unless it was too cold. Then they sat in the living room and talked about horses, cars, or politics. Matt was good at horseshoes. He could throw a ringer one out of three times and sometimes as many as five ringers in a row. The women played Chinese checkers or gossiped while doing handy work. Those Sunday outings were a nice change for both, Matt and Julie.

Chapter 11

INVASION OF TARAWA, LESTER'S VIEW

*P*rior to 0500 hours the next morning, the Japanese shot a red star cluster into the air on Tarawa. Twenty minutes later the enemy gun installations commenced firing. The battleships in the attack force returned fire. The escort carriers were about three miles off shore. Les was on the bridge of *Resolute* and the sight was magnificent. The atoll was lit up with the continuous firing of the big guns and the invasion ships could be seen easily. There was a steady rumble like thunder that never stopped. Les was looking through his binoculars and he could see the Marines climbing down the sides of the transports and getting into the Higgins boats. After the boats filled with men, they circled, waiting for the signal to head for shore. American fighter aircraft were already airborne providing air cover in anticipation of being attacked by enemy planes.

They didn't have to wait long. At daybreak, the sky was full of aircraft engaged in mortal combat. Parachutes started to blossom with those who had lost their individual battles. One landed near the *Resolute* and it was an enemy pilot. He refused to take the line they threw to him. Les fired his forty-five pistol over the head of the man and pointed at the line. He still made no move to grab the line. Les fired again and the round hit the water right next to the man. He took the line and they pulled him in. He spoke English and admitted to attending the University of Southern California. They picked up two American pilots.

Les kept his binoculars trained towards the beach. The destroyers, cruisers, and battleships kept a continuous barrage on the atoll defenses. The Japanese sustained their return fire, seemingly with no lessening amount. At about 0900, the landing boats were heading towards the beaches. It looked like the water was full of them. Many Marines were dreadfully seasick in those boats. They had been bobbing around for more than two hours. Some boats received direct hits and sank in less than a minute. When the boats started dropping their ramps at the beach, the Navy barrage stopped. Planes were taking off from the carriers to bomb and strafe the enemy positions. Some of the boat coxswains dropped their ramps too soon and the men charged off the boat into deep water and drowned. The tank commanders applied maximum power to get out of the boats as soon as possible.

Most of the boats kept going until they scraped bottom before dropping their ramps. Marines were dying from machine gun fire before they were out of the water. Those who could make a fifty to one hundred foot run across the beach got some protection from a three-foot sea wall. There were two reinforced machine gun nests on the dock north of the Marines. They were raking the beach with 50 caliber projectiles and inflicting serious casualties. Les noticed a Higgins boat headed for the dock. The enemy gunners were so engrossed firing down the beach, they did not see the boat. When the boat arrived just short of the machine gun nests, two men with flame-throwers appeared at the boat rails. The murderous flames engulfed both machine gun nests and put them out of commission.

The Japanese defenses were made up of big block houses and lines of dug-in machine gun nests. These were cross connected with trenches of riflemen. There was a steady flow of bullets going over the sea wall. If a Marine raised his head, it was instant death. The American tanks climbed the sea wall and were effective blowing out the enemy defenses. Marines with flame-throwers followed close behind and applied their deadly flame to emplacements left and right of the tank. It was a bitter fight for every foot of ground, paid for in Marine lives. Men who lived through this battle would shed tears for the rest of their lives when they thought of those terrible hours. They would also wonder why they lived when so many of their buddies died. It was horror of a magnitude beyond belief.

Les had the ship's radio tuned to a tactical command net. The radio transmissions caused great frustration and anxiety to hear but they couldn't turn it off. They heard desperate requests for ammunition, a medic, or plasma. It never stopped and always in the background was machine gun fire, screams, and the noise of big guns going off. Suddenly, Les saw a huge ball of fire go up followed by billowing black smoke. A few seconds later, the sound of the explosion reached them. Apparently the enemy ammunition dump exploded. If any Marine there had been asked if the intensity of the enemy fire was decreasing, he would have denied it. Actually, it was by a considerable amount.

It was well into the third day before the battle of Tarawa was over. There were still some tunnels with Japanese soldiers who refused to come out. The flame-throwers relieved them of their fears. A few snipers were tied in the tops of coconut palms. Some Marines, who lived through the invasion, were killed by them. The sniper would immediately be shot out of the tree and they hung from their attached rope. Most of the enemy soldiers would not surrender because they believed that it was honorable to die for their Emperor.

The week following the invasion, the *Resolute* took on supplies and ammunition from one of the transport ships. Mr. Walters was transferred to a hospital ship and a Lt.(jg) Delvan Garrison came aboard as the new skipper. He was an Annapolis graduate and he seemed very trim and proper.

Two days later, the *Resolute* received a radio message from the flagship. The message directed its attachment to the U.S.S. *Tabberer*, DE-418. The two vessels would accompany three transport ships crowded with wounded Marines en route to Hawaii. Lt. Garrison announced the news over the intercom and the crew cheered with great enthusiasm. Their morale went into orbit.

Large red crosses with white backgrounds were painted on the sides of the hospital ships. At night, these crosses were illuminated to be plainly visible to enemy submarines, and the ships had their running lights on. Les wondered if the Japanese would honor the fact that they were hospital ships. Lt. Garrison apparently was thinking the same thing. He said to Les, "Chief, we will have a safe ride to Hawaii or we will be beautiful targets. I don't know which it will be."

The trip would have taken five days steaming at sixteen knots but they were zigzagging. This meant a course change every eight minutes.

In the event an enemy submarine did attack, the course changes would make a torpedo shot more difficult. It also added two days to the trip.

Everything was routine during the first two days. Mr. Garrison spent a lot of time reading the ship's log or looking into every compartment, including the bilge. He carried a small notebook and wrote in it frequently. At 0800 hours on the third morning, he told the two chiefs to have the ship's company, not on duty, fall into formation on the fantail. At 0815 hours, he stepped in front of the men who were standing at attention. Garrison said in a loud staccato voice, "Crew members of the *United States Ship Resolute*, PCS 715, this ship is an absolute pig pen. It will not remain a pigpen and action will take place with diligence to make the transition as soon as possible. When I dismiss you, I want all personnel in leadership positions to remain on the fantail. You are dismissed."

The formation broke up and the men walked away mumbling. Fifteen petty officers and three seamen first class remained. He then said, "Men, five days from today I will inspect the ship in detail. In the event that an area does not measure up to proper United States Navy standards, the particular leader responsible will be disciplined. Are there any questions?....You are dismissed."

Within an hour, one could hear the thump thump of paint being chipped off and the metal being wire-brushed. A lot of the superstructure above the main deck was made of wood and men were scraping the paint off all wooden surfaces. The torpedoes were being cleaned to be painted navy gray. Men were mumbling that they hoped a Zero would show up and burn Garrison's ass. During each meal, the men had never eaten with such gusto.

At night if they were not on duty, they were in their bunks sleeping. The all-night pinochle games stopped. By the third day, it seemed like everyone aboard ship was swinging a paintbrush. On the fourth day, the ship looked like it had just rolled out of dry dock with a complete overhaul. It glimmered in fresh navy gray and all the brass looked new. Arguments broke out as to what areas looked the best. A message was sent from the skipper of the *Tabberer*. *To C O Resolute. Have you traded for a new ship during the night?* The afternoon of the fourth day, Garrison told the two chief petty officers to have the ship ready for inspection at 0900 hours the next morning. The uniform for all hands would be whites with shined shoes. That evening, the men were sitting on the deck, in their sleeping quarters, or on their bunks polishing their shoes. They seemed in good spirits although worried how the inspection would turn out.

At 0900 hours sharp the next day, Lt. Garrison started his inspection. It took two and a half hours to cover the ship from stem to stern. In each area, he had specific questions for the man in charge. When he left that section, he complimented the job that had been done. He had Chief Baker pass the word to have all hands form on the fantail. Garrison stepped in front of the men and he said, "Crew members of the *United States Ship Resolute*, you have done a magnificent job of sprucing up the look of this great ship. It will be kept in this condition. In the future, all personnel above decks will be in the proper uniform of the day, including headgear. You are dismissed." The sailors departed once again, mumbling. They were not pleased with that last order but they were proud with how the ship looked.

Les learned something from the ship-cleaning ordeal. The men did the work and complained constantly, but they seemed pleased with the improved look of things. He noticed that they were now keeping the areas policed up. There were complaints about staying in uniform all day above decks, but they did it. He even heard two of the lower ranking enlisted men talking about how sloppy the crew on the *Tabberer* looked. Diligence made time pass quickly. It seemed like no time at all and the Hawaiian Islands were in view. The skipper had the word passed that all personnel would be in dress-white uniform for entry into port. Those without special sea details would be in formation on the fantail. Les looked at the men as they approached their anchor point in the harbor. Every man was standing proudly at attention and he realized the value of good order and discipline.

The day before they entered port, Seaman 2nd Class Calvin Hickenbottom, from the Bronx, shouted, "Crew members of the *United States Ship Resolute* 715, your ass is grass and I am the lawn mower! YOU HEAR THAT?" He was on the fantail and never dreamed the skipper could hear him. Lt. Garrison happened to be walking back on the fantail and about three steps behind Hickenbottom at the time. The other men could see the skipper and they were trying not to grin as they looked from one to the other. Hickenbottom said, "What in hell's the matter!" as he turned and saw Garrison. He immediately went stiffly to attention and saluted. The skipper returned the salute, smiled, and walked away. When he was out of sight, the rest of the sailors burst out laughing.

Les and Phillips went to the naval clothing store at Barber Point. They showed a copy of their official orders promoting them to chief petty officer and they received a complete set of uniforms. When Les looked at himself in the mirror at the store, he couldn't believe all that had happened in a few months. He and Phil returned to the ship to stash their new uniforms then signed out on liberty. It was Friday and the skipper had given them the weekend off for R&R. They rode the liberty boat to the fleet landing and took a cab to the Royal Hawaiian Hotel.

The hostess in the hotel restaurant was the most beautiful woman that Les had ever seen. She was tall, slender, with jet-black hair and olive skin. She had slightly slanted eyes, perfect white teeth, and a dimple in each cheek when she smiled, a Betty Grable figure and a low mellow voice. She enamored Les and he felt butterflies in his stomach as she led them to a table. As she placed a menu in front of them she said, "Your waitress will be with you in a minute." Les couldn't keep his eyes off her and he said, "Wow." She smiled showing those remarkable teeth, batted her eyelids at him, giggled, and walked away. Her hips had a most appealing sway as she took each step. When she was out of sight, Les said to Phil, "I don't think I'll be able to eat. For the first time in my life I think I'm in love." Phil laughed and said, "You're just suffering from too much sea duty."

The hostess had a name tag on which spelled Lilanii. Each time she appeared, bringing dinner guests to a table, Les froze keeping his eyes on her every moment. After seating the people, she looked over at him and smiled. He blushed, but managed to give a little wave with his hand. The food was excellent but Les was not aware of it. When they left the restaurant, Les said to Lilanii, "Is there any chance a sailor from Massachusetts could take you to a movie?"

She smiled and said, "I don't know you."

"How do I take care of that problem?"

"I go to church at the chapel on Fort Shafter each Sunday, eleven o'clock."

"I will be there."

Once he went out to where Lilanii waited for customers. She told him that her boss wouldn't like it if he hung around. He said, "Okay," and went back to the bar. The restaurant closed at 2100 hours and he walked to the men's room. He saw Lilanii leaving with an Army lieutenant colonel. He hoped that he was her father.

Les and Phil took a cab to the Anchor Bar and Restaurant in town. It had a large dance floor with a lot of pretty women available. The music was excellent with the Tony Martin Orchestra. Most of the ships were in the Pacific fighting the war so it wasn't nearly as crowded as Les thought it would be. Within minutes Phil was on the floor dancing with a beautiful native girl. When he came back to the table, he said, "Come on, Les. Get your mind off Lilanii and pick out a partner."

Les did dance three or four times, but he couldn't get his mind off Lilanii. Most of the couples on the dance floor looked as if they were glued together. Some were passionately kissing as well. Each time Les danced, he didn't hold the girl close and talked to her like she was his sister. He did not feel a physical attraction because the thoughts of Lilanii were always present.

The most popular girl in the room was a gorgeous blonde. When she wasn't dancing, there was a ring of sailors competing for her attention and obviously she enjoyed it. She frequently looked over at Les. He was not aware of her attraction to him with his thoughts of going to the chapel on Sunday. He was sitting there in his Chief's uniform looking as if he had stepped off a movie set. He, like many of the crewmembers aboard the *Resolute*, did push-ups, deep knee bends, pull-ups, and running in place nearly every day. He filled out his uniform perfectly, topping it off with a handsome face, light brown hair, blue eyes, and a neatly trimmed mustache.

The blonde excused herself from the men around her and walked away. They thought she was going to the ladies room. She went directly to Les and said, "Hey swabbie, is there room for me at your table?" As he got up, he bumped his table and knocked his beer over. "Sure. Have a seat." He thought, wow, she *is* a beautiful woman.

"I'm Melanie and it appears that your thoughts are elsewhere. Am I right?" Les blushed and she continued. "I'll bet you have a sweetheart back home. She wouldn't mind if you danced a little, would she?" Melanie's gregarious personality got Les talking. He finally asked her if she knew Lilanii. Melanie said, "Lilanii and I are good friends. We graduated from high school together. Has she stolen your heart?"

Les blushed, "I met her the first time today."

"Let me tell you about her. She is 21 and single. She broke up with her boy friend less than a month ago because he wouldn't take no for an answer. You know what I mean?" He nodded. "Her father is an Army lieutenant colonel and her mother is Hawaiian. He married her mother when he was assigned here years ago as a second lieutenant. Lilanii is what is known on the island as a "nice girl". If you are looking for someone to take to bed, you'll have to go to Mom's Tea Room."

Les had heard plenty about Mom's Tea Room. The crew aboard ship talked about their escapades there in the most descriptive terms. It was a whorehouse at an old hotel just outside the Fort Shafter gate. Les often wondered if the females who worked there would continue if they heard how the men talked about them. Each one had a derogatory nickname. Two of the deck hands were twin brothers. They shacked up with one of the whores all night. When they were not having sex in bed, they had her dancing the hula naked while they drank beer and watched. Les couldn't believe that they would boast about it, even in front of the skipper. Going to Mom's Tea Room did not appeal to Les in the slightest degree.

Melanie said that the girls he saw here would not leave with a man alone, but would go out as two or more couples. She said, "If you want to be alone with one of these girls, you will have to do some courting." They danced the last two dances of the evening together. Melanie wished him luck when she left with three of the girls.

On Saturday, Les was disappointed when he found out that Lilanii wasn't working. He and Phil spent most of the day snorkeling. They went to the Island Steak House for their evening meal and then headed for the Anchor Bar. At about 2045 hours, Lilanii walked into the dance hall with Melanie. Goose bumps came over Les as he smiled and waved. The two girls joined Les and Phil at their table.

Les and Lilanii danced every slow dance number. They barely moved their feet. Les held her close and he loved the smell of her perfume. He had never had the feelings for anyone that he felt for her. He liked her smile, her hair, her voice, her body, and her eyes. He knew he was in love and he would not be able to function without this gorgeous woman. Half way through the evening, he said, "Lilanii, do you believe in love at first sight?"

"Why do you ask?"

He continued, "If I have ever known anything in my life, I know that I love you."

She blinked, "My, you do move fast!"

Les blushed, "Please take me serious. I have never told anyone that before tonight."

She was obviously flattered and he did sound sincere. He felt her body relax more against his during the rest of the evening. When the girls said they had to go home, Les gave her a prolonged kiss. Finally, Melanie said, "Hey you two, we have to go!"

The U.S.S. *Tabberer*, DE 418

Chapter 12

RESOLUTE SAILS INTO A TYPHOON

The *Resolute* received sailing orders December 1. Once again, it was attached to the *Tabberer*, DE 418, and they were to accompany the same three hospital ships to Long Beach, California. The entire crew was happy except for Les.

He had been courting Lilanii and had even been to her house for Sunday dinner twice. He liked her parents and they seemed to like him. He realized that the sailing orders could have been worse. War in the Pacific was still raging and thousands would lose their lives before it ended. Les and Lilanii were deeply in love and when they were apart, he could think of little else. When they parted company the night before he left, a stream of tears rolled down Lilanii's cheeks. Les felt a tightening in his throat and he had trouble speaking.

While they were in port, replacements had reported aboard including a Lt.(jg) Barry Gregg. The skipper had been promoted to full lieutenant. It would take seven days cruising at twenty knots to reach Long Beach. The weather the first two days was nothing short of beautiful and morale aboard ship was high. There was a running dialog among the crew members detailing their liberties in Hawaii.

The morning of the third day, there were huge clouds on the horizon directly in front of them. As they sailed on, the clouds looked more and more threatening. The *Tabberer* signaled the other ships to increase spacing to two thousand yards or more. As they proceeded under the clouds, it was starting to get dark and the cloud bottoms looked black.

They did not know it, but they were entering into the center of a full-blown typhoon. The barometer had dropped several points in less than two hours. The sea had been getting more churned up until they were now dipping the bow under water at the bottom of each wave. The ship was also rolling from side to side 45 degrees each way. The skipper had ordered a speed of five knots to reduce the hammering they were taking. It was hard below decks trying to keep from falling. Half of the men were seasick and in their bunks holding on for dear life. Les and Swicegood had tied themselves to stanchions in the engine room to keep from being thrown against the bulkheads.

When the crew had rigged for rough seas, everyone donned their life preservers. All assigned positions on the bridge required each person to be secured to his station. Waves were washing over the entire ship.

The screws were coming out of the water when the bow went to the bottom of a wave. Each time, the ship shook violently. When a huge wave broke over the entire ship, the crew on the bridge wondered if they were sinking. Without the tie ropes, they would have been washed overboard. The helmsman diligently worked to maintain his easterly heading, but it was next to hopeless. The ship swung at least 30 degrees off course with each passing wave. They were being tossed around like a child's toy and it was as dark as night. In the compartments below deck, the men felt like they were in a box that was being shaken by a monster. Those who had taken to their bunks from seasickness were fighting to keep from being thrown to the deck. They were all moaning and groaning as their muscles ached from holding on to their bunks. The ship was making strange noises as it was being stressed to nearly breaking apart. Everyone from the skipper on down thought the ship would finally break up and sink.

It was more than two hours before the screws stopped coming out of the water. In another hour, the bow stopped going under and it was getting light again. Finally, the skipper passed the word to secure from heavy sea status and all divisions were required to make a damage report. One life raft had been torn loose and washed away, but there was no other serious damage. During the storm, all five ships had been scattered as much as five miles apart. When they reformed to continue towards the States, the crew of the *Resolute* could see that the main mast of the *Tabberer* had snapped off during the storm. Les wondered how the wounded aboard the transports came through it. It was after 1500 hours before the cooks were able to feed the famished crew. The next day, everything was back to normal.

December 7, 1943, two years after Pearl Harbor, the small convoy entered the port of Long Beach. Both the *Tabberer* and *Resolute* were scheduled for overhaul in dry dock. Both ships needed careful inspections for potential structural failure. Once the *Resolute* was in dry dock, the crew was moved into barracks and offered two weeks' leave.

Les got three different hops aboard military aircraft to arrive at Fort Devens, Massachusetts. He took a Greyhound Bus to Greenfield and surprised his folks with a call from the bus terminal. Matt and Julie were there to pick him up in their 39 Ford four-door convertible, twenty minutes later. It was the first time Les had been home since joining the Navy and his folks were overwhelmed seeing him in his chief's uniform. It was a happy reunion for the three of them.

Sam had been drafted into the Army and he was playing the trombone in Major Glenn Miller's military band. Rumor had it that the band would be going overseas, but they didn't know when or where. Les was shocked to learn that Charlie had joined the Marines and was with the 2nd Marine Division. The thought that Charlie was in one of those Higgins boats Les watched the day of the invasion gave him the chills. The look on his face made both of his folks say at the same time, "What's wrong, Les?"

He explained about the invasion, trying not to make it nearly as terrible as it actually was. The folks had not heard from Charles for weeks. The last letter they had received from him, he mentioned that he would be shipping out. There were no details and he said not to worry. They had not seen him since he left on the train for basic training at Paris Island. In one letter, he mentioned learning to use a flame-thrower and that it was a vicious weapon.

Les told his folks about Lilanii and that he planned to marry her. "Les, that means your children will be one quarter Polynesian. Are you sure you want that?"

"Dad, I love that girl with all my heart and that is all that matters to me. I hope it doesn't bother you and Mom." They said that it was fine with them if that was what he wanted.

Two other servicemen were on leave in town, Arthur Brown and one of the Deane boys. The three of them had a great time together. No matter where they went, they couldn't pay for food or drinks. They swapped uniforms one night for the fun of it. Les used his Dad's 39 Ford to come and go as he wished. He spent one evening at Mr. Latfield's house.

He told his folks that he would be at Latfield's for about an hour, but stayed there nearly four hours. Mr. Latfield was in his late seventies by now and he asked Les if he would like to hear the rest of the story about the McHenrys. Melissa was Latfield's niece and she had gotten a job performing at the Copa Cabana nightclub, which was owned by New York mobster, Frank Costello. She became his girl friend even though he was much older. He set her up in a furnished apartment. Everything went fine until she fell in love with Josh McHenry, the host at the Copa Cabana. They knew they were on dangerous ground with Costello.

When Mr. Latfield moved to Bernardston, Melissa called him and asked if she and Josh could join him after they got married. Josh kept returning to New York to work at his job. They didn't think anyone knew about his trips to New England or that he had married Melissa. He planned to work for at least six months to avoid suspicion. Mr. Latfield assumed that someone squealed on Josh and that is how they located Melissa. He also figured that Josh had met with a violent death. He had never heard from him.

A letter came from Charlie the day before Christmas. There wasn't much specific in it. He said that he was on a troop transport and that it was crowded with Marines. It was a hassle getting a shower when they were authorized one every three days. He thought that anything would be better than being aboard ship.

Les guessed that Charlie had written a day or two before the invasion of Tarawa. They were probably told to write so the letters could be gotten off the ship. Between worrying about Charlie and his thoughts of Lilanii, Les had a difficult time going to sleep each night. Every time his folks brought up the subject of Charlie and the invasion, Les tried to imply that he must have come through it okay. He said that they would have notified them by now if Charlie had been hurt. Les knew that it could take a long time to figure out who had been killed. It had been total chaos on the beach with units all intermingled. It didn't take a dead body in the tropics long to start decomposing. All the dead were probably buried in mass graves dug by bulldozers. On the other hand, Charlie might be all right, so he couldn't see making his folks worry needlessly.

Les phoned Lilanii and it took more than four hours to get through to Hawaii. Calls were limited to two minutes due to wartime priorities. It was a bittersweet conversation. He knew she started to cry when he hung up. He was supposed to start back to duty the day after Christmas. He called the skipper and got a week's extension. He finally left for the West Coast January 3, after a wonderful leave at home. There was no further word from Charlie.

Chapter 13

INVASION OF TARAWA, CHARLES' VIEW

Charlie joined the Marine Corps two weeks after Les left for the navy. He completed basic training August 22, 1943. He qualified as a Marksman with the M-1 rifle and qualified on the 50 caliber machine-gun and flame-thrower. His entire class was flown by military air transport to San Diego where it was assigned to the 2nd Marine Division. They were quartered in tents on the navy base. It was a boring interim with inspections, close order drill, classes on survival in the tropics as well as hand to hand combat training. Finally, the entire division was loaded onto transport ships.

Charlie found the conditions crowded on board and wished they were back in tent city. He stood in line to wash, eat, and take a shower. All the time he showered, the next men in line were yelling, "Hurry up with those showers." The shower wasn't refreshing because it was salt water pumped right out of the Pacific Ocean. He shared his bunk with two other Marines, each one having the bunk for eight hours a day. He had the 0400 to 1200 shift and it was difficult to sleep in that stuffy compartment which smelled like a sweaty locker room. He had no idea where they were going, but he would be glad to get there if it let them off the damn ship.

He had joined with Ray Bateman from North Adams, Massachusetts. They stayed together most of the time aboard ship. Ray had a great sense of humor with a knack of keeping those around him laughing. He pointed out that this would be a wonderful way to live if they had women Marines. He said, "When our turn came to have a bunk, you might not make the other marine get out. Those females would get a lot of volunteers to help them shower, too."

The convoy anchored at Hawaii for two days. When it departed to the southwest, several more ships were joined up. There was a ring of submarine detection ships around the perimeter of the convoy. Five escort carriers were now in the group. They were told nothing but it was obvious that they were part of an invasion force. After ten days at sea, ammunition was issued for their rifles. The men were told over and over again to keep their weapons clean. It was too crowded to have inspections. Charlie and Ray were designated as a flame-thrower team. The men were lined up in the order that they would load into the Higgins boats and told to stay in those positions. Sandwiches were passed out to them at mealtime; everyone knew that it was the eve of the invasion.

The next morning at daybreak, they started climbing down the sides of the transports to board the landing boats. The Japanese had already started firing heavy weapons at the convoy. The Navy ships commenced their barrage on the Tarawa atoll to soften up the enemy defenses. The noise was worse than a rock crusher and it didn't stop. The smell of burned gunpowder permeated the air. Ray and Charlie loaded into the fourth Higgins boat and they joined the other boats circling, loaded with Marines. They wondered how things could keep getting worse. They wanted off the ship and now they were seasick and wished for the crowded decks of the transport. Half the Marines got sick due to the boat's motion and the others got sick watching the first ones throw up. The smell was noxious, the boat deck became slippery, and they continued to circle.

After close to two hours, the boats received the signal to head for the beach. There were several boats ahead of the one that Ray and Charlie were on. The coxswain of their boat yelled that two enemy machine gun nests were blasting the marines who were on the beach. They were on the dock, north of the beach, in two sandbag pillboxes. A marine staff sergeant told the coxswain to head for the dock. He then yelled at the two teams of flame-throwers to get on the port side of the boat ready to fire. The boat got closer and closer and the Japanese were so busy firing down the beach, they didn't see the boat coming. The

The Pacific, 1945

This Japanese snapshot of an officer about to behead an Australian flier was passed hand to hand by GIs in the Pacific, and finally reached LIFE near war's end.

Sergeant waited until they were nearly in front of the enemy then yelled, "Fire...Fire...Fire." Both flame-throwers blanketed the machine gun nests with flames and put them out of commission. The boat continued on and dropped the ramp. The men ran for the sea wall where they were pinned down.

About half the men in that boat made it to the sea wall. The sergeant made it and he yelled, "Keep your heads down. We'll follow the tanks when they get here." Charlie looked back at the water and sure enough, tanks were coming across the beach. The sergeant said, "One flame thrower team and five riflemen behind each tank as it goes over the sea wall."

Ray and Charlie got behind the second tank and stayed close to it. As they came to machine gun nests, they blasted flames at them. Even with the continuous loud noise of the weapons firing, they could hear the screams of the enemy machine gunners. It would bother Charlie later, but right now, it was kill or be killed. A mortar hit the tank they were following and the right track came off. The tankers stayed inside and kept firing their weapons. Ray and Charlie stayed crouched down behind the disabled tank. If they had stepped to one side, it would have been instant death.

In about twenty minutes, another tank came lumbering close by and they got behind it. They were getting into the growth of coconut palm trees. They gave some protection, but there were snipers in some of the trees. Charlie felt a hard tug on the flame thrower hose and he looked back. Ray was on his knees and falling sideways. A sniper's bullet had caught him in the throat. He was dead before his face hit the sand Charlie yelled, "Oh no, Ray. RAY!" One of the marine riflemen shot the sniper out of the tree and said to Charlie, "I'll carry your gas bottle. Let's go or we'll be dead too."

The tank would stop for as long as thirty minutes until all the other tanks were on line, then they started ahead again. Finally it got dark and it was a welcome relief to both sides. There was sporadic firing through the night but nothing like it had been all day. Word was passed that the enemy would counterattack but that didn't happen. The men took turns sleeping for two hours at a time. They were all dead tired, dirty, and sick of the hell called war. Charlie thought about Ray and the hundreds of others who were killed fighting for a pile of sand and palm trees. Some of the wounded were moaning for help all night. At daybreak, they were on the move again. Enemy resistance seemed less intense; however, the Japanese refused to come out of their bunkers and surrender. A few of them had stuck their rifles into their mouths and fired them with their toes. Hand grenades and the flame-throwers were the only sure way to clear the enemy out.

It was three miserable days and two nights before they had taken the Tarawa Atoll with a heavy cost in American lives. The flame-thrower teams were about finished with their gruesome task. Charlie, like all the others, was filthy, dead tired, and hungry. He was wondering about all the enemy soldiers he had killed. He had never really considered the possibility of killing one human being up until three days ago.

During the last 72 hours, he had devoted himself to killing the enemy and he hated it. During the two nights, he would doze off then wake up dreaming of killing with his flame-thrower. He thought about home. It had been only a few weeks since he left, yet it seemed like an eternity. He wondered what his mom and dad were doing at that moment. He had dated Debra Puffer from Vernon, Vermont, for more than a year. He thought of the wonderful times they had enjoyed together and he could see her perfectly in his mind's eye. During the first night on that terrible island, he realized that he loved her very much. He decided he would ask her to marry him when this mess was over. He tried to imagine them with their own home and a couple of kids.

Guns fired sporadically through each night, but the worse part was hearing the moans and groans of the wounded. He wished the whole event was a bad dream. When he went through Marine basic and heard the talk about killing the enemy, he didn't actually think that it would come to this. He hadn't been ready for the loss of Ray Bateman. He could have had a long, enjoyable life and now he was gone. Was this small island in the Pacific Ocean really worth it?

Finally, the staff sergeant who came ashore with Charlie said, "PFC Baker, turn in your flame thrower at the supply point on the beach. You won't be needing it for awhile."

Charlie said, "Roger." He turned towards the beach and before he completed the first step, two shots rang out and Charlie fell face first in the sand. A sniper had put one bullet between his shoulder blades and another through his heart. Charlie had lived through one of the most fearsome battles in the history of mankind and the last enemy sniper killed him after it was over.

At the moment Charlie died, his mom was dusting his picture in the marine uniform. Julie said out loud, "That boy sure is handsome in his uniform." She placed it carefully back on the sideboard.

Chapter 14

LILANII IS CAPTURED BY JAPS

On January 5, 1944, Matt and Julie Baker received the message from the Defense Department that Charlie had been killed in action. They were devastated. Matt's brother Larry sent telegrams to Sam and Les. Sam was still at Fort Knox, Kentucky, and Les had just gotten back to the West Coast. They both got hops on military aircraft to Westover Field near Springfield, Massachusetts. It was a sad reunion for all of them. Paul, the youngest of the four Baker brothers appeared to be the most upset. He was sixteen years old and he loved and admired all of his brothers. Sam had ten days emergency leave and Les left after five days. Reverend Truesdale conducted a memorial service at the Goodale Memorial Church even though Charlie's body had not yet arrived home.

Sam Baker left the port of New York with the Glenn Miller military band February 24, 1944. They arrived in England eight days later. The band was entertaining the troops at military installations on a non-stop tour. When a band member complained about the routine, Glen pointed out that they were damn lucky. All they had to do was play instruments. The men they played for would be risking their lives and many would not live through the war. He would end by saying, "If you want a transfer to the infantry, put in the papers." None were submitted.

Les felt like his world had been turned upside down. Charlie was on his mind a lot and he dreamed about him at night. Some times the dreams were so real, he woke up thinking for a moment that Charlie was still alive. He wished that he had known his brother was in the invasion he had watched so closely. He might have been able to see him on the transport ship before the invasion. He thought of Lilanii too, but losing Charlie dominated his mind most of the time. Letters were slow between Hawaii and San Francisco. Getting a phone line was impossible. The *Resolute* was scheduled to be out of dry dock the end of February and Les hoped he would return to Hawaii.

His wish was not to be. They made two shakedown cruises to Catalina Island to check out all the modifications that were made in dry dock. Their orders then directed them to sail to Key West, Florida. They would be attached to the sonar school as a training vessel. At the time, Les wondered why they were installing the latest state-of-the-art sonar equipment in a PCS. The two torpedo launching tubes and the forward three-inch gun had been removed. In place of the gun, a device called a *hedgehog*, a weapon against submerged submarines, was installed. It was a rack of forward firing rockets. They were fired in unison at a specific range and landed in a widely dispersed pattern. The *Resolute* would be training sonar conning officers and equipment operators in the proper procedures to detect and sink enemy submarines.

That assignment was welcome to most of the crew, but Les wanted to go back to Hawaii. He asked the skipper if it was possible to transfer to a destroyer before the PCS left Long Beach. He said Les could apply, but he would recommend disapproval.

He said, "Chief, you are good at what you do and I don't want to lose you. I'm sorry." Les was down in the dumps for a couple of days. The skipper noticed it but he didn't say anything. He knew that Les was still having problems with the death of his brother at Tarawa. Three days later, he noticed that Les was out of his doldrums. He said, "Chief Baker, you look like you're back on the bright side again."

"Yes sir. When we reach Key West, I'm going to see about having my girl friend join me there. I'll probably propose marriage."

When Lilanii received the letter from Les proposing marriage and asking her to move to Key West, she was thrilled. Her parents were not pleased with the idea, but she was twenty-one. She looked into a way to make the trip, but every plane and surface ship was booked ahead for non-priority passengers. She put her name on the waiting lists and it appeared that it would be months before her turn came.

Her father was chief of staff for the commanding general of Fort Shafter. She asked him to help her find a way to make the trip. Her dad explained that travel space was limited and priorities always filled the manifests. He did know Nathan Haliby, the general manager of Pan American Airways, in Hawaii. He presented the problem to Haliby and it appeared that no seat could be made available. Two days later, Haliby called back and said, "We can list her on the manifest as a stewardess trainee for a flight to Los Angeles. She will have to perform those duties en route."

Lilanii was scheduled to depart on a Pan American Clipper flying boat on March 31. That was a 72,000lb aircraft with four 1,200 horse power Pratt & Whitney radial engines. It was an ideal aircraft for carrying heavy loads over long distances with the capability of landing in the water. She put a letter in the mail to Les the day before she left Hawaii. When she dropped the letter in the box, she thought, "I will probably be in Key West before the letter arrives." The next day, it was a tearful time leaving her parents. They had no idea when they would be back together again. Once she got on the plane, the excitement of the trip made her feel much better. The entire crew treated her well and one stewardess started briefing her on her duties. She noticed that men or women in uniform occupied nearly all the seats. There were four army nurses and one Red Cross lady.

An hour after Lilanii boarded, they were airborne. Once the plane reached twenty thousand feet, engine power was reduced to the normal cruise settings and it was much quieter inside. The weather was nice with a few high cirrus clouds. The aircraft was flying at 165 knots and it would be about an eighteen-hour flight to Los Angeles. At 1415 hours, they had been en route seven hours. The number three engine started running rough, backfired, and quit. In less than a minute, the other three engines started running rough, backfired in succession and they all died. They were losing altitude fast. The co-pilot transmitted, "May day. May day. Pan American Clipper, flight number 802, is in an emergency descent with all four engines stopped. Flight number 802 is seven hours out of Hawaii headed for Los Angeles." He continued to transmit that message over and over again. The pilot had the plane in a glide attitude to maintain 120 knots and they were descending at 1,500 feet per minute. He tried to re-start number two engine on the way down, to no avail. He had feathered the other three propellers to reduce drag. At 2,000 feet above the Pacific Ocean, he concentrated on preparing to land the aircraft. He started leveling the plane and decelerating forward speed at a hundred feet. He made contact with the water just as the aircraft was about to stall and made a perfect landing.

Attempts were made to start each one of the engines without success. Radio calls were made in vain to contact another aircraft. The maintenance chief climbed out on the superstructure to draw fuel from the number two-engine carburetor and he discovered that water in the fuel had shut down the engines. They were on the ocean about four hours when it started getting dark. An hour later, the navigator had made star sites to pinpoint their location. He waited two hours and repeated the process. He reported that they were drifting in a northerly direction at five knots. By morning, their position would be about sixty miles north of the regular air route to Los Angeles. They had shut down all electrical equipment and lights to conserve battery power. It was totally dark inside the plane and one could hear the waves slapping against the sides.

The crewmembers discussed their options. They decided to make radio calls at fifteen-minute intervals after daybreak. They would also attempt to rig a sail and establish a course for California. The prevailing winds were out of the northwest and they would make better time in that direction. They would use the plane's rudder to maintain a specific heading. Blankets would be tied together for a makeshift sail. Two of the fifteen foot docking staffs would be erected on top of the plane to attach the sail between. The next morning, it took close to four hours to get the sail of blankets erected. The huge plane immediately started moving in an easterly direction. The plane's rudder held the desired course. The navigator estimated the course for the rest of the day. He fixed their location by the stars that night and calculated an accurate course to steer for Long Beach. The first day, they averaged eleven knots per hour, which would put them in Long Beach in five to six days. The second day the wind stopped and they were drifting with the current.

Food and fresh water were in short supply. Fishing hooks and lines were found in the emergency equipment on board. Some of the passengers got busy fishing. They managed to catch some small fish with treble hooks. These were used for fish bait to catch larger fish. By the third day, everyone was eating raw seafood.

No one aboard the clipper was aware of it, but a Japanese submarine had come to periscope depth the morning of the third day. They were about a half mile distant when the submarine commander spotted the flying boat. At first, the commander was puzzled to see that big aircraft sitting dead in the water hundreds of miles from any landmass. He finally realized that the blankets strung between the poles were supposed to be a sail. It hung limp because the wind was calm. The commander lowered the periscope and discussed the situation with his officers. His operations officer wanted to fire a torpedo at the plane. That idea was rejected because the plane looked like a civil transport aircraft. They decided to surface an hour before dark close to the plane, man their deck gun, place two machine guns on deck, and then maneuver close enough to board the plane. If the people on the plane started to shoot, they would blow it out of the water.

The submarine surfaced less than two hundred feet from the plane at 1730 hours. The men fishing spotted the sub first and alerted the others. Everyone was hoping that it was American, but they realized that it was Japanese as soon as the deck gun was manned. In a few minutes, two machine gun teams were set up with the guns pointing at the plane. Once the sub got close enough, two sailors swung ropes over an inboard engine nacelle and pulled the plane and sub together. There were no defensive weapons aboard the plane so the passengers had to submit to the Japanese.

An officer and two sailors boarded the aircraft with pistols in hand. They pointed at each of the females, four nurses, the Red Cross woman, and three stewardesses. The officer motioned for them to go to the side door of the plane. The sailors pushed and shoved the women until they were on the submarine deck. Once they were all aboard, they were herded down one of the open hatches of the submarine.

They untied the ropes and pushed the plane away from the sub. The engines were engaged and the sub circled away. Once it was broadside to the plane and about three hundred feet away, they opened fire with the deck gun. The first shot fell short and a little left. The second shot went over the plane but was on line. The next three shots hit the plane and it blew up. The plane sunk in less than a minute. Some survivors were in the water alive with their life preservers on. The submarine moved closer and machine-gunned them. The plane's flight officer, Howard Evans had been an Olympic swimmer. When he realized that the Japanese meant to kill everyone, he slipped out of his preserver and swam under water as far as he could. He came up long enough to take a breath and went under again. He was the only survivor when the Japanese submerged.

The sub commander positioned the boat twenty-five fathoms below the surface and stopped the engines. The eight American women were forced to strip naked and participate in an orgy. Lilanii and the Red Cross woman were taken to the officers' quarters and experienced the same treatment there. At first the women tried to resist and were slapped and punched into submission. This continued for an hour and a half. The women were in stupors or unconscious. The Jap commander barked a command.

Each female was knocked in the head with a large wrench. Unconscious, they were slid into torpedo tubes and blown into the sea by compressed air. Not one survived.

Flight Officer Evans found several yellow life preservers which he fastened together. He fashioned a raft that measured four feet by fifteen feet. Being large allowed more chance of being seen by an airplane. The distress signal sent out by the clipper had been picked up. Two PBY search planes had been dispatched, but they had been searching south of the actual location. The day after the Japanese sunk the plane, the pilot in one of the PBYs flew north for an hour before heading back to Pearl Harbor. At the end of that leg, he banked left towards Hawaii and spotted the life preservers. Evans was on the way to Pearl in a few minutes. He lived to make a detailed report of an event that would be investigated by a board of inquiry after the war.

April 18, 1944, Les received the letter from Lilanii that she would be departing on March 31. When he read it, he let out a yell of delight that startled the crewmembers near him. He thought she would undoubtedly be there any day, possibly at any moment. He and Phillips went to Sloppy Joe's Bar on Duval Street to celebrate the good news.

Les found a small one-bedroom apartment with a balcony on the south side of town on Atlantic Blvd. He bought groceries and made the place ship-shape for Lilanii's arrival. He vacuumed and mopped the floors. He scrubbed the sinks and bathtub and purchased new pillows, sheets, pillowcases, and a bright flowery bed spread. The apartment hadn't been as clean since it was new.

There was an unobstructed view of the ocean and the wash of the waves on the beach could be heard at night. When he didn't have duty, he stayed at the apartment. He was anxious thinking about Lilanii joining him there. Each night as he sat on the balcony drinking beer, he knew that she would arrive the next day. He watched the evening sun set and he could hardly wait for her see to it with him. The sunrays reflected off the water to the high cirrus clouds and back to the water. He thought that the only thing on earth he had seen more beautiful was Lilanii. He bought fresh cut flowers every day for her expected arrival.

After a week went by, he started to be concerned. He went to the telephone office on Main Street and asked for assistance in making a call to Hawaii. In less than an hour, they had Lilanii's Mother on the line. She had trouble talking and then Les realized that she was sobbing deeply. Finally, she managed to tell him that the enemy submarine had captured Lilanii.

Les returned to the apartment. He grabbed the flowers and threw them off the balcony, vase and all. He fell on the bed and cried like a baby and kept saying, "Why, Lord? Why, Lord?" Two days later, Phillips found Les in the apartment passed out and smelling like a brewery. He looked terrible and he was almost incoherent. Phil walked him up and down the street in an attempt to sober him up. He eventually got him straightened out enough to take back to the ship.

Chapter 15

LESTER & PAUL IN KEY WEST

Paul Allen Baker was born January 6, 1928, in the Cushman mansion on South Street in Bernardston. Matt and Julie saw that he was exceptionally bright. He talked at eight months, walked at ten months, and could write the alphabet in the correct order at two years. He had an uncommon interest in books. Julie taught him to read his older brother's first grade books in his third year. By the time he was five, Paul was reading at the third grade level. He started first grade at Green School, one of the small district schools near the country store. His teacher, Lillian B. Richmond, recognized his advanced aptitude and moved him to the third grade after consulting with Julie.

At age twelve, Paul had completed the eighth grade with honors. Julie attempted to enroll him at Mount Hermon School for boys. The admissions department rejected him based on a standing rule requiring all freshmen be at least fourteen years old. Matt and Julie made an appointment with Dr. Howard Kirkendoll, Dean of Mount Hermon. He agreed to make an exception for Paul as a day student at an annual fee of $150.00

The academic load at Hermon taxed Paul's ability; however, he continued to stay on the honor roll. He did three to four hours of homework each night. His interest in school and overall attitude were outstanding into his senior year, until the family was notified that Charles had been killed in the war. It was as if Paul's switch had been turned off. No one thought much about it for the first few weeks. It wasn't unusual for a sixteen-year-old to react as he did. After four weeks, Matt tried to encourage him to concentrate on his studies again. He seemed unduly passive and indifferent.

No one in the family knew it, but Paul had tried to join the marines the day before his dad talked with him. The recruiter in Greenfield told him he had to be seventeen to qualify and then only with his parents permission. Two days later, the Navy recruiter called. When Paul answered, the recruiter said, "Are you Paul Baker?"

"Yes."

"If you are eighteen years old, I can sign you up in the U.S. Navy right away. Are you eighteen?"

"Well, I...."

"Are you eighteen or not?"

"Yes, I am eighteen and I'll be down tomorrow."

The next morning, he was on the Vermont Transit Bus headed for Springfield. The last thing the recruiter said was, "Don't forget your age and you were born in 1926." With a group of forty-eight men, Paul was taken to the post office building in Springfield. They received physical examinations, filled out numerous papers, and were sworn in as sea-men recruits. At four p.m., they were all on a train for Bainbridge, Maryland, for basic training. He mailed a note to his folks from Springfield to explain what he had done and asked them to refrain from trying to stop him. Matt and Julie got Paul's letter the next day. Their first impulse was to get him released due to his age. After a lot of dis-cussion, they decided to let it alone. At least he was in the navy, which seemed safer than the marines. Surely the navy would realize that he was under age and release him.

Paul completed eight weeks of basic training and he was assigned to the USS *Charles R. Ware*, DD-865, at Norfolk, Virginia. His orders indicated a six-month delay en route to attend sonar school at Key West. For the first time since he heard about Charlie's death, he laughed out loud as he read the orders. Les was at Key West.

Les had known about Lilanii's capture less than two weeks when Paul arrived. Paul found the *Resolute* tied to a dock at the fleet landing. He walked aboard, saluted the colors, the Junior Officer of the Day (JOD), and requested permission to come aboard. The duty petty officer was Chief Phillips and he said, "I'll be dammed. You look like Chief Baker."

Paul said, "Yes sir. He's my brother. Is he aboard?" The reunion was emotional for both brothers. Les signed out on liberty and they went to Sloppy Joe's. Les ordered a beer and a coke for Paul. Les told Paul about Lilanii. He said that he prayed every night that she was safe. He had checked out of the apartment, not being able to stand the place without sharing it with her. When Matt and Julie found out that the boys were together at Key West, they felt that Paul's joining the Navy was for the best.

When Paul reached the sea training phase in school, he was assigned to the *Resolute* each day. Les had asked the scheduling clerk for that favor. The brothers were together every night when neither of them had duty. On the nights that Les was JOD, Paul came aboard for the evening meal. Lt. Garrison noticed how the brothers got along as well as the improved affect on Chief Baker. He went to the sonar school commandant and requested that Seaman Baker be assigned to the *Resolute* when he graduated.

Paul had been promoted to seaman 2nd class when he graduated from boot camp. The sonar school had a test every Friday. He achieved a perfect score each time. He also studied the Navy's seamanship manuals to prepare for the thirteen examinations required to be promoted to seaman 1st. He completed the requirement and was promoted in three months. In another three months, Paul graduated from sonar school, first in his class. It was a great surprise when he received orders diverting him from the destroyer assignment to the USS *Resolute*, PCS 715.

During sonar school, Paul went to the USO Club when his brother had duty. There was always some activity going on there for the men in uniform. Many young ladies from Key West were usually present as well as some mothers to act as chaperons. They played table tennis, checkers, chess, and danced to records. Soft drinks and light snacks were furnished. Leaving the USO with a girl was not possible. About the closest thing was to be invited to one of the girl's homes for Sunday dinner. Paul's navy record indicated that he was eighteen, two years older than his actual age. He was attracted to a shapely blonde by the name of Yvonne Cannon. She was twenty and of course she thought he was eighteen. She made a concerted effort to teach him to dance and Paul enjoyed her company very much.

It wasn't long before he was invited to Yvonne's house for Sunday dinner. He was invited again and soon it became a routine. He stayed longer and longer each week until the evening meal was included as well. Yvonne had two older sisters, Janet and Marie. Marie, the oldest, played the piano beautifully and they all had great fun singing popular songs. Sometimes, all three girls and Paul went downtown to a movie. The first time, Janet said, "Yvonne, why don't you and Paul sit together in the back row? Marie and I will sit further down so we can see better." The two older sisters both laughed and went ahead into the theater.

In a few minutes, Paul and Yvonne were necking with enthusiasm and paying little attention to the movie. At the end of the show, he had more lipstick on his face than she did. When they got out in the lobby, she said, "Paul, you better go into the men's room and get that stuff off your face!" He blushed. "Okay."

During the time that Paul was at the Cannon house, he told them about his own family including the death of his brother, Charlie, and that Les was stationed right there at Key West. He mentioned the fact that Lilanii was en route to marry Les when the enemy captured her. After hearing the story, Mrs. Cannon said, "Paul, ask your brother to come with you for Sunday dinner next week."

Les reluctantly agreed to accept the invitation after a lot of urging by Paul. He had been spending his Sunday afternoons snorkeling with Phillips. Key West beaches were some of the best in the world. The water was crystal clear and full of a wide variety of fish. The different species varied from pure white to every color imaginable. Les and Phil had chipped in together to buy a rubber boat which they rowed out to the coral reef.

Before Les' first Sunday visit was over, the two older sisters had him laughing, singing, and thoroughly enjoying himself. He had a natural ability for singing harmony and he was a big hit with the entire family. Both boys were invited the next Sunday and it was obvious that Les was more than willing to accept. Mrs. Cannon was a persuasive lady and before long, the brothers were attending church services too. Paul noticed a change for the better in Les. He talked less about the loss of Charlie and Lilanii. Marie could sing and play the piano equally well and Les enjoyed harmonizing with her. It wasn't long before Mrs. Cannon had them singing specials in church. The boys felt like members of the family and it was seldom that Les went to the chief's club to drink beer.

Within the first three months of Les joining the family gatherings, it was clear to everyone that he and Marie were sweet on each other. When they sang a special at church, the glances they gave each other were of love and affection. Les wanted to buy Marie an engagement ring, but the thoughts of Lilanii made him feel guilty. He discussed the dilemma with Paul and Phil. They both gave him the same message. It was most likely that he would never see Lilanii again.

The Japanese treated American prisoners of war cruelly. Information and pictures had been smuggled out to the States describing the inhumane treatment doled out to allied servicemen. The stories told of starvation, beatings, and murder by public beheading. *Life* magazine published some photos of the brutality.

Marie was twenty-four and she worked at Music Unlimited in town. She taught piano there as well as being a sales person in the store. She owned a 1939 Buick two-door sedan. As time went on, the two of them along with Paul and Yvonne double dated in the Buick. Les drove her car and the last stop most evenings was at a secluded spot near the boat docks. A couple of times, Les tried to take Marie parking when the two of them were alone and she refused to let him. When he asked why, she said, "You know what will happen and I won't be able to wear a white dress at our wedding. Please, Please don't ask me to do that again." Les was disappointed but he went along with her restriction.

Les bought her a beautiful diamond ring for $128.00 at the Base Exchange. She was thrilled and she went straight home and showed the family. They were happy, too, and all of them wanted to know when the wedding date would be. Les and Marie picked April 11, 1945.

Marie wanted to buy her wedding dress in Miami. It was a hundred and fifty seven miles to the city on US-1 over many miles of narrow bridges connecting the Florida Keys. She had driven there once and vowed that she would never do it again. Each time she met an oncoming truck or bus, she was terrified. Les offered to drive her, but she said she didn't want him to see her dress until the wedding day. She said, "I'll ride the early Greyhound Bus next Saturday and be back on the bus late that night." Both of her sisters were busy on that day so she went alone.

Those bridges were extremely narrow. When one rode a bus and looked out a curbside window, it looked like the bus was riding on water. The guardrails could only be seen by pressing one's face against the window and looking straight down. The driver had to stay alert constantly to keep his bus on his side of the bridge while not side-swiping the guardrail. Marie was on the six a.m. bus just two weeks before her wedding day. Five hours and fifteen minutes later, the bus arrived at the terminal in Miami. She took a cab to the New Elite Restaurant on First Avenue for lunch. The restaurant was a short walk from the Wedding Boutique. It took more than three hours to select her dress, accessories, and have the dress altered. She went to Edward's Jewelers, 38 NE First Avenue, and picked out matching wedding rings. Each ring was inscribed inside, *forget me not.*

She took a cab back to the bus terminal and there was enough time for a sandwich and coffee at the snack bar. The bus departed a few minutes after six p.m. for Key West. After the stop at Key Largo, Marie tilted her seat back and dozed off. When she woke up, it was dark and she noticed a sign, "Marathon 28 mi." She was sitting three rows back from the front and she heard the bus driver complaining about the on-coming vehicle with headlights on high beam.

Suddenly, she heard him yell, "The damn fool is in the middle of the road!" The bus started rubbing against the railing and the driver was blowing his air horns and applying the brakes. Seconds later, the car hit the left front corner of the bus, glanced off and the two vehicles passed one another. The impact had driven the bumper on the bus against the tire and it blew out causing the bus to swerve across the road against the opposite guardrail at a forty-five degree angle. The speed and weight of the bus broke the rail easily and it went into the ocean. The two-piece windshield popped out when the bus hit the water nose first.

The screams of the passengers lasted a few seconds until the bus filled with water and sank twenty feet to the bottom. The driver and four sailors were the only survivors. The driver of the car was a drunken seaman 1st class off the submarine, *SailFish,* stationed at Key West. His car, a 1939 Hudson, rolled over and blocked both lanes when it came to rest. He had been thrown out and was crushed to death.

Chapter 16

DOROTHY LANE IN LOVE WITH LES

On April 30th, 1945, it was believed that Adolf Hitler committed suicide in his Berlin bunker. His last official act was to designate Grand Admiral Karl Doenitz to succeed him as chief of state. Doenitz sent General Alfred Jodl, as his representative, to sign Germany's unconditional surrender at Eisenhower's headquarters in Reims, May 7th, 1945. May 8th was designated VE Day. Twice in the twentieth century, the United States of America had sacrificed hundreds of thousands of American lives to save England and deliver France back to the French, Holland back to the Dutch, Poland back to the Poles and Denmark back to the Danes.

The end of World War II came when the Japanese agreed to unconditional surrender on August 14, 1945. Vice-president Harry S. Truman had become President of the United States after Roosevelt's death. Truman made the decision to drop the first two atomic bombs. Each bomb killed thousands of people and led to the war's end. The requirement to invade Japan's homeland was avoided; which most military minds believed it would have taken several hundred thousand lives on both sides.

Les and Paul were both discharged from the Navy on September 1st, 1945. Les had gone through a terrible time during the months following Marie's tragic accident. He had stayed sloppy drunk for days and no one could get through to him. He kept mumbling that he was a curse to the women he loved. If Lt. Garrison had not had a great amount of tolerance, he would have been reduced in rank and sent to the brig. The wedding rings that Marie had bought were found and Mrs. Cannon gave them to Les. He wore them both around his neck with his dog tags.

The relationship between Paul and Yvonne had been dampened considerably due to the bus accident. Life for her had been wonderful up to that point. Even the war had been distant to her because she knew no one directly involved in the fighting. Her sister's death slammed her into reality with no notice and she was having a hard time trying to cope. The fun times Paul had experienced at the Cannon house did not return. The month before he was discharged, Paul had seen Yvonne three times, including the day before he left. They both promised to write.

The two brothers arrived at the Greenfield railroad station on September 4th and their folks were delighted to have them home. There was a gold star on a red, white, and blue banner hanging in the living room window signifying the loss of Charlie at Tarawa. They had received a letter from Sam and he was to be released from the Army the first of October. Sam had written that he was saddened over the loss of Glenn Miller a few months prior to the end of the war. Miller departed England by plane on a trip to France in bad weather. It didn't make its destination and was never found.

The Navy Department expended the time and money necessary to determine the fate of the eight women captured by the Japanese submarine. Captain Sado Asanuma commanded the submarine. He and his crew survived the war. Lengthy interrogations produced the criminal facts in detail. The captain and his officers were executed and the crewmembers were given life in prison at hard labor. The families of the women were notified that, *"their loved ones died in captivity"*.

A few days after he got home, Les learned that Hershall Latfield had died during the summer. Mr. Stoddard, a lawyer in Greenfield, called and told him that Latfield left everything he owned including his savings and checking accounts to Les. He was stunned and said. "My God! I can't believe it. How much money did he have?"

"Ah. Let me see here… Yes, here it is. The combined total in cash is two hundred fifty-eight thousand, three hundred forty-three dollars, and nine cents. I need you to come to my office to sign the papers necessary to transfer the assets to you." Les felt an enormous mental lift due to Latfield's generosity. Three people he had cherished died tragic deaths. He had a dismal outlook on life that he couldn't shake. The news from Mr. Stoddard was like a shot in the arm of a miracle drug.

Paul Baker was honorably discharged from the Navy as a sonarman 3rd class before his eighteenth birthday. He and Les had developed a very close relationship while they were together at Key West. Paul never gave up trying to lift his brother's spirits after the bus accident. Les was aware of his brotherly dedication. He invited Paul to move into Latfield's house with him. Les had received the 1932 Packard and a 1939 Chevrolet four-door sedan as part of his inheritance. He gave Paul the Chevy and Les bought a 1941 Lincoln for his personal car. Mr. Lunt in Greenfield had owned it and it was in excellent condition. The gas mileage was poor at 12 miles to the gallon, but that didn't bother Les. Texaco high-test gas was only eighteen cents a gallon.

Les frequented the Hollywood Inn and the Chase House to drink and eat most evening meals. Both establishments were in north Bernardston. Bill Forbes and his wife at the Hollywood served as fine a meal as could be purchased anywhere in the area. He didn't go to the Bernardston Inn very often because his dad owned it and they always insisted that he not pay for anything. Occasionally he drove to Greenfield and ate at Bill's Restaurant on Federal Street. He loved their fried clams. He always sat at the bar before ordering off the menu. He usually drank a beer followed by two Bloody Marys. Mike, the bartender, had the latest funny story to tell plus the atmosphere was great. It was a most relaxing event and the food couldn't be better.

There was dancing to a jukebox at the two places in north Bernardston. Single girls and boys from the local towns filled both places each Friday and Saturday nights. Les enjoyed dancing but he tried to avoid becoming attached to any one girl. Sometimes the bartender would say that he noticed a particular female was all eyes for Les. He would not look at that girl or dance with her again. Dorothy Lane, a very pretty girl from Newfane, Vermont, was attracted to him. She tried her best to get his attention, to no avail. After what happened to Lilanii and Marie, he would not let himself get seriously involved.

Les left the Chase House if Dorothy was there. He would drive south down route 5 to the Hollywood. In a few minutes, Dorothy and her girl friends would show up. Les would finish his beer and drive to the Moose Club in Greenfield. He developed a routine that confused many a nice looking female. He would make a dinner date with a girl, take her dancing after they ate, drive to the pumping station for some passionate activities in the car, take her home, and never ask her out again. He never took one to his home on Hoe Shop Road because of the talk it would cause. He didn't want to offend his parents.

The first winter after the war, Les couldn't decide what to do with his new found wealth. He banked most of the money in a savings account at the Franklin County Trust Company and he maintained a checking account with a balance of a thousand dollars or more. He wanted to be busy at something, so he took a job as a mechanic for Spencer Brothers' Ford in Northfield. The starting pay was $40.00 a week. Les wouldn't work Saturdays because he had things to do at home. In two months, the Spencers gave him a raise to $50.00 then gave him a hundred-dollar bonus at Christmas time. He had been turning out twice as much work as any two of the other mechanics.

Les contacted Jarvis Construction in Turners Falls for a bid on a three-stall garage to be built on his property. After working out the details and cost, the job was scheduled to start as soon as the frost was out of the ground. Les decided to look for old cars to restore and the garage would provide the place to do it. He gave Spencer Brothers notice that he would terminate his employment on June 1st. They immediately offered him a pay hike to $75.00 a week, if he would stay. That was more money than they had ever paid.

Soon after he had gone to work for Spencer's, Dorothy Lane showed up for a tune-up on her 1937 Ford convertible. She told the service manager that she wanted Les Baker to do the work. She stayed nearby while Les made the repairs. He was distracted by her because of how beautiful she looked and she kept asking him questions. She was in high heels with silk stockings and the bottom of her dress was knee level. Les thought that he had never seen prettier legs on a woman. Her bosom was a perfect size for the rest of her body and she had a low cut dress. Les was tightening a spark plug when Dorothy said, "Les, will I get better gas mileage after this tune-up?" He looked up from his work. She was leaning over with her elbows on the car fender. He could see her full cleavage. He blushed and looked back at the spark plug and said,

"Yes, you will probably get a little better gas mileage. Would you mind waiting in the office area for me to finish this job? You might get hurt."

"Oh…Okay, I'm sorry. I've been a nuisance, haven't I?" Les heard the clicking of her high heels as she walked away.

Dorothy worked in Brattleboro and she had Wednesday afternoons off. Each Wednesday she drove into Spencer's yard and said there was some problem with her car. She insisted that Les do the work. "I think my tire pressure is low…I can't seem to get the top down. I think my fan belt is loose…my engine is making a funny noise … One of my tires needs balancing." She would be dressed like a New York model and always tell Les how smart he was. All the employees at Spencer's would start grinning when they spotted the car driving in the yard. He took a lot of kidding about it. Tom Russell, who also worked there said, "Les, you need to take that car out at night with her in it and see if it parks properly. If you do that, you won't be bothered with these Wednesday visits." Two other mechanics heard the comment and all three men burst out laughing. Les grinned, blushed, and said nothing.

Les finally decided that the way to stop this embarrassing situation was to ask her out for a date. He took her to dinner at Bill's restaurant. They had a couple of gin and 7ups before ordering. During the second one, he said, "Are you aware of what you are doing coming to Spencer's every week?"

"Yes. I am trying to date a guy that I like very much."

"If I take you out one night a week, will you stop coming to Spencer's?"

"If you take me out one night a week, I know that I will forget how to find Spencer Brothers' Garage in Northfield, Massachusetts."

"I don't expect to see you this next Wednesday." She lifted her glass, He lifted his and said, "No more Wednesdays!"

By the middle of June 1946, the garage was finished with a full basement. It was partitioned off with a wood burning furnace on one side and a lounge, toilet, and shower on the other. Les stocked the garage with the best automotive repair tools available. One stall was partitioned off exclusively for painting. Les remembered during his years in school Mr. Packard's words, "If you want professional results, don't mix painting with other automotive work."

The entire facility cost Les a little over $23,000.00 and it was a great feeling to be able to write a check for the full amount. He talked with Mr. Haigus at the bank about investing most of his money in something with a better return than the 3% his savings account paid. From that conversation, Les bought shares in the amount of $70,000.00 each in General Motors, General Electric, and Sears Roebuck. That left him nearly $45,000.00 cash on hand for running his business. He hired Paul at seventy-five dollars a week, his room and board, and ten percent of the profit netted on each car they sold. That was tremendous pay for anyone in those days and Paul was only eighteen.

Les put ads in *the Springfield Union* and *Boston Globe* advertising for restorable old cars. The first car he bought was located in Ayer, and it was a 1926 Model-T station-wagon. The wood was in excellent condition and there was very little rust. It was in a hay barn covered with dust with four flat tires. He bought it for fifty dollars.

He was taking Dorothy Lane out regularly every week, usually on Saturday night. He never asked her out more than once a week. She asked him several times if she could come by to see his garage. Each time he answered that she must wait until it was finished. Finally he agreed to let her come by on a Saturday afternoon. He and Paul had just finished cleaning up and had put away the tools. Paul immediately excused himself and left for the house. Les gave her a tour of the upstairs, which took about five minutes. She said, "What's down there?" She pointed at the stairs.

She was really impressed with the lounge. She put her arms around his neck and kissed him passionately. He wrapped his arms around her waist and pulled her tightly against him. After a few minutes they sat on the couch and entwined themselves together again. She broke off their kiss and whispered in his ear, "I love you, Les." She attempted to kiss him again and he pushed her away and got up. She said, "What's wrong? What's wrong?"

"You need to go."

"What did I do?"

He went into the bathroom, shut the door, and locked it. She started crying hysterically and yelled, "I don't understand you at all. What kind of a guy are you, anyhow? I thought you were falling in love with me." She ran up the stairs and out to her car. She drove out of the yard with tears rolling down her cheeks.

Les showered and shaved and went to the Moose Club. He woke up the next morning with a terrible hangover. He couldn't remember how he got home. With a throbbing headache, he managed to get downstairs to the kitchen. Paul poured him a large glass of tomato juice. Les drank the whole thing right down. Five seconds later, he jumped up and ran for the toilet. He threw up the juice and dry-heaved for several minutes. Then he flopped down on the bathroom floor. Paul checked on him about a half-hour later and he was asleep. An hour and a half later, Paul was having another cup of coffee and reading the Sunday paper. He jumped and almost fell over backwards when he heard Les suddenly yell, "PAUL! How did I get home last night?"

"Two of your Moose buddies brought you home. We had a hell of a time getting you in bed. You kept mumbling the same thing you said in Key West. I'm a curse to the women I love. Are we going to have to go through another spell of you getting drunk every night?"

Chapter 17

THE KOREAN WAR

During the summer of 1947, Les bought a new dark-green Lincoln V-12 convertible. He couldn't believe it drove so much better than the old one. He and Paul had restored eighteen cars since he opened for business. They made a good profit on all of them except the first two. Both those vehicles came out fine, but they were not popular models. He still had the Model-T Ford station wagon. His Mother had driven it in the last two Memorial Day parades.

Paul attended Mount Hermon and graduated with honors. He had considered going to college, but he liked working for his brother in the new garage. He had become so proficient painting the reconditioned vehicles; Les had turned that phase of the operation over to him. Les told him that all the other work was important, but it is an excellent paint job that sells the car. Each one looked like it had just rolled out of the factory.

Dorothy had bumped into Paul at Sears in Greenfield and they had a long talk. He explained why his brother was skittish about getting serious with another girl. She called Les a week later without telling him about her talk with Paul, and asked if they could go out occasionally. He said that he thought it would be okay and they went to a dance or a movie about three times a month. Paul found Les much easier to work with after he went back to dating Dorothy. He didn't drink nearly as much either.

In the fall of 1948, Paul traded his Chevy for a new 1949 Mercury two-door sedan. It was a new body style with the fenders integrated seamlessly into the car's design. It was built lower to the ground and held the road on corners much better. For the first several months, it pleased him to see people look at the car wherever he went. He and Yvonne Cannon had written back and forth for a couple of years, but he had not heard from her in a while. He had been dating Beverly Stokes from east Bernardston for nearly a year.

Les struck up a friendship with John Hodgeskins. He had moved to town with his parents and lived on Depot Street across the road from the train station. The two of them often went to look at an old car that had been advertised for sale. He had talked Les into joining a reserve US Army combat engineer battalion in Springfield. Paul couldn't believe that his brother would join a reserve unit. Les had to attend a six-week intensive course at Fort Dix, New Jersey to learn how to be a soldier. They did promote him to master sergeant when he completed the training. They had to spend one weekend a month at the unit in Springfield and two weeks of summer camp at Fort Dix, but Les did look sharp marching in the Memorial Day parade.

On June 25th, 1950, North Korea invaded South Korea with intentions of unifying both into one nation. Problems had been smoldering between the two since they were liberated from Japanese control in 1945. The Russians and Americans had designated the 38th parallel as the dividing line between North and South Korea. The north under Russian influence became a communist nation. The result of the invasion eventually put US Forces in a so-called "police action"; however, the troops who fought in Korea resented that label. For those who served it was war in its purest sense.

The engineer battalion in Springfield was activated with orders to Fort Dix, New Jersey. Les was bewildered. He had joined the unit for two reasons: his friendship with John Hodgeskins and the fact that he wanted to learn to use heavy equipment. It never crossed his mind that they would ever go to war. Paul mentioned joining up so he could go too. Les flew into a rage, saying, "Like hell you will. You are staying here and running this business. If I find out that you joined after I leave, you will never work for me again." The 79th Engineer Battalion was flown out of Westover Field aboard Military Air Transport Command aircraft for refitting and combat training. It was a heartbreaking event for the entire Baker family.

After arriving at Fort Dix, a board of Army officers evaluated the organizational status of the unit. It was short on commissioned officers and overstaffed with master sergeants. Les was one of five selected for a direct appointment to second lieutenant. The next two months consisted of rigorous combat training. It was tough on every person in the unit, but it would pay off once they reached Korea.

The 79th Engineer Battalion was attached to General Walker's 8th Army and joined up with those forces south of Pyongyang on the West Coast of Korea. It was the end of October 1950, and the U.S. Forces were not aware that large numbers of Chinese soldiers were crossing the Yalu River. MacArthur had bragged to President Truman at Wake Island, October 14, that if the Chinese dared to cross the Yalu, they would be slaughtered. He believed that they were incapable of effectively engaging a modern equipped military force. He planned to attack north, take Pyongyang, and the North Koreans would sue for peace. He stated that, "Our troops will be home for Christmas." By November, 300,000 Chinese had crossed the river undetected.

The Chinese were well aware of their lack of air power and modern equipment. Their strategy was to fight on their own terms. Their units occupied the hills over-looking the roads that followed the narrow valley floors where a modern military force would have to travel. They planned a huge ambush near the Chongchon River. They hid during the day and traveled at night carrying all their equipment with them. The Allies continued to underestimate the Asians' determination, dedication, and ability. Once the Chinese did attack, the size of their force was estimated at less than a quarter of its actual size.

The first ambush that the 79th Engineers experienced was devastating. In a matter of minutes the convoy of trucks and equipment could not advance or retreat. The bullets and mortars rained down upon them from above and there was no real cover for the troops. Flat open terrain was only a half-mile behind them, but they couldn't turn around. It was obvious to all the troops that they were in a trap. A trailer truck behind Les' jeep was on fire. There was a large dozer on the trailer. Les ran back and climbed onto the dozer seat. Once he got it started, he drove it off the trailer and immediately pushed the truck and trailer off the road. Then, he headed towards the rear and started pushing another disabled vehicle out of the way.

Other men followed his lead and they cleared the way to retreat. Vehicles were turning around, and the convoy started to inch back out of the valley and out of harm's way. Nearly half of the men and equipment were lost before they managed to evacuate the area exposed to the intense fire from the Chinese. Staff Sergeant John Hodgeskins was one of the casualties. He and two of his men were killed by machine-gun fire.

Other 8th Army units were coming out of the valley including tanks and armored personnel carriers. They fared much better than the Engineer and Infantry units. Defensive lines were set up along a wide front facing the north. If the Chinese attacked the new positions, allied air support would provide a cover. Once again, the enemy fooled them by attacking with mortars at 0300 hours two days later. Under the cover of darkness, they set up all along the defensive front. They maintained a barrage of mortar fire for thirty minutes and raised havoc among the American troops. By daylight, they were back in the hills. It was frustrating and demoralizing for the 8th Army troops.

Les knew his battalion commander personally. Lt. Col. Jankowitz had purchased a restored 1932 Model-B Ford from him a few months back. Les asked him if he could take a ten-man patrol with him after dark. The idea was to locate the Chinese positions and radio back the coordinates for air attacks. He planned to locate a spot to operate from in the mountains and scout from there each day. Jankowitz said, "Les, you have already earned a Silver Star for your performance during the ambush. Are you sure you want to go on what is actually an infantry type mission?"

"It sure beats sitting here waiting for a mortar to drop in my lap. We need to give them something to worry about."

The eleven-man patrol left that night with rations for a week, a radio, personal weapons, and one Browning Automatic Rifle (BAR). It took more than two hours to reach the foothills. They found that it was difficult to impossible to walk quietly in the thick woods once they were in the hills. They decided to get some sleep and attempt to find a secure place in the morning. By mid-morning the next day they found an ideal location. At the bottom of a steep ledge, there was a natural cave that was not apparent until one was a few feet in front of it. They made radio contact with their base and spent the rest of the day improving the cave for their operational quarters.

At first light the next morning, two four-man patrols departed the cave. Three men stayed at the cave with the radio and BAR. Les took one patrol and headed northeast. Sergeant First Class Burrows, from Hatfield, took the other and they headed due north. Both patrols were back at the cave before noon. Each had located large numbers of Chinese camped in the woods. They radioed the encoded information to their base operations. In less than an hour, aircraft were bombing and strafing both locations. That night, the Chinese did not mortar the American units. The two scouting parties went back to the same locations the next day. Both units had moved and it was easy to follow their trails. The Chinese unit to the north had gone west about three kilometers and the other had moved east-southeast about five kilometers. Les estimated each unit to be of division size. Back at the cave, the new locations were radioed back to base and soon navy Sky Raiders were attacking once again.

After the second attack, the Chinese perceived that they were being scouted by allied patrols. The bombers were accurate and they knew they were not visible from the air. They sent out their own patrols and found where Les and his men had taken a smoke break. The U.S. Amy combat boot had a diamond print on the sole and the cigarette butts were on the ground. The Chinese backtracked the trail for quite a distance and then set up an ambush in case the Americans came again.

Just after 0800 hours the next morning, Les and his men walked into the trap. All four went down with the first volley. Two of the men were killed instantly. Les and PFC Shores were both wounded. Shores got hit in the left side and he was in a lot of pain. Les was hit in the left arm and right ear lobe. Both were flesh wounds and not life threatening. The Chinese soldiers took all equipment and personal items from the GIs including their boots. They showed no sympathy for the two prisoners. They tied their hands behind their backs and ropes around their necks to lead them like dogs. It wasn't long before Shores passed out. They made a makeshift stretcher and four Chinese carried him.

When they got to the enemy field location, the two Americans were split up. Les was tied to a tree and a young soldier cleaned and bandaged his wounds. He never saw Shores again.

December 15, 1950, Matt and Julie were notified by the Department of the Army that Les was missing in action. It was a sad holiday season for the Baker family. Matt and Julie were both in their fifties and having another son missing in action weighed heavily on their minds. Julie kept herself busy cooking and cleaning but her thoughts were mainly on Charlie and Les. She thought, they were such fine boys and it didn't seem right to have lost them to wars far away from home. Matt had always enjoyed washing and polishing his automobiles but now his heart wasn't in it. He just couldn't motivate himself after this latest news. One day he got ready to wash the old Franklin. Suddenly he dropped the sponge into the water bucket and walked up on West Mountain behind the house. He sat under an apple tree for several hours thinking about his missing sons. Occasionally, tears were impossible to keep back. He had hoped his sons would take over the Bernardston Inn. He was looking forward to the time when he could cut back to just buying and selling cars. He had never lost his love for automobiles. There was nothing he enjoyed better than getting a car washed and polished to put on his sales lot.

It was near dark before he came off the hill. When Julie saw him, she said, "Honey, where have you been? A couple of men stopped to look at your cars."

"I took a walk up on the hill. I couldn't stop thinking about Les and Charlie. I hope and pray that Les is still alive!"

"Yes. I keep busy all day but I can't stop thinking about them either. Matt, I feel in my heart that Les is alive and will return some day. I really believe it!"

Chapter 18

PAUL IS TAKEN PRISONER IN LIEPZIG

*P*aul continued to run the business for his absent brother. By 1953, when hostilities ceased in Korea, the Baker family had not heard anything from Les or the government. He was listed as missing in action. Paul had hired two men to work with him in the garage and it was doing well. Les had given Paul full power of attorney when he left.

Paul was still dating Beverly Stokes, but they had not made definite wedding plans. She was in nurse's training and they wanted to wait until she graduated. They had wonderful times together. Most of their activities depended on the time of year. They both enjoyed going on long drives Sunday afternoons in the spring and fall. The view along the roads in the New England countryside was very appealing. It was a joy to see the new leaves on the big hardwood trees mixed in with white birch and evergreen trees. During these drives, they were in the shade of over hanging branches for hours at a time. They would put the Lincoln's top down and the fresh air was exhilarating. When they drove past logging operations, the smell of fresh cut pine trees permeated the air.

In late spring, farmers had cut their first crop of hay. Quite often they stopped to observe them gathering up the hay to store in their barns for winter-feed. Paul and Beverly both loved the aroma of fresh cut hay. One day on one of these outings Beverly asked, "Where did all those rocks come from for the stone fences?"

"Each year when the farmers plow their fields for planting, they turn up a new batch of stones. Some of the stones are quite large and would be a nuisance during cultivation of crops. For a couple of hundred years, the first thing a farmer did after plowing was to pick up the stones. They used them to make fences, which never deteriorate or need repair."

"Where did the stone come from for the fences around the areas with large trees?"

"That is a good question. Those plots were once cleared fields. In later years, people let the trees grow back. The individuals who cleared those fields would be sick to see large trees growing where they worked so hard to clear them out."

Their drives in the fall were nothing short of spectacular. The green leaves change color to bright reds, yellows, and browns and are beautiful beyond imagination. Each weekend during this annual event, people come from cities like New York and Boston to enjoy the sight of nature's artistry in brilliant colors. Paul and Beverly had wonderful times together and they seemed to be a perfect couple. Paul knew that she assumed they would eventually marry. But Paul had something more on his mind he hadn't shared with her. He thought a lot about the loss of his two brothers and he had an urge to return to military service. Sometimes he thought, I must be stupid to even consider re-enlistment. At other times he was taken over by the desire to go back in the service.

When Bev passed her qualification tests and became a nurse, she brought up the subject of marriage. During the discussion it became obvious that Paul was not going to set a firm date and he would not give any reason.

"If you are not willing to set a date, call me when you are." She walked out with tears in her eyes.

Several weeks went by and Paul heard that Bev was dating Walter Barnes from Greenfield. Walter was the son of W. Hunter Barnes, owner of Barnes Motor Express. It seemed like those trucks were everywhere. Paul had not called and had not seen her since she walked out with hurt feelings. In January, three days after his twenty-sixth birthday, he read in the paper that Beverly had gotten married. It really bothered him and he knew it was his fault.

From the moment he knew Bev was another man's wife, he felt emptiness in his stomach. She was the only female with whom he had felt what he assumed was love. He had enjoyed the company of Yvonne

Cannon, in Key West, but he never developed the strong feelings he had for Beverly. He didn't feel that Yvonne really loved him either. The *Resolute* stayed out to sea for a week each month conducting anti-sub-marine warfare exercises. Paul was at the Cannon home the first day after their return from each of those trips. One day, Yvonne seemed a little distant rather than thrilled to see him. He had been there about an hour when a marine walked up on the porch and knocked. Yvonne's mother answered the door and yelled, "Yvonne, it's Sandy." She excused herself and went outside and talked to the marine for several minutes. When she returned, she giggled and said, "He met me at the USO Club a while back." Paul felt sure she had been dating that marine while he was out to sea.

He continued to operate the business on Hoe Shop Road and the profits were very good. He had a feeling of loss that never left him and it had a negative affect on his life. He dated several girls but they never quite measured up when he compared them to Beverly. Paul finally admitted to himself that he had been a fool to let her go. He missed her almost as much as he did his brothers and especially on the weekends. He had not appreciated how much he enjoyed those drives with her. He went on one alone and it was no fun at all. He asked a girl from South Deerfield to go with him on a drive. She became carsick from those winding roads and threw up on the floor of the Lincoln. It was a hell of a job getting that mess cleaned out.

The first part of December, 1954, he started visiting the military recruiters in Greenfield. He thought that the Air Force would provide the opportunity to learn to fly. He was informed that without a college degree there would be little hope of him attending flight school. The recruiter said, "Why don't you check out the army? They have a war-rant officer flight program." He learned that with his high school diplo-ma plus high grades, he could enlist for that flight-training program. He went by his parent's house to tell them about his plans. As soon as he walked in the door his mom said, "Paul guess who I saw in Foster's Market yesterday?"

"Who?"

"Beverly and she looks more beautiful than ever. Paul I think she is still in love with you. She asked about you and said to say Hi when I saw you. She is married to that rich guy in the trucking business." Matt and Julie were shocked when he told them about his decision to return to military service. He said, "I have put a lot of thought into it. I'll be going to flight school in Alabama. Working at the shop hasn't been much fun since Les left."

Matt said, "When will you be leaving, Paul?"

"After the first of the year, Dad. I'm looking forward to learning to fly."

On January 3rd, 1955, Paul enlisted in the army with orders to flight school, after eight weeks of basic training. He had shut down the business in Bernardston much to the chagrin of his parents. They wanted him to attend college if he was dissatisfied doing automotive work. It was heart wrenching for them to see their fourth and youngest son bent on going back into the service. They seldom saw Sam because he was a professor at Boston College. He and his family were only a hundred miles away but they were busy on weekends with their kid's activities. They got together some in the summer and for Christmas. They had been enjoying having Paul right there in town.

In December, Paul graduated first in his flight school class and was appointed warrant officer W-1. He loved to fly and there was not the slightest feeling of regret about being back in the service. He stayed at Fort Rucker in southern Alabama to fly the U-6 Beaver. He was assigned as an instrument flight instructor due to his class standing. The plane is manufactured by De Havilland of Canada and has a single radial engine with excellent short field capability. He had three students at a time in the aircraft with him, one in the pilot's seat and the other two in the back, observing.

During the following two years, Paul became a proficient flight instructor. He enjoyed the work more than anything he had ever done. He also became an expert at flying the Beaver and if a person can love an object, he loved that airplane. He enjoyed working with the students although they thought he was a tough taskmaster. He taught them well but he never let up on the students throughout the course. The more they improved in proficiency, the more Paul put on the pressure. It was the scheme of the program to make it hard to become an army pilot.

It was the goal of flight school to turn out pilots who could cope under adverse conditions. They wanted pilots who would keep trying to fly planes regardless of what happened during missions like receiving hostile fire, the aircraft catching on fire, the pilot being wounded, or severe weather. Instructors covered instrument dials, made students read books, talked to them like they were stupid, and applied any and all distractions they could think of while students tried to fly the planes. At times they hit them on the side of their heads with the Federal Aviation Rules book. Instructors felt that if they could make a student quit the course, he might quit trying to fly in stressful situations when it would cost lives and an aircraft.

A year and a half after Paul graduated; he was promoted to chief warrant officer. Another instructor, Craig Lukas and he became good friends. Craig and his wife Jean frequently entertained Paul at their quarters on Harris Drive West. Jean often tried to fix him up with one of the local females. When he came to dinner, a woman *just happened* to be invited at the same time. Paul did take some of them out to dine and dance at the club or in Dothan. On occasion, they went to his room for fun and games. He wondered why he always compared them to Beverly and found them coming up short.

In 1959, he was promoted to chief warrant officer (CWO) W-3. He was bored with his job and he felt it was time do something different. He applied for a transfer to Germany, which was approved and he went on a thirty-day leave. He flew from Dothan, Alabama, on Southern Airways to Atlanta. From there, he flew Delta to Bradley Field in Hartford, Connecticut. He rented a car and drove to his folks' house in Bernardston.

They were surprised and happy to see him. Matt and Julie were both in their sixties. Paul noticed they had aged considerably since he left to join the army. There had never been any word concerning Les' fate in the Korean War. That situation and the loss of Charlie in World War II no doubt had a negative affect on his parents. Matt was still crazy about automobiles. He had sold the Bernardston Inn and his interest in the grocery store after Paul joined the Army. He was operating a used car lot right beside their house, the old Cushman Mansion. Matt said, "It got to be too much managing those businesses and we don't need the money. I do enjoy buying and selling automobiles. Livermore's Garage does most of my mechanical work."

After Paul was home a couple of days, Julie said, "Paul, we have not heard one bit of news about what happened to Les." They had contacted an official in the State Department and he said there was no Lt. Lester Baker listed as a prisoner of war by the North Koreans. There were many individuals still listed as missing in action from that war. Matt continued, "Are you aware that Les made a will before he left? He left everything to you, Paul."

Paul stopped at Bill's Restaurant just before lunch the next day. He sat at the bar and ordered a beer. Mike, the bartender, went after the draft and Paul felt a tap on his shoulder. He turned to see who it was and there stood the most beautiful woman he had ever seen, Beverly Stokes Barnes. She had a mile-wide smile. He stood up and they hugged. She said, "I stopped for lunch. Would you join me at a booth?" They had a lot of fun talking about old times and what had happened to various people. That lunch took more than two hours and it seemed like neither one wanted it to end. She didn't mention her marriage at all. Just before they parted, in front of the restaurant, Bev asked him if he would like to meet for lunch again. He said, "Yes."

She gave him a hug and whispered, "I'll call you."

The very next morning, before eight, Julie answered the phone. She said, "Paul, it's for you." It was Beverly and she said, "Can you meet me at the Whately Inn for lunch today?" They had another long lunch, which lasted for more than three hours. She did discuss her marriage and she said that she wasn't really happy. She had three wonderful children, but her husband had become a bore. They got along okay, but he had no enthusiasm for doing anything exciting. She thought that he cared for her, but he demonstrated almost no affection in recent months. Finally, she said, "Paul, I'm going on a shopping trip to New York this weekend. Would you like to meet me there?"

They shared a room at the Hilton Hotel in downtown New York and had a wonderful time. They went dancing, to a Broadway show, and to fine restaurants. Saturday night they were at the Rainbow Room in the NBC Building. From that lounge, there's the most magnificent view of New York City. Paul admitted that he had made a terrible mistake when he let her get away years before. They both felt guilty about what they were doing, but they were still madly in love with each other. She got on a Trailways bus at the Port Authority Terminal with tears rolling down her cheeks. The day after Paul got home from New York; he left to turn in his rental car at Bradley Field. He reported to McGuire Air Force Base in New Jersey for a military flight to Germany, three weeks early.

Paul was assigned to the Seventh Army Flight Detachment at Nelligen, Germany. He was qualified in the Cessna, L-19 Bird-dog and the U-6 Beaver. The weather was chronically bad for flying in Europe but his years as an instrument instructor offset that problem. He volunteered for any mission that came up regardless of the weather. He wanted to stay busy, but the flights still gave him a lot of time to think about Beverly. He was reading the *Army Times* one day and found an article referring to the army's need for signal corps officers. Individuals having related experience could apply for a commission from enlisted or warrant officer ranks. At first he didn't give it much thought, then on a flight to Mannheim it came to him that his experience as a navy sonarman might be enough to qualify.

He went to the Seventh Army personnel section and filled out an application for appointment to first lieutenant as a signal corps officer, based on the circular quoted in the *Army Times*. Several weeks later, the flight operations officer, Captain Dan Evans, said, "Chief Baker, call Specialist Peacock at personnel." He called and when he identified himself as, "CWO Baker," Peacock said, "No, you are wrong. You are First Lieutenant Paul A. Baker, sir." The appointment included orders assigning him to the 379th Signal Battalion at Boebligen, Germany.

Paul reported to Major Thomas Bennett, Commanding Officer, 379th Signal Battalion. Major Bennett asked Paul for a synopsis of his military experience. He smiled when Paul finished and said, "Lt. Baker, I have a great need for a mature lieutenant." He picked up his phone and dialed a number, "Ralph, I have sitting in front of me a man that should be a lot of help to you. We will be in your office in just a few minutes." A few minutes later, they were in the office of Captain Ralph Shelton, Commanding Officer of the 585 Signal Company. After some preliminary introductory conversation, Major Bennett said, "Captain

Shelton I want you to designate the lieutenant here, your motor offi-cer." He then looked at Paul; "I want you to put a man on your motor pool gate each day. He will inspect each and every vehicle that attempts to leave the motor pool. Any vehicle not passing his inspection will not be allowed to leave. Don't let one vehicle leave the motor pool, even if the driver says it is for Colonel Van Houston, the group commander or me. Do you understand that, Baker?"

"Yes, sir."

Paul thought to himself, I don't know the first thing about running a motor pool. Maybe I was better off as a warrant officer. I knew my job there without a doubt. He found out later that the 585th Company was most unusual. Most companies had 150 to 180 men. The 585th had more than four hundred. One mission was to maintain fixed commu-nications throughout the Southern Area Command, in essence, the entire southern half of Germany. Another mission was to provide con-trol communications for field exercises for all Seventh Army units. The 585th also had their own field exercises, almost monthly. The compa-ny was short of officers and NCOs. All personnel worked twelve to fourteen hours a day, including Sundays.

Captain Shelton had taken command one week before Paul arrived. He was the third company commander in three months. The two pre-vious ones had been relieved for inefficiency. All the news Paul received about the 585th was dismal and discouraging. The officers talked of resigning their commissions. The 585th was not a happy assignment. When he got to bed in his bachelor officer quarters (BOQ) that night, he couldn't sleep. If he had only known how well off he had been at Fort Rucker. Being bored seemed like a wonderful state of mind.

Seventh Army conducted alerts on a regular basis. They simulated going to war and the alerts were taken seriously. A commander could ruin his career if his unit performed poorly. All personnel and equip-ment had to leave their barracks. They would go to a pre-assigned loca-tion and there was a time limit to get there. Any equipment or vehicles left behind would have to be explained in writing. The 585th had the worst unit record for alert performance.

The day Paul assumed the job of motor officer, he held his first staff meeting. He had two NCOs and the senior man was his motor sergeant.

Buck Sergeant Waters was a husky black man with a good attitude. He assigned Waters to the gate as the official inspector and they connected a field phone from the gate to Paul's desk. Within an hour the phone rang and Waters said, "Sir, could you come to the gate right away?"

When Paul arrived, Lt. Andrews was there with his jeep and driver. Andrews shouted, "Baker, tell this NCO to open the gate. I have a mission." Paul asked Waters for the inspection sheet. There were more than twenty discrepancies.

He said to Andrews, "When the items on this list are corrected, you can take this jeep out of the motor pool."

Andrews looked at him in utter amazement; "You mean that?"

"Exactly."

Andrews looked at Paul for several seconds, then looked at his driver and said, "Park it and get to work on those discrepancies."

Within a week, not one of the officers in the company would talk to Paul except Captain Shelton. Drivers were seen working on their vehicles every time they had the opportunity. On the next alert, one ton and a half trailer was left behind. On the next alert, nothing was left behind. The gate inspections had produced superior results.

Captain Shelton implemented a policy that improved morale. He directed that all personnel, not on duty, would have Sundays off. It had an immediate positive affect on the troops. They had been working seven days a week for months. When Shelton saw the improved morale, he added a further benefit. The platoon with the best ratings for Saturday inspections would be off at 1200 hours that day. The 585th was reborn with new life and an upbeat attitude. The officers and men lost their hangdog look, the entire unit improved daily, and spirits were up.

Captain Shelton made good use of Paul's aviation qualifications. A massive field exercise, Winter Shield II, was planned for the near future in the Graffenvor area near the East German border. Paul flew Shelton and his Executive Officer, Lt. Johnson, there to reconnoiter the 585th's assigned field location. The two planned to stay for three days so Paul returned to Boeblingen. He had borrowed a U-6 from the 7th Army Flight Detachment at Nelligen.

The day he needed to return and pick up the two officers, the weather forecast was not good. That was not unusual in Europe. It did cause concern because he would be flying close to East Germany. If he accidentally strayed across the border, he might be shot down. He stopped to refuel at Nurenburg. An operations sergeant told him that the navigational VOR was unreliable to the north and east of their location. That meant that he would have to use the automatic direction finder (ADF) to navigate. It was a system developed in the thirties and still used as a backup. The weather was forecast to be deteriorating, with possible thunderstorms, the closer he got to his destination.

Paul filed his instrument flight plan and took off. He climbed into the solid overcast. In about thirty minutes the visual omni range (VOR) needle started to jitter and then it became erratic. He tuned the ADF to a station southwest of Graffenvor. It did not hold stable and he knew that it was still too far away to lock on. He held the course expecting the ADF to settle down when he got closer. He was at four thousand feet in solid instrument flight rules (IFR) conditions.

About an hour into the flight, the aircraft started into rough air. In another few minutes, it was much worse and it was difficult to maintain his heading. Then he saw lightning with the plane bouncing up two or three hundred feet, followed by dropping that much or more. He heard the thunder above the engine noise. He flew from updrafts to downdrafts so fast that it was hard keeping the wings level. He could feel the tremendous strain put on the airframe and wings. He wasn't sure of his heading, but he hoped he was flying due north. He had filed his flight plan for four thousand feet and now he was fluctuating above and below five thousand. There was nothing he could do but ride it out and hope for the best. This condition continued for another two hours and he became concerned about how much fuel he had left.

Paul was in a severe thunderstorm that was moving east at more than forty miles an hour. The turbulence finally diminished when his fuel guage was bouncing on empty. A few minutes later he was out of the clouds and in clear skies. He knew that in a short time he would be out of fuel. He spotted a large town on the horizon to his right and headed for it. As he approached the outskirts of the city, he saw an airport. After landing, he taxied to a spot near the control tower and shut down the plane. A vehicle drove up with two policemen and they immediately arrested him. He was in Leipzig, East Germany.

He was pushed into the rear seat of the police car. As the car departed the airport, Paul thought, "It has been nearly ten years since Les was listed as missing in action. Now I am a prisoner in East Germany and no one will know what happened to me." He also realized that it would be another devastating blow to his folks.

Chapter 19

LESTER A PRISONER FOR TEN YEARS

Ten years earlier and half way around the world, Lt. Lester M. Baker had been captured by the Red Chinese. He suffered through his first day hungry, tired, and hurting from his wounds. His hands were bound behind his back and his legs at the ankles. There was a short rope from his hands tied to a tree. It was not long enough for him to see how it was fastened, but it did allow him to move and change positions a little. He ached all over, especially where the rope rubbed his feet and hands. The Chinese soldiers ignored him except for the young soldier who administered first aid. He untied him twice during the day and marched him to the latrine. The second time he re-tied Les, it seemed like the ropes were not quite as tight. It was several hours into the night before he fell asleep from pure exhaustion.

The next morning, after he was taken to the latrine, the young soldier brought him some hard bread and strong tea in a metal cup. It made Les feel much better and being free of the ropes for a while was a relief. When he was bound up again, they tied his hands in front of him. Then two additional ropes about ten feet long were tied to him. One was hitched to the rope at his hands and the other was around his neck. A group of six soldiers in a line started off through the North Korean woods with Les in the center. A soldier in front of him and one behind held the long ropes. The man who had treated his wounds was in the group.

They moved at a fast rate along a narrow trail for two or three hours and came to a cleared area that was obviously a landing strip. Les was given a piece of hard bread and some dried fish. Within an hour, a small single engine plane landed. Les and the young soldier got aboard and they were airborne in minutes. He realized that his chances of escaping were nearly zero. They landed two more times at remote places to refuel. The third place, was an airport at the city of Omsk in southeastern Siberian Russia. He was turned over to Russian soldiers there, loaded into a truck, and driven to a prison on the outskirts of the city.

He was put in a cell that had a wooden bunk and a thin mattress. He was dead tired and immediately lay on the bunk. Before he could go to sleep, a large female unlocked the cell door and redressed his wounds. She spoke a little English and said that he would be on a train the next day. The next morning, he was allowed a sponge bath in cold water and was given a fresh change of clothes. He felt the best since he was first captured. About noon, two Russian soldiers took him to the railroad station. One of them spoke heavy accented English and he told Les that they would be heading west on the Trans-Siberian Railroad. He said, "My name, Yakev. Relax for long trip. Try escape. I kill you." He smiled and added, "I mean it. Don't try."

The train was primitive and the hard seats were uncomfortable. He sat next to a window, beside Yakev with his right wrist handcuffed to the metal armrest. The backs of the seats were hinged and could be positioned facing forward or backward. Another soldier sat facing them. They borrowed a food tray from the trainman and played a card game similar to hearts. Yakev taught Les the game and it helped pass the time. Yakev liked speaking English and asked about the States. He couldn't comprehend much of what Les told him. When Les said that most adults owned their own cars, Yakev responded with disbelief. He said, "Can't be. Can't be." Les understood his response. Most of the people in each town the train passed through were on bicycles or horse drawn wagons. There were a few automobiles in the large towns and cities. As they progressed further west, everything looked more modern and cars were more plentiful. It was obvious to Les the soldiers had never been west. They were as interested as little kids watching the sights as the train passed through the large cities.

The train stopped at Lake Baikal, a popular tourist spot, for several hours to take on water and coal. It is the largest and deepest freshwater lake in the world and a tourist spot. The soldiers got off the train with Les and they ate in the terminal building. There were numerous

Russian families arriving or waiting to depart the train station. They were much better dressed than the people Les had seen to this point on the trip. Additional passenger cars were added to the train and many of the people in the terminal got on board.

Days later, the soldiers took him off the train at Izhevsk, a city in East European Russia on the Izh River, west of the Ural Mountains. The mountains run generally north and south and divide European and Asiatic Russia. Yakev said it was a large steel mill center. Les was taken to a prison and interrogated at length.

At first, he stated only his name, rank, and service number but he would not answer any questions. He was sitting on a chair in front of a Russian officer. There was a guard standing to his left holding a three-foot rubber hose. The officer said, "You are not a prisoner of war. Russia and the United States are not at war so you must answer my questions." Les stared at the officer for several seconds. The officer glanced at the guard and nodded his head slightly. The guard swung the hose and hit Les with so much force, he fell on the floor. He had struck him on the shoulder of the wounded arm and the pain was agonizing. The officer yelled at him to get back on the chair. They went through the same routine several times and it took Les longer and longer to get up off the floor. Finally, he was knocked unconscious. He awoke some time later in his cell in agony. Every move he tried to make resulted in shooting pains. He was left in his cell for a few days and fed potato soup with stale hard bread. One morning, he was taken to a steel mill and put to work with other men from the prison.

Under any conditions, the work would have been tough, but the pain from the beating made it much worse. They worked six days a week from 0700 until 1900 hours at night. It was a month before Les totally recovered from the beating and he kept wondering if it would happen again. He worked with other prisoners loading heavy lengths of steel from the mill onto a trailer. The trailer was towed by a tractor to the rail yard where they unloaded it near train tracks. One day the tractor wouldn't start. A Russian mechanic worked for more than an hour with no luck. Les made motions to the mechanic, indicating that he would try to start the tractor. The mechanic moved to the side and let Les work on the tractor. In a few minutes, he found the distributor cap was cracked. He showed it to the mechanic who smiled and walked off carrying the broken part.

The next day, Les was brought to the maintenance Foreman. He told Les through an interpreter he would be working for him. In less than a week, he could sense the other maintenance men liked him. Les was able to fix nearly all the problems that developed on the motorized equipment at the plant. At times, repair parts were not on hand, which was the only hang-up. He was moved to a better part of the jail with a bunk bed and mattress. He was fed much better food and allowed to shower once a week.

After a few months, Les was bored and yearned for Bernardston. He would lay in bed at night and try to picture how things looked there. In his mind's eye he could clearly see his folks and he regretted joining the National Guard. He even imagined hearing the big clock on the town hall striking. He mentioned to the other prisoners the possibility of getting a message smuggled out of the country. They scoffed at the idea as being impossible and no one would risk the possible consequences of helping him. Dubchek, a political prisoner, advised him, "Accept your status as it is. We are much better off than most."

One day, he was ushered into the front office and brought to the commandant. He motioned for Les to follow him and they went outside. It was cold and the ground was coated with freezing rain. They walked to the commandant's car, which was damaged badly all along one side. It had apparently slid off the road and sideswiped a tree. He asked Les if he could fix it. Les said that he could and for the better part of two weeks he worked on the car. There was some trouble getting materials he needed, but he finally had the vehicle looking nearly as good as new.

Living conditions for Les greatly improved from that day forward. He was moved into a walled compound with long apartment buildings. The apartments were similar to a stateside efficiency apartment without modern appliances. There was a coal burning cook stove in the small kitchen and a coal burning space heater in the tiny living room. He had this apartment to himself. Most of the units had two or more men with bunk beds in the small bedrooms. There were two cot-sized beds in the one Les occupied and he expected that he would eventually have a roommate.

As the years went by, Les was given more and more freedom; however, each night, he had to be inside the compound. He got to know several of the other inmates who were assigned to the compound. Some of them spoke a little English and Les learned to speak Russian. They visited and played cards together. One game was cribbage without a board with four players. It was played with partners and Les liked it better than playing with just two people. It was a more challenging game. Inmates were allowed to associate as they wished inside the compound. Everything allotted was in bulk quantities and divided up equally among them.

The idea of escaping was always on his mind. Listening to the other prisoners talk was the main reason he didn't make an attempt. There was so much checking of credentials in Russian society; it would be next to impossible to get out of the country. They would be suspicious of anyone who couldn't speak the language fluently. The general public would report him to the authorities being afraid not to. It was a society kept in fear all the time. They didn't trust anyone including their own relatives. In all probability, if Les tried to escape he would be captured and sent to Siberia forever. He lost all hope of getting back home, but things could be worse.

One evening while playing cards, one of the men said that he had talked with a friend at the mill that day. His friend told him that an American pilot had been brought into the prison. Les became immediately interested but the man didn't know any details. Les had gained the confidence of the mill commandant over the years. The next time he saw him, he asked, "Is it true that there is another American here in the prison?"

"Yes."

"Sir, is it possible to have the man assigned to my apartment?"

"We are not sure what the disposition of that man will be. I will look into the matter."

Nearly two weeks went by and Les figured that he would not be seeing the American. He walked into his apartment one evening and there was a person sleeping in one of the cots. His face was turned towards the wall and Les thought, well, I have lost my privacy after all this time. He started heating water to take a sponge bath and he heard the new man moving around in the bedroom. Les looked towards the doorway of the kitchen just as the man appeared.

Les started to speak, stopped, and stared. "Can it be you?.. Is it you, PAUL!.."

Paul didn't recognize Les at all and just stood there. He was shocked to be called by his first name. He thought, how could this skinny foul-smelling person know my name?

"Paul, it's me, Lester, your brother. Don't you recognize me?"

Paul saw a slight resemblance and then said, "Les, it is you. My God, what have they done to you? How could this be?"

They hugged one another and tears rolled down their cheeks. Les started sobbing. He finally managed to say, "I had lost all hope of seeing any of you again. There is a God. There must be. OH, thank God." As he said the words, his voice was high pitched and near breaking. They talked all night and Les hung onto every word as Paul told him all that had happened since he left for Korea in 1950. When Les told him that Dorothy Lane had never married, Les became overwhelmed and he couldn't speak for several minutes. Paul could see the deep impact his words had on Les. He lowered his voice and said, "She stops in to see mom and dad two or three times a month. If a woman ever loved a man, she loves you."

Chapter 20

PAUL & LES IN SAME PRISON

The Russians hit the jackpot. When 1st Lt. Paul A. Baker landed in East Germany, they knew there would be a propaganda benefit. They didn't report the event because they had not decided what approach to use. When Paul was transported to the prison, which held Les, the Russians had no idea of putting the two men together or that they were brothers. When the Steel Mill Commandant, Vladimir Rurik, asked permission to put the two Americans together, mill security decided to install a listening device first. That was the reason for the two-week delay. They wired the bug to an empty apartment to listen and record what the two Americans would say.

When they heard the fact that the two were brothers, it was like fishing for a minnow and catching a whale. The first thing they did was to tell Commandant Rurik to give Paul an administrative job. They didn't want the brothers together during the day. Better food was put on the menu for that prison compound. They speculated that the pilot would eventually be released and they wanted him looking trim. The information was reported to the KGB and within two days an agent, Igor Godunov, arrived to take charge of the surveillance.

The brothers slept very little the first night. Les wanted to hear all the news since his capture ten years ago in 1950. He was pleased to hear that his folks were well. He was surprised to learn that Dorothy Lane had never married and that his stock investment was now worth more than a million dollars. Les reminded Paul what he had told him when the Engineer unit was activated, "If you join the service, you will never work for me again." They both laughed. Each night, they talked for hours about the events in each other's lives over the lost years. It never crossed their minds that every word was being recorded.

A week went by and Paul was taken to an interrogation room and told to sit at a table. In a few minutes, Agent Godunov sat down across from him. He smiled and said in perfect English, "You will sign this statement." He slid a piece of paper across the table and it said:

> I, 1st Lt. Paul A. Baker, do hereby swear and affirm that I illegally entered into East Germany to become a spy for the United States of America. I regret my actions and apologize to the East German people. I have written this statement of my own free will and I believe the United States should make a public apology as well. I was following the orders of my Country.

Paul looked at the agent and said, "I'm sorry, sir, I refuse to sign that statement or any other." The agent smiled and said, "Lieutenant, you will sign that statement if you want to see your brother again. You will also be sending him to a camp in Siberia to work at hard labor for the rest of his life. You see, Lieutenant, no one knows that your brother is here. You have one minute to make up your mind." Paul thought of the ten years that Les already had been incarcerated. How could he be responsible for making life much worse for him? He grabbed the paper and signed it. Within twenty-four hours, the statement was major news around the world.

The Baker family had not received word of Paul's disappearance and they were shocked at the headlines in the Springfield Union:

"ARMY PILOT FROM BERNARDSTON ADMITS SPYING"

There was a front-page article along with a picture of Paul in uniform. It was covered on radio and TV. Matt and Julie were sick to their stomachs. They did not feel concerned about the statement by Paul. They felt ill because he was a prisoner behind the Iron Curtain. Matt thought, why did one family have to suffer so much grief?

In the apartment that night, Paul told Les what he had done. They agreed that it would probably not end with just the statement. The idea also came to their minds that they were being monitored. They went into the tiny bathroom and closed the door to talk. Paul said that he would not be leaving unless Les went too. Les tried to talk him out of it, to no avail. The brothers were filled with anxiety and at a loss as to what they should try to do. Les said, "Paul, there is no need of you ruining your life. Do whatever they ask to get yourself released."

Another week went by before Paul was brought back to Agent Godunov. He said, "Come with me." They left the building and climbed into the back seat of a black sedan. They rode for about twenty minutes and pulled into a parking lot near a large brick building. When they got inside, it was obvious to Paul that they were in a TV studio. Godunov turned to Paul and said, "You will be making a statement on television. If you care for your brother, you will fully cooperate and do as you are told." Paul was videotaped making the following statement:

> *"I am First Lieutenant Paul A. Baker. I was ordered by the United States Army to enter East Germany. My mission was to spy for my Country and I know that I can be shot for this serious deed. The East German authorities have been very good to me. They have informed me that if the United States makes a public apology for what I was sent to do, they will negotiate my release. Thank you."*

The video clip was released around the world. The Bakers were pleased to see that Paul looked well but they were still full of grief. Matt called the Department of the Army and pleaded with them to get a public apology out so Paul could come home. He was told that the situation was under consideration and he would be kept informed. Matt and Julie received numerous phone calls and cards offering sympathy and support. Everyone seemed to think that an apology would be a small price to pay for Paul's release.

After ten days another televised statement by Paul was released:

"I am First Lieutenant Paul A. Baker. If the United States of America does not apologize for sending me to East Germany as a spy, I will be committed to a Siberian Prison Camp for the rest of my natural life. They have one week to respond favorably to my message. Thank you."

Four days later, the U.S. Secretary of State made this televised statement:

"The United States of America regrets sending First Lieutenant Paul A. Baker to East Germany to function as a spy. It was a bad decision and we apologize to the East German government and people for the unfortunate event."

As soon as the Russians heard the apology on television, Paul was brought to the KGB agent. He said, "Lieutenant, you will be released in two days. When you arrive back with your people, you will not change your story in any way. You will not report that you saw your brother. You will be contacted by one of our agents in the near future. You will cooperate with him. Any infraction of these guidelines and your brother will be on his way to Siberia. Do you understand?"

That evening and through the night, the brothers felt the dismal thought of parting the next day. They knew there was not even a remote chance of them seeing each other again. It was heartwrenching and they both ached inside. They felt like they should do something constructive with the time they had left, but what could be done. Several times, Les said, "Don't do anything to mess up the chance you have of being released." Paul had never experienced such frustration. He kept thinking, there must be a solution to this problem. What is it, Lord? A prison guard brought Paul's flight suit to him early the next morning and told him to put it on. He was then ushered into a vehicle and driven to the airport. He was flown in a small jet aircraft to Berlin with the KGB agent. During the flight, Godunov amplified the problems his brother would have if he did not follow instructions.

The morning after his arrival in Berlin, Paul was at a crossing point between the Russian and American sectors, still in the company of the KGB agent. He could see American military officers waiting across the fifty meters of no-man's land. Godunov told him to go across. Paul started on his way to freedom. When he was two thirds of the way across, he pulled something out of his flight jacket pocket. He wound up like a baseball pitcher and threw something towards the Americans. He then turned and ran back towards the Russian side. An expression of shock and disbelief was on the face of Godunov. Paul was immediately hustled into the guard building. The agent said in a high pitched voice, "You are stupid. You have just signed your death warrant along with your brother's."

The Americans were highly confused too. One of them picked up the item that Paul had thrown. It was a stone with paper wrapped around it. The paper was read aloud by an army major: "My brother, Lt. Lester M. Baker, is being held in the same prison I was in. He has been a prisoner since being captured by the Chinese in the Korean War. They threatened to send him to Siberia if I don't follow their instructions and become an agent for them. I don't know if I have done the right thing, but I will not leave here without my brother." They all looked across to the Russian sector. Paul was no where in sight.

The decision was made by the State Department to release the contents of Paul's note to the worldwide press. They hoped, through diplomatic diplomacy, they could gain the release of the brothers. There was a huge reaction throughout the world against the cruelty by the Russians for holding a man prisoner for so long after the Korean War had ceased. Newspaper headlines demanded the release of the two brothers. Articles pointed out the billions of dollars of aid the Americans had provided the Russians during World War II. The newspapers asked the question in two inch headlines:

"IS THIS HOW THE
SOVIET UNION SAYS THANK YOU?"

The furor continued for days over news media throughout the world. Paul and Les got the impression they were going to be released soon. They were moved to nicer quarters and the food was better including Vodka and orange juice. Within a day of their improved conditions, a lady came by with a tape measure. After taking and recording numerous measurements of Lester's body, she left indicating she would return. Two days later, she was back with a totally new outfit for Les.

Premier Nikita S. Khrushchev made a public statement on television: "It has been brought to my attention, that an American soldier has been located in a Russian prison. It has been a regrettable oversight which will be corrected." Three days later, Paul and Les were both released at the same junction where Paul threw the rock nearly two weeks before. Just before Godunov told them to go, he said, "Lieutenant Baker, will you be coming back this time?" Paul laughed and said, "No, sir. Not this time." As the two walked across no-man's land, (Les in his new clothes and Paul in his flight suit) Les said, "There really is a God, and thank you, Paul!"

Chapter 21

LESTER & DOROTHY GET MARRIED

The brothers were flown to Andrews Air Force Base, near Washington, DC. The red carpet was rolled out for their arrival accompanied by a military band. Matt, Julie, Sam and his wife Nora, were among the greeting party. The family huddled together for several minutes on the tarmac. It was a tearful, heart-warming event. Les and Paul were taken away for debriefing and physical examinations for the next two days. The family members were given VIP quarters while they waited.

Paul was promoted to captain and Les to major with a backdated date of rank. Les had accrued a large sum of money in back pay plus ten percent interest. They were given thirty-day leaves upon arrival at Westover Air Force Base near Springfield. They spent the first week with their folks in the Cushman Mansion. Matt gave them the pick of his car lot for transportation. By the end of the week, the boys had the house and garage opened on Hoe Shop Road. They spent several hours of each day in the basement lounge below the garage. Les said often, "For many years, I thought I would never see this place again."

Dorothy Lane came by the mansion the second day after they returned. Les gave her a hug and kiss then they went into the living room together. They kissed for a long time. Their eyes were full of tears and they couldn't speak. Finally, Les said, "Why haven't you gotten married?" She looked up at him with tear filled eyes and said, "I've been waiting for you." He thought to himself, how could she wait when there was no word about me for all those years? She thought to herself, he has aged so much. He must have gone through hell. They made a date for that night.

Les found out that his stock had increased in value to 1.3 million dollars. He transferred half the stock to Paul's name. When he told Paul, he said, "If it wasn't for you, I would still be in prison. You had full power of attorney. You could have taken all of it."

The second week home, the boys had moved into the house on Hoe Shop Road. Les and Dorothy had been out every night together. He was putting on weight and his face showed less strain and had better color. He was extremely thin and looked haggard when he first got home. Les called Fort Devens and informed the post adjutant that he wanted to resign his commission. The adjutant said the papers would be ready when he came off leave.

The organizations in town formed a committee. A Welcome Home Day was established for Les. A stage was constructed in Cushman Park. The Bernardston Band played March music and popular songs. The high point of the day was the speech by Paul relating the events leading up to their release from East Germany. The committee chairman read a proclamation designating the *Lester M. Baker Drive* in place of South Street.

Les and Dorothy announced their engagement. The couple seemed consumed by total happiness. Les was still overwhelmed with the undying love and loyalty she maintained while he was in prison. They planned to build a beautiful home on Fox Hill overlooking the town of Bernardston. He had not decided what he would do, but he knew it would not involve leaving his hometown.

Paul told Les that he would remain in the army for the foreseeable future. He planned to apply for a transition course to fly helicopters. Bell Helicopter had developed a turbine-engine helicopter, model UH-1. It was anticipated that the industry was on the threshold of a new era in rotary aircraft and Paul wanted to be in on it.

Paul and Beverly met for lunch twice during his leave. Neither of them mentioned going on another secret weekend together. He was deeply in love with her, but he didn't want to be responsible for breaking up her marriage. He knew that if he got out of the army and stayed home, they would not be able to stay apart. Learning to fly helicopters would keep him busy and help to occupy his thoughts.

Les and Dorothy were married the Saturday before Paul had to return to duty. He was the best man. The wedding took place in the Goodale Memorial Church with standing room only and the reception was at the Bernardston Inn. It was a joyful event. Matt and Julie had not been so happy in years. Sam played the organ at church for the wedding ceremony and entertained on the grand piano at the Inn. He had been a professor at Boston College for several years. The newlyweds went to Maine for their honeymoon.

Paul drove to the Department of the Army offices in Washington, D.C. They cut orders sending him to helicopter transition at Fort Rucker, Alabama. It was a ten-week course and he was selected to be an instructor pilot in the H-13 after graduation. Many of the civilians he had known before were still there and some of his army friends as well. Craig Lucas had been killed in a mid-air collision while Paul was in Germany. Jean was living nearby. She learned from a friend that Paul was back at Rucker. She called and invited him for dinner.

When he came through the door, she wrapped her arms around his neck and gave him a passionate kiss. There were tears of joy on her checks and she was too choked up to talk. He felt the emotion too and they were half way through their first highball before they started a conversation. She said the first year after Craig's accident was miserable beyond belief. Her two sons had been good students and it took months before they were back on the honor roll. Paul could relate to that, remembering the time Charlie was killed at Tarawa. Both boys were visiting friends that evening. Jean knew she would break down when she saw him and she thought it would have a negative effect on her sons. She said she had been out to dinner with a couple of guys, but there had been nothing serious.

Paul had envied Craig Lucas being married to such a beautiful woman. The two of them seemed to have it all. She obviously adored him and the natural harmony between them was evident. Paul appreciated her beauty. She had an exceptional bust line, small waist, ample hips, and long legs. When Jean smiled, a dimple in each cheek added to her loveliness. She seemed unaware of how gorgeous she was. Jean was also intelligent and well educated.

They had fun talking about the past at Rucker. Paul related the events about finding Les in a Russian prison. When he started to leave,

UH-1D Troop Carrying Helicopters

they became locked in each other's arms for several minutes. They made a date for dinner at the officers' club on Friday night. Paul felt a little dismayed over the obvious passion that radiated from Jean. He never felt she had any feelings for him other than a good friend during their previous relationship. She was so devoted to Craig. He knew that she must be very lonely and he did not want to take advantage of her. When he took her home from the club Friday night, he declined her invitation to go in the house. They kissed on the front porch. They dated two or three times a month and they enjoyed each other's company. Paul refused to get too involved because he couldn't get Beverly Stokes out of his thoughts. He knew that Jean was looking for a husband to help raise her sons and he didn't want to take that responsibility on.

After eighteen months of teaching in the H-13, Paul requested a transfer to the Bell UH-1 which was approved. Once again he was teaching instruments and found it enjoyable. He was content for two more years until he heard about the 11th Air Assault Division at Fort Benning, Georgia. That division was testing a new concept of war using helicopters to transport troops to the battlefield. He volunteered for assignment and was accepted. He became a platoon leader which meant he was in charge of four UH-1 Helicopters and crews. They conducted simulated combat assaults on and around the military reservation. Paul became a proficient flight leader and he thoroughly enjoyed flying helicopters.

Two months had gone by since he left Fort Rucker when he walked into flight operations on a Friday and found a message for him to call the Holiday Inn, room number 115. A female voice answered. "Good afternoon, Jean Lucas."

"Hi Jean. What are you doing in town?"

"My sons are off on a camping trip. I thought if you are not busy, we might have dinner together. It's my treat."

"That sounds great. I'll pick you up about six?"

They went to the Officer's club. After dinner they went to the bar for a drink. Jean had a strapless cocktail dress on and at least a third of her breasts were visible above it. The other officers at the bar kept glancing in her direction but she was all eyes for Paul and vivacious in her conversation with him. After a couple of drinks, Paul heard himself say, "Let's go to a more private place."

A few minutes later, they pulled up outside of his BOQ. His car was a 1964 Thunderbird with the shifting console dividing the front seat. She had her hand resting on his right knee on the way there. As soon as the door closed behind them in his room, they were in each other's arms. Jean whispered in his ear, "Oh Paul, I've fallen in love with you." He didn't answer and they were kissing passionately again. She looked so beautiful and her body felt wonderful pressed against his. It had been a long time since either one had been intimate with anyone.

The phone rang and he answered it. A voice said, "Hi Paul, this is Beverly."

"Really. Where are you?"

"I'm at the Columbus air terminal."

"I'll be there in less than an hour." He hung up the phone and said, "Jean, an old friend just arrived at the airport."

"What's her name, Paul?"

"Beverly. We went to school together."

Chapter 22

BEVERLY MARRIES WALTER BARNES

*B*everly Stokes had completed nurses' training, passed her exams to become a registered nurse, and expected to marry Paul A. Baker. They had been in love for a long time and she had found it more and more of a chore to resist Paul's advances. She knew that she loved him without reservation; however, going to bed with a man before marriage was against her principles. She had been raised with an ethical code, which placed that idea off limits. Single girls, who succumbed, lost their dignity and they were talked about in the ugliest terms. She was looking forward to becoming Mrs. Paul Baker and enjoy the benefits of being a respected married woman.

The night she tried to get Paul to set a date for the wedding, it became evident that he was not ready to do it. A feeling of hurt swept over her. She told him to call her when he was ready and left. He never called. When she was not at the hospital, she found herself looking at the phone every few minutes, wanting it to ring. She felt depressed most of her free time.

Several weeks after she walked out on Paul, Walter Barnes was admitted to the hospital. He had been in a serious automobile accident. He had been traveling at a high rate of speed in his Corvette, hit an icy spot on a sharp corner beyond the French King Bridge, and slid off the road. The car was totaled and he was lucky to be alive. He was placed in a private room on Beverly's floor when he came out of intensive care.

He was semi-conscious for nearly a week. The nurses had to do everything for him to include brushing his teeth. Beverly was giving him a sponge bath when Walter's eyes blinked open, fully alert. He smiled and said, "I'm in heaven and you're an angel." She blushed and couldn't help grinning. He said, "Oh. A beautiful smile too." He had a gregarious personality and she loved his sense of humor. It was the first time she had really laughed in weeks. Two days after he woke up, he said, "Isn't it time for another of your wonderful baths?"

"I'm sorry, Mr. Barnes. You have a shower right here and you are fully capable of taking advantage of it."

"Please call me Walt."

"Okay, Mr. Barnes."

Walter Barnes was the only son of W. Hunter Barnes, the owner of Barnes Motor Express. They had thirty-eight trailer trucks and hauled freight all over the United States. The business operated out of Turners Falls and Walter had been the General Manager since he was twenty five. He lived with his parents in a mansion on the Bernardston Road in Greenfield. He was good at running the trucking business, and on weekends he was a typical playboy. His mother kept urging him to find a nice girl, get married, and settle down. His dad told her to be happy that he was doing so well in the family business.

Beverly enjoyed the banter from Walt when she was in his room. One day, she leaned over to pick up his food tray and he reached up and put his hand on her breast. She jumped back, startled. She stood for a moment with a hurt look on her face then she said in a rigid voice, "Mr. Barnes, I resent what you did. I know you are wealthy. I know that you have dated every female in Franklin County at one time or another; however, you have no right to fondle me." She turned and walked out of the room with tears in her eyes.

Walt was taken aback at her reaction and he regretted what he had done. By mid-afternoon the next day Beverly had not been in his room once. A much older nurse had come in two or three times. Walt asked her, "Is Miss Stokes off for the day?" She said, "No. She works on another floor now." Walt was disappointed. He looked out the window and thought, I am really stupid. She is not just beautiful; she is a very nice lady. I have probably blown my chances of taking her out.

He was released from the hospital three days later and he had not seen Beverly since the incident. He went to Yetters Florist and ordered a dozen roses to be sent to the hospital, addressed to Beverly. The accompanying note said, "Please, please, please forgive me. What I did was in poor taste and I am truly sorry." Every day for two weeks, he sent a dozen roses asking for forgiveness. She called his home and asked him to stop sending the roses. He said, "Do I have your forgiveness?"

"Yes."

"May I take you out to dinner?"

"Let me think about it." He said, "Okay."

Walt called Beverly a few days later and said, "Are you going to let me take you out to dinner? I promise to be a perfect gentleman and I will bring you home directly after."

"I am only twenty-one."

"I know that you did a lot for me in the hospital. I want to show my appreciation and you have my total respect." She finally agreed and she did enjoy herself. He made no unwanted moves at all, and he kept her laughing much of the time. She didn't hear from him for a week and she felt a little disappointed. Then he called. They went out to dinner at the Greenfield Hotel and to a movie at the Garden Theater. He didn't even attempt to hold her hand. She thought, I have really turned him off.

A routine developed. They went out for dinner and the movies every Saturday night. After nearly two months, Walt said during dinner, "Tex Benecke and his orchestra are at the Sweetheart Lounge in Springfield tonight. Would you like to go?"

"Sure."

When they got up to dance, it was the first time he had physically touched her since he was in the hospital. She felt goose bumps and she liked being in his arms. By the third number, they were dancing close. When he dropped her at the house, they kissed passionately at the front door. She had trouble going to sleep that night. She had fallen in love with Walt and she kept thinking about their age difference. He was twelve years older.

The following Sunday, he brought her home for dinner with his folks and that was added to their routine. His parents liked her and she felt at home with them. They started trading off Sunday dinners between her folks and his. As the weeks increased to months, Walt had not done one thing to offend her. One Saturday night during dinner, he slid a small wrapped box across the table to her. She unwrapped it and saw a beautiful diamond ring. She looked at him and tears flooded her eyes.

They were married the following September and they went on a cruise to Europe for a month. They had a glorious time. It was obvious to everyone on the trip that they were totally in love with each other. The glitter of their love did not diminish throughout the entire trip. One evening after the QE2 departed for the States, Walt looked at Beverly with a serious expression on his face.

She said, "What is it, Honey?"

"I didn't think I would ever find a woman that I would want to spend my life with. I have now and you are it. I have a request."

"What is it, Walt?"

He explained that the job of running the family trucking business was no easy task. Two people were presently capable of doing it, his dad and him. "Would you let me teach you how to manage the business to give us more flexibility? Dad is ready to retire and it is poor business to have only one key person."

"If you think I can handle it, I will do my best to learn."

Within a couple of months Beverly had learned the trucking business. She knew the status of all thirty-eight trucks. Where they were, what loads they carried, and she knew most of the drivers by name. Within six months, she had learned to coordinate trips to gain maximum use of the trucks. Few of them returned from a long haul empty. W. Hunter Barnes designated her Assistant General Manager and he loved her like his own daughter. He spent less and less time at the office.

As the years passed, Walt and Beverly had two boys and a girl. They had a nanny to take care of the children while they worked as a team running the business. Over a ten-year period, they had purchased twenty-one more trucks as well as replacing most of the thirty-eight with new rigs. They were living the American dream and life couldn't be better.

In the early 1960s, Walt became less attentive towards Beverly. Neither of them knew it, but he was in the early stages of prostrate cancer. He had a dull pain in the lower back. He didn't mention it to her and took painkillers to get through each day. She was only conscious of his passiveness towards her. At night, he fell asleep in his recliner and went from there to bed and asleep. She laid awake many nights yearning for his love and affection.

The day she walked into Bill's restaurant and saw Paul Baker, she felt ashamed at the desire she experienced for him. After all the years had passed, she knew that she still loved him. She felt giddy during the hours between the two lunch dates and wished the hours away so they could be together again. She was ill at ease riding the bus to New York due to mixed emotions between wanting to be with Paul and feelings of guilt. She enjoyed every minute of their hours together and felt a huge sense of loss on the ride home. She called the Baker residence the next afternoon and felt hurt when Paul's Mother said he had left for Germany. She knew he had three weeks of leave left. She blamed herself for arranging the weekend in New York and driving him off. He had said that he didn't want to break up her marriage.

It was almost a year later when the family doctor discovered that Walt had cancer. He told Beverly that it was advanced beyond hope and he had less than four months to live. It was a miserable time until Walt finally died in his sleep, heavily sedated. She felt a great deal of guilt for not realizing his problem sooner. Eight months after Walt died, she met Paul's mother at Foster's Market in Greenfield. She gave Beverly his address at Fort Benning, Georgia. She told Walt's folks that she wanted to get away for awhile and her father-in-law agreed to run the business for her. She flew to Columbus via Atlanta on Delta Airlines.

He arrived at the airport in forty-five minutes after her call. They greeted each other with a big hug and a warm kiss. While they waited for her baggage, Beverly told him that she had a reservation at the Holiday Inn. Paul wondered what would happen if they met Jean there. Beverly brought him up to date on Walt's terminal cancer and death. She conveyed her guilt feelings for meeting him in New York even though she did not know that Walt had cancer at the time. She said, "Paul, I would like nothing better than to marry you right away, but I can't. I feel that I should wait at least a year after Walt's death." He said he understood her reasons.

On the way to the Inn, Paul told Beverly that he had to be on duty for twenty-four hours starting at 0800 the next morning. He was scheduled as staff duty officer and it would be nearly impossible to get a replacement this late on a Friday. She indicated that it would provide her a chance to get a long needed rest.

Paul parked in front of the Holiday Inn and he carried Beverly's bags into the lobby. The clerk handed her a key after she checked in and said, "Ms. Barnes, you are in room 116 and we have a continental breakfast starting at six a.m." Paul thought, my God, she is in the room next to Jean. He dropped her bags after they entered the room and they immediately locked together in a fervent kiss. They couldn't get enough of each other during the next several hours. Paul finally left a few minutes after six o'clock.

At precisely 9:02 a.m., Beverly walked out of her motel room. At exactly 9:02 a.m., Jean Craig walked out of her room. The two looked at each other and in unison said, "Hi." Jean said, "I am going for a late breakfast. Would you join me?" Beverly said. "Can you believe that I am about to do the same thing?" They introduced themselves. When Jean heard the name, Beverly, she thought, could this really be the gal Paul picked up at the airport? Jean said, "Did you arrive at the Columbus airport yesterday?"

"How did you know?" The girls spent the day together and had a great time relating their relationship to Paul. They both admitted that they loved the same guy.

Jean said, "It appears to me that I am 'Jeannie come lately'."

Beverly said, "We have to check with the 'object of our affection'. Do you agree?" They both laughed.

They had a lot in common intellectually, and similar taste in clothing, food, and drink. By the end of the day it seemed they had known each other for years. After dinner at the officer's club, they went back to the motel to discuss their predicament. Paul was picking up Beverly at ten o'clock Sunday morning for brunch at the club. The two rooms were adjoining and they decided to pull a little practical joke on Paul. Beverly said, "We could become great friends, if we were not in love with the same man."

"I believe you are way out in front of the competition and I think we should be friends, regardless."

At 1001 hours Sunday morning, Paul knocked on the door of room 116. Beverly was in Jean's room when she heard the knock. She went into her own room and closed the door connecting the two rooms. She was dressed in a soft pink dress, nylon stockings, medium high heels and she looked like a million dollars. She opened the door.

Paul said, "Wow. You look gorgeous. How was your day yesterday?"

"I kept busy and I have someone I want you to meet." As she walked to the door between the rooms and opened it, Jean walked through wearing a blue dress, nylon stockings, medium high heels, and she looked like a million dollars. He said, "Wow. What am I going to do with two beautiful women?" All three of them laughed. They went to brunch and had a hilarious time talking about their alternatives...for awhile.

Finally, Paul said, "It is serious time." The girls looked at him with smiles that faded when they realized he meant it. He continued, "I cannot relate the details, but I will be leaving the States soon for an indefinite period of time. A confidential message came in last night while I was on duty. Today is the only time I will have to spend with either of you for the foreseeable future. Forgive me for watering down these unusual circumstances."

Jean said, "I can see that you are telling the truth, Paul. I am the odd one out. I wish you both the best." She got up to leave.

Beverly said, "Sit down, Jean. If Paul wants one of us to leave, he should say so. Right?"

He said, "At this point in time, I am not able to make a firm commitment to anyone. If the two of you agree, we will try to enjoy the day together." The three of them had a smashing good time until the wee hours of the next morning. Monday morning, Jean took Beverly to the airport before she drove back to Alabama.

Chapter 23

PAUL GOES TO VIETNAM

While serving as staff duty officer, on May 23rd, 1965, Paul read a high priority teletype message from the Department of the Army. The message re-designated the 11th Air Assault Division and the 2nd Infantry Division into the famous First Cavalry Division (Airmobile). Once the new division was established, expeditious preparations would be made for relocation to the Republic of Vietnam.

This was the information that he had alluded to when he told Beverly and Jean that he had one day to enjoy their company. He knew the message implied maximum urgency to comply with the directive. There would be little else on anyone's agenda for the near future. He was correct in his assessment. The next two months were nothing short of chaos, preparing and then transporting all the men and equipment to the port of debarkation at Charleston, South Carolina. It was well into September before the transport ships, carrying the bulk of the First Cavalry Division, arrived at the port of Qui Nhon, Vietnam. The final destination was An Khe, due west, in the central highlands. The helicopters flew to the An Khe airstrip. The vehicles drove in convoy over highway 19.

Immediate activity commenced to clear an area large enough to establish a home base. The huge parking space for the helicopters cut out of the jungle was named "The Golf Course." It occupied several acres. The combat engineers began erecting a security fence to enclose the entire facility. While these projects were ongoing, General Westmoreland ordered the division into action west of Pleiku in the Ia Drang Valley. Intelligence reports indicated that a large North Vietnam Army (NVA) force was in that location preparing to attack east in an attempt to cut South Vietnam in half. The First Cavalry Division's mission was to search and destroy all NVA forces in that area.

The time had arrived to test the months of training at Fort Benning, Georgia. There was apprehension on both sides. The NVA was aware of the cavalry's arrival into the country. They were concerned as to their ability to function effectively against a modern superior force.

Paul was an assault helicopter flight leader in "C" Company, 227th Assault Helicopter Battalion (AHB). There were four flight leaders in each of three companies, A, B, and C. "D" was the Gunship Company which provided direct support to the troop lift companies. The gunships were B model Hueys. Machine guns and rocket launchers were installed and the crew consisted of a pilot, co-pilot and two door gunners. One of the door gunners was the crew chief. He had the additional duty of maintaining the helicopter between missions. It was a struggle for these choppers to take off with the weight of the crew, weapons, ammunition, and fuel. Their support of the troop lift helicopters was essential for the successful completion of combat assaults.

The flight leader, Yellow One, was the key individual responsible for the vital phases of each combat assault. The four flight leaders in each company took turns being Yellow One, for a day. Paul's flight of four choppers would be in the lead on that day. The other flight leaders would follow with their four choppers in line depending on how many helicopters were involved. Each flight of four were designated a color to distinguish each one for communication purposes. The first flight was always yellow one, two, three, and four; the second, white one, two, three, and four; the third green one, two, three, and four; etc. There was no limit to how many helicopters could be involved in an assault force.

All combat assaults were conducted according to an established procedure developed at Fort Benning. The Yellow One flight leader was given the mission of arriving at a set of co-ordinates at a specific time with assault troops, labeled a Combat Assault. He would then determine his take-off time to meet the requirement. The Vietnam maps had a scale whereby it was five minutes flight time between the tip of his thumb and the tip of his middle finger with his hand spread wide open against a map. In this manner, it was easy to estimate the time en route to the assigned destination of the assault. The flight path was always planned in an arc rather than a straight line. This afforded the option of increasing or decreasing the time en route. A couple of easily identified terrain features were noted along the flight path. If the flight leader arrived early at one of these points, he could extend the arc thereby increasing the flight time. Conversely, if he arrived late, he reduced the arc and decreased the time. This procedure made it possible for the flight leaders to become very good at arriving at the designated assault location on time.

An artillery barrage, of at least ten minutes, was usually laid on the landing zone (LZ) to be assaulted. It was the responsibility of Yellow One to confirm that the last round had been fired a minimum of two minutes prior to his arrival at the LZ. Once he received that information, on the Artillery Radio Net, he switched to the Aerial Rocket Artillery Helicopters (ARA) radio net and reported, "This is Yellow One. Last round is on the ground. Make your run." The ARA choppers orbited near the LZ at four thousand feet waiting to shoot forty-eight rockets each at the LZ. It took them less than one minute to complete their task and report, "Mission complete." Yellow One immediately switched to his command net and gave the order to his supporting gunships to commence firing. As the troop-lift helicopters approached the edge of the LZ, the door gunners opened fire. Just prior to the troops jumping off the choppers, Yellow one transmitted over the radio, "Cease fire. Cease fire." The troops started jumping off the skids four or five feet above the ground. They were off-loaded by the time the choppers reached a two-foot hover. The pilot applied take-off power and the helicopters left the LZ.

The massive firepower applied to each LZ just prior to the arrival of the assault troops was "standard operating procedure" for the First Calvary Division. It saved untold numbers of American lives. The helicopter crews were involved in as many as six combat assaults each day, seven days a week. Without the artillery barrage, few crewmembers would have survived their tour in Vietnam. Paul was good at performing his duties as flight leader even while receiving intense hostile fire. In fact, he was amazed to find himself as calm as he had been during the months of training at Fort Benning. His voice over the radio did not

reflect the inherent danger of the mission at hand. It resulted in a set-
tling effect for the other pilots in the flight. The 227ᵗʰ AHB commander
realized how well Paul led flights and he often designated him as flight
leader when it was not his turn.

Night operations were much more dangerous. Tracers filled the sky
and added to the anxiety of everyone. When a chopper received a disabling hit, it was next to impossible to make a safe auto-rotation. Flares
illuminated each assaulted LZ. They were dropped from fixed-wing aircraft or shot from artillery batteries. It was as light as day under the
canopy of the flare. The light was necessary to put the troops safely on
the ground, but it also made the choppers an excellent target.

The Ia Drang Valley campaign raged for three days. Frequently, the
Americans were nearly over-run by the enemy. Aerial fire support was
called in as close as one hundred feet in front of friendly troops. The
NVA finally retreated west into Cambodia leaving more than three
thousand casualties. American loss of life was about one tenth that
number. There were dead bodies throughout the operational area.
Many American lives were saved due to being quickly evacuated via
helicopter to a field hospital.

Paul experienced a close call when his co-pilot, CWO Fletcher, was
shot in the neck. Fletcher's reaction was to pull back on the cyclic,
putting the helicopter in a steep climb. They were near stalling before
Paul got him off the controls. Being fully loaded and just above the
trees, recovering from a stall would have been impossible. Fletcher bled
to death before they completed the flight. Paul was Yellow One during
one of the days of the battle. During the after action briefing, the
Battalion Commander said, "Captain Baker, your method of leading
flights is excellent. You have developed a standard that all flight leaders should strive to match."

Paul appreciated the BC's comment, but he was also aware that he
had screwed up on one of the approaches to a ridgeline. His flight of
four was second behind the Yellow flight and he did not maintain
enough spacing. They arrived while the Yellow flight was off-loading
troops and the distance between helicopters was dangerously close. He
related the incident during the briefing when the BC asked for lessons
learned.

Chapter 24

GUNSHIP GETS SHOT DOWN

December 1st, 1965, Paul was assigned a gaggle of eight helicopters to provide a "ready reaction force." Since returning from the Ia Drang Valley, the 227th AHB had been conducting combat assaults around the First Cavalry home base at An Khe. The objective was to clear out NVA units to a radius of thirty miles and reduce the chances of mortar attacks. Paul's flight took off at 0610, heading northeast for LZ Trenton. He carried troops from the 1st of the 7th cavalry Battalion. The LZ was thirty-two kilometers (km) from An Khe and less than six km from the scheduled assaults for the day. He would spend the day monitoring the infantry command net, ready to respond if he received a call for re-enforcement.

Once the flight arrived at LZ Trenton, the troops off-loaded from the choppers. They had to stay in close proximity and ready for a mission at a moment's notice. It was a long, boring day in the extreme heat and high humidity. Even with no physical activity, sweat poured off the men. They carried plastic canteens full of warm water. Cool drinks were seldom available in the jungles of Vietnam.

The troops' uniforms must have seemed strange to the natives, who wore loincloths and most of the children wore nothing. The troops were fully dressed with their sleeves rolled down. The flight crews also wore bulletproof flack vests and gloves when they flew. If a chopper crashed and caught fire, the clothing provided a few seconds of burn protection. That brief time was critical and saved many soldiers from serious injury or death.

The troops ate C Rations, a great improvement over WW II K Rations. They were often eaten right out of the container. If the situation allowed the time, heating improved the taste enormously. An easy way to build a small fire was to draw a small amount of JP-4 fuel from a helicopter into an empty ration can, converting it to a small stove.

Approximately a third of the troops wrote letters during the time spent waiting for an emergency call. They used the butt of their rifles for desks and attempted to keep sweat off the paper. Mail was probably the single most important item on the mind of each soldier. Letters were read and re-read many times. The women who wrote "Dear John" letters to their men in combat, could have no idea of the negative impact they inflicted.

The combat soldier is not on the verge of being killed every day. He may not have been under enemy attack for weeks at a time and then he would go through hell for ten or twelve days. During these periods, he saw his fellow soldiers killed or wounded. Some were close friends, who had been sharing the hardships of life in combat with him. One minute they were vibrant and joking and the next minute a dead body. The soldier wonders if he will be next. He keeps doing his job because he wants to survive and that is the bottom line of living through combat operations.

At 1800 hours, Paul loaded up the troops and cranked up the gaggle to return to home base. They were airborne, turning southwest, when Captain Bill Goodyear reported, "Yellow One, this is Devil Three-six, I have lost engine power and I'm going down." An enemy sniper had put a disabling round into the engine compartment of Goodyear's helicopter. Goodyear made a successful autorotation (landing without engine power) at the base of a steep hill. Paul circled his flight keeping the descending gunship in sight. He reported over the Command Net, "This is Yellow One, Romeo Romeo Fox-trot (ready reaction force), one of my gunships is making a forced landing. I will put the troops we are carrying on the ground to secure the downed chopper." There was enough room near the gunship to land one helicopter at a time. In a matter of minutes, the infantry troops had a perimeter defense set up.

As Paul's flight of eight choppers formed up to return to LZ Trenton, he was ordered to pick up another load of troops to further strengthen the security force on the ground. It took less than thirty minutes to complete that task. He returned to the LZ with his gaggle to await orders to pick up the troops. A Pipe Smoke Company CH-47 Chinook Helicopter would lift the disabled gunship out. The company's primary mission was to recover downed helicopters. The radio call sign had developed because their first company commander smoked a pipe. Paul hoped they would be able to extract the troops before it became totally dark. He monitored the command net and heard that the security troops were receiving hostile fire.

When Paul heard on the radio that the Chinook was lifting out the gunship, he was pleased. They would have some daylight to make the extraction of the troops. When he heard the next transmission he became as mad as hell. Major Gruesome, the infantry battalion's executive officer, told his operation's officer, Captain Dexter, to delay the troop pickup. He said, "I will give you the word when to make the troop lift. The Bravo Charlie (battalion commander) and I are going to eat chow first. We want to see 'Rattlesnake' (227th's call sign) make the extraction of troops." The pickup would have been precarious enough with some daylight and now it would have to be done in the dark. There would be three adversities: darkness, landing at the base of a steep hill, and hostile fire. There would be a fourth when they arrived, the elephant grass was on fire ignited by the tracers.

Paul was fuming. He said to his co-pilot, "If we lose one ship, I'll kill that bastard!"

Major Gruesome had caused problems in the past. He was what was commonly referred to as a "glory boy." He was always looking for something spectacular to do and earn a medal for it. He would put others as well as himself at risk in the pursuit of his desire. The 227th provided command and control aircraft for the infantry. If a single NVA suspect was sighted on the ground, Gruesome would order the pilot to land. He would then run after the suspect with his rifle. This was against normal operating procedures. There could be a large enemy force not in view, putting the helicopter and personnel at risk. The 227th's battalion commander finally got that stopped.

Forty-five minutes later, Paul received the order to pick up the troops. They had to make two trips, landing one ship at a time. Not only was the area on fire, there was a brisk wind blowing towards the base of the hill. They had to make their approach along the side of the hill and then turn into the wind just prior to landing. During the approach, they flew in and out of smoke, which increased the difficulty. While in the smoke, visibility was zero. Tracers seemed to be everywhere. As the helicopters climbed out loaded, they received heavy automatic weapons fire. The tracers passed right in front of the windshield and the sound of the enemy weapon was loud, coming from the right. The slightest adjustment of the gun sighting would have put the projectiles into the cockpit.

All eight choppers made their first individual pickups without taking a hit. After Paul made it clear on his first trip, he listened apprehensively for the potential call of a chopper in distress. They dropped off the troops and returned for the second lift. There was less smoke in their approach path, but the hostile fire was more intense. Paul made it in and out without getting hit. The second chopper made it too. Then he heard on the radio what he feared, but expected, "This is Yellow Three. We are hit, BAD. We're going in. Oh God. We're upside down. Oh mom....Mom!!" Paul looked back just as a ball of fire appeared in the vicinity of the pickup point. The next five choppers made it out taking non-lethal hits. One door gunner got shot in the foot.

As soon as the troops were clear of the crash site, gunships made strafing runs against the enemy strong points. US Navy Crusaders dropped bombs and napalm. The NVA unit was wiped out.

Paul was fit to be tied. The entire crew and troops of the third chopper were killed on impact. The two pilots were personal friends; they had been together since the days of the 11th Air Assault test at Fort Benning, Georgia. It was obvious to Major Milton, the Commanding Officer that Paul was terribly upset and he blamed Major Gruesome for the loss of the men on the destroyed helicopter. Major Milton said, "Captain Baker, simmer down. We all feel bad about the loss of those people, but you can't blame it on anyone. Who knows, if you had made the pickup in daylight, we may have had more shot down. You are grounded until further notice." Two days later, Paul's anger had cooled down and he was put back on flight status.

He had been corresponding with both Beverly Barnes and Jean Lucas since they were all together at Fort Benning. He received five times as many letters from Jean as he did from Beverly. Jean had time on her hands and Beverly was busy running the trucking company. He tried to write to each of them about twice a month. He felt that his relationship with them was most peculiar. Neither woman pressured him and they always asked if he had heard from the other one. He could tell that the women were writing to one another as well. They both sprinkled perfume on their letters and each had their own special fragrance.

Jean Lucas returned to her lonesome routine at her home in Enterprise. At times, it was frustrating trying to be both father and mother to her two sons. She knew that she was much easier on them than Craig would have been. Life seemed so easy before he was killed. They were living the American dream and she never thought that it would end so abruptly. The times that Paul was at their home, she thought of him only as a good friend. She wondered how that feeling had developed into the love she now felt. There were plenty of single good looking men available and she had been out a few times. She often asked herself, Why did I have to fall in love with a man who has someone else near and dear to him?

She had been writing to Paul at least once a week. She would start a letter Sunday afternoon and write some each day during the week. She felt a strong urge to write flowery love letters, but she was afraid that they would turn him off. She did end each one with "I love you." She received one or two letters from him each month and he always ended with "Lotsa love."

Candy Monroe, one of Jean's friends from flight school, called and asked her to go with her to a dance at the Officer's Club on a Saturday night in November. Her husband, Jerry, was on TDY (temporary duty) at Fort Walters, Texas. Jean liked the idea. Candy said she would pick her up about eight thirty p.m. It was Thursday morning and Jean was happily looking forward to the dance. After lunch, she drove thirty miles to Dothan to shop for a new cocktail dress. She picked out a flowered dress with a full skirt that reached just above her knees. It had a plunging neckline and exposed a fair amount of cleavage. The sales clerk said that it was perfect for her and she added, "Every man that sees you in this will wish he was with you."

Saturday afternoon, Jean started getting ready for the dance. She went to Cherry's Beauty Shop in Enterprise. Cherry gave her a facial, manicured her nails, and shampooed and set her hair. When she got home, she took a leisurely bath, shaved her legs, and got dressed. She used her favorite lilac scented perfume. She looked in the mirror and approved of what she saw. Then she thought, why am I doing this? Paul is in Vietnam. She considered calling Candy and backing out of going. Then she thought, she is counting on me to go with her. Maybe it will be fun.

Candy arrived a few minutes early and she looked gorgeous with a light green cocktail dress that matched her eyes. It had a deep plunging neckline, which was obscured by fancy lace. A longer look revealed her large breasts, which were voluptuous and ravishing in proportion with her build. Her high heels made her look much taller and brought out the beautiful shape of her long legs in nylon stockings. She wore a triple-string necklace of cultured pearls with matching earrings, bracelet, and an emerald ring on her right hand. Jean thought, she looks like she just stepped out of Saks Fifth Avenue.

She said, "Candy, I'm not sure I want to go to a dance with such a stunning lady. They will think I'm one of Cinderella's sisters."

Candy laughed and said, "You are going with me and I could say the same about you."

Both women wore mink stoles that added just the right finishing touch for their night out. They climbed into Candy's Mercedes convertible and off they went. They walked into the Officer's Club and every eye in the place watched as they were escorted to a table just off the dance floor. They each ordered a margarita. When the drinks arrived, Candy picked up her glass and said, "Here is to a wonderful evening." Jean started to raise her glass and stopped halfway between the table and her mouth. Her expression changed drastically. She looked like she had seen a ghost. Candy noticed immediately and said, "What's wrong, Jean?"

"Paul Baker is standing at the bar." Candy turned just as the man looked in their direction. They both said at the same time, "No. It's not him."

He was a major wearing dress blues, three rows of ribbons and senior pilot's wings. It was obvious to him that both women were staring in his direction. He grabbed his drink and walked toward their table. Jean thought, he even walks like Paul. When he got to their table, he stopped and said, "I have never had the pleasure of seeing two more beautiful women. That is not a line. It's the truth." The girls laughed and asked him to join them.

He said, "My name is Clark Walker and I have a friend, Ben Tullos, at the bar. Could he join us as well?" The girls introduced themselves to him and Candy said, "Please bring your friend to our table if you wish?" Once all four were seated at the table, Clark ordered a round of drinks. Before the waitress returned, the music started and Clark asked Jean to dance. Ben and Candy followed them onto the dance floor. After three or four more dances, the four of them were visiting together like they had known each other for years.

Jean felt a strong attraction towards Clark and she thought that he liked her. She noticed that he was not wearing a wedding band. She finally got up enough courage to say, "Clark, do you mind if I ask you a personal question?"

"Fire away."

"I was wondering if you are married?"

"I was married for nearly eight years. She didn't like being hitched to a military pilot and the continuous moves. She felt that she was always waiting for me to come home. Fortunately, we had no children. I have been single for more than five years."

Jean explained her situation to him, including the fact that she had two sons. Towards the end of the evening, they were holding each other close and Jean thought to herself, I really like this man.

The bandleader announced that they would play one more three-song set for the evening. Clark had danced all evening with Jean. During the last dance, he said, "Jean, may I take you home?"

"No. Candy is married and I promised to stay with her the entire evening. Her husband is away on TDY. He doesn't mind if she goes dancing as long as she is with one or more lady friends all evening."

"May I take you to dinner tomorrow evening?"

"No. I try to be home the nights before a school day. The boys do their homework better if I am there. Really, I am not just making excuses." She gave him her phone number and asked him to call her later in the week.

The men walked the girls to Candy's car. Ben gave Candy a hug and a quick kiss on the cheek. Clark pulled Jean tight against him and looked into her eyes. She liked the feel of him against her and they kissed each other on the lips. They held the kiss a few moments then he said, "I'll call you Thursday night about seven." They kissed again. By this time, Ben was walking towards the club and Candy was in the car with the motor running. As they pulled onto the road, Candy said, "Hey, lady! It looked to me like the two of you were getting along. Am I right?"

"Other than Paul, he is the first man I have felt attracted to since Craig died." It took Jean a long time to go to sleep. She couldn't get her mind off Clark Walker.

Ben and Clark went to the bar for another drink. Ben said with a big grin, "Clark, it looked to me like you and Jean found some common ground. I wish I could have taken a picture of the way you two looked at each other."

"I have to admit it. I like her very much. Until tonight, I didn't think I would ever marry again. She is not a woman interested in a one night stand. I respect her for that, too."

Clark and Jean went out both Friday and Saturday nights the following weekend. Jean invited him for Sunday dinner as well. She wanted to see his reaction to her sons. During the meal, Clark asked the boys how school was going. Richard, the oldest, mentioned he was having difficulty with his math. When they got up from the table, Clark said, "Richard, may I have a look at your math homework?"

He hesitated then said, "Yes, sir. I guess." In a few minutes, the two of them were totally engrossed and Clark was tutoring Richard. It was obvious that Richard was understanding the instruction and enjoying the help. When they finished, he said, "Thanks a lot, Major Walker." Jean could tell that her son was really pleased.

The following weekend was pretty much of a carbon copy of the first. Clark helped both boys with their homework on Sunday. The third weekend, all four spent Saturday on Clark's boat in the Gulf. The boat was a nineteen-foot Chrysler with an aluminum hull designed especially for fishing or water skiing. It had a 75 horse-power outboard motor. Both boys took turns steering the boat and it was obvious to Jean that her sons liked Clark. They spent the last half of the day bottom fishing and caught two red snapper and a large grouper. They all had a wonderful feast that evening after Clark cooked the fish over charcoal. Jean had not seen her boys as happy since Craig died.

That evening after the boys went to bed, Jean said, "You seem to have made a big hit with my sons."

"They are fine boys. I have always thought how nice it would be to have a family."

The boys had hinted about going out on the boat next Saturday so Jean said, "Don't feel you have to take us out on the boat next week-end."

"Jean, I had a wonderful time and we will go again on Saturday if the weather is good. We were lucky it was warm today." He put his arms around her and they kissed passionately for a long time. Jean finally pushed him away and got up.

"Clark, it has been wonderful, but I think you better go."

"What's wrong. Did I offend you in some way?"

"No, you have been a perfect gentleman, but I may be falling in love with you and I don't want to get hurt."

"Jean, I know I am falling in love with you. I just don't want to rush into marriage and then find out it was a mistake. One of those is enough. I want to see you every possible minute as long as you enjoy my company. In other words, don't agree to spend time with me if you are not one hundred percent for it, okay?"

"What about my sons?"

"If this relationship goes where I think it's going, I'll want them to be my sons." They were in each other's arms again. Jean leaned her head back and looked at Clark with tears in her eyes.

She whispered, "Clark, I do love you."

"I love you too."

Their relationship continued, and their feelings for each other grew stronger. They refrained from going to bed together. Jean explained that she would be sick with regret if they let nature take its course.

Clark said, "You may not believe this, but I am glad you maintain such a high standard for yourself."

"There are so many reasons, my upbringing, my sons, and my respect for Craig even though he is dead."

The boys seemed to totally accept Clark around the house every weekend. He not only helped with their homework, he fixed various things for them as well as normal household items that break or quit working. By late spring, both boys had learned to water ski and they seemed content spending the time as a family. Richard, who was fourteen, surprised Jean one Monday morning by asking, "Is it possible that you and Clark will get married?"

"There is a possibility that we will, some time. What do you think about that idea?"

"Tommie and I have talked about it. We think he would be a great stepdad." With that, he grabbed his books and went out the door.

Jean's letters to Paul had decreased considerably from one each week. She decided it was time to clue him in on her relationship with Clark.

May 23rd, 1966

My dear Paul,

Something extraordinary has happened to me and I think you will understand. Last November, I met a wonderful man. Candy Monroe and I went to a dance at the Officer's Club. We were there only a few minutes, when I actually thought I saw you at the bar. After a few seconds, I realized that he was not you. He caught me looking at him and we ended up dancing all evening together.

We have been going steady for months now and it looks like we are made for each other. He adores my sons and they seem to like him equally well. He is the only other man that I have felt a real attraction to since Craig died. I assume you know that you are the first. If he asks me to marry him, I plan to accept.

I have been thinking of writing to you for weeks. I hope you, Beverly, and I remain friends because I cherish you both. Our relationship and the way

*Bev and I met is one for the books. You will always have a special place in
my heart.*

> *Love,*
> *Jean*

She mailed the letter and felt better because of it. She wrote to Bev
and told her basically the same thing. Four days later, Bev called and
enthusiastically told her how happy she was for her. She said, "I do feel
a little let down. I thought that we were going to share the same guy."
She laughed and added, "I am so pleased that you have found a good
man for yourself and one who likes your sons, too. You deserve to be
happy again."

On June 15th, 1966, Jean became Mrs. Clark Alfred Walker. They
were married at the Fort Rucker Chapel. During the reception, both
boys went up to Clark. Richard said, "Do you mind if we call you Pop,
Pop?" Everyone within hearing range laughed.

Chapter 25

THE RAPPELING MISSION

Less than a month after Paul's supporting gunship was shot down, the commander of the 1st of the 7th Infantry was killed when his unit came under mortar attack. Major Gruesome was on the promotion list to lieutenant colonel so he was designated the new commander. Paul read about it in the *Stars & Stripes*, the newspaper published by the U.S. military. We will have more trouble supporting that unit was the first thought that came to his mind.

It was only a few days before his prediction came true. Gruesome submitted a request to 227th Flight Operations for rappelling a platoon of soldiers onto a mountaintop east of Kontum. This was to be followed by a combat assault into a small clearing five kilometers further north along the ridgeline. The assault troops would arrive an hour after the rappelling operation was complete. One of Gruesome's long range reconnaissance patrols (LRRP) reported a company size NVA unit south of the clearing. The plan was for a two-pronged attack from the north and south.

Paul and his flight platoon were assigned the rappelling mission. He checked his map of the area and didn't like what he saw. He went to Major White, the battalion operations officer, and discussed the mission's misgivings. Rappelling from a helicopter is probably the most dangerous mission for a chopper pilot. The helicopter must hover, out of ground affect, while the troops rappel to the ground. It puts the entire operation at risk to potential enemy fire. During the operation if the chopper engine loses power, for whatever reason, it will crash killing all aboard as well as those on the ropes. A helicopter cannot make a successful auto-rotation without forward travel.

Paul said, "Major White, you are well aware of the inherent problems when conducting rappelling operations. Added to those difficulties, the troops will be dropping down through the jungle canopy. If a rope becomes tangled in the trees, it is nearly certain we will lose the chopper it is hitched to. I recommend that we reject the mission request." White answered, "Our BC has accepted the mission. I checked with him as soon as it came in. War is hell, Paul."

Paul countered, "Yes and we are doing this to make our 'glory boy' (Gruesome) look spectacular. It is a happy day for him when he can observe us in the worst possible situations. Remember, I am doing this mission under protest."

He called his flight crews together and did his best to brief them without showing his doubts for the mission. He said to the door gunners, "Stay alert and report the slightest drift to the pilot. It is imperative that each chopper stay stationary to avoid tangling a rope in the trees." He was well aware that the artillery, rocket, and machine-gun fire applied to each LZ prior to a combat assault usually neutralized enemy resistance. But there was to be none of that for this operation. If the NVA troops were on the ground under them, it would be like shooting frogs in a well. Especially, if the enemy troops waited until the ropes were dangling down through the trees. Paul thought, it would be a miracle if we accomplish this mission without a serious problem.

Paul had his flight, loaded with troops, in position to commence rappelling at daybreak. Each chopper was about two hundred feet apart, in line. The top of the jungle canopy was nearly eighty feet above the ground. Two troops on each helicopter started down through the trees, one on each side. It was slow because they had to work themselves down through the thick foliage while keeping their ropes from becoming tangled. All their equipment, including weapons and ammunition, made the job extremely cumbersome. It seemed to take forever before the first eight troops were on the ground.

While the second group of troops was descending, a door gunner in the third chopper reported forward drift. The pilot was confused and corrected in the wrong direction. The door gunner shouted over the intercom, "You're drifting forward! You're drifting forward!" The pilot, still confused, added more correction in the wrong direction. One of the troops on his rappelling rope was pulled against a tree branch. The rope slid towards the tree trunk and became wedged in the fork of another branch causing the chopper to be pulled down. The pilot applied more power, which accelerated the downward pull and, in seconds, they were in the trees. The main rotor blade sliced into the treetops. About ten inches of one blade tip broke off. This imbalance of centrifugal force ripped the transmission out of the chopper frame. A broken brace sliced into the fuel cell and the chopper burst into flames. In a matter of seconds the machine became a fireball as it burned its way towards the ground.

The chopper hung in the trees thirty-five to forty feet above the ground and continued to burn. Three of the infantry soldiers jumped and grabbed onto branches, then lost their grip due to the intense heat. The two troops rappelling and all aboard were killed. Paul grasped the impact of the situation from reports from his door gunners. A feeling of panic came over him, followed by the thought that he had to take control of himself. After a moment, he said, with no noticeable emotion in his voice, "Stop the rappelling. Have those men on the ground monitor their radio for further instructions." There had been one man equipped with a radio among the first eight troops on the ground. Six more men made it to the ground, making a total of fourteen.

If the enemy force was close by, they were in extreme danger. The burning chopper would pinpoint their location with ammunition exploding due to the heat generated by the fire. The operation had turned into a disaster and it wasn't over yet. Paul made a full report, en route to their temporary base of operations. He recommended that the scheduled combat assault be conducted immediately to divert the enemy away from the burning chopper.

As it turned out, there was no sign of the NVA. The assault troops combed the area for a day and a half. They found the fourteen troops who had rappelled in as well as the remains of those killed in the accident. They also recovered the back third of the helicopter tail boom and rotor. Everything else was destroyed by fire. Paul blamed Gruesome for the tragedy. He wondered how long they would have to put up with him. The two pilots lost in the debacle had replaced those killed during the troop extraction, three weeks back. They had come to the unit fresh from flight school.

Colonel Caster, Brigade Commander, took a dim view of the rappelling accident. He felt that he was wide open for a congressional investigation. He discussed it with the First Cavalry Division Commander. The result of that meeting was a directive: "Rappelling operations will never be conducted through the jungle canopy without the approval of a Brigade Commander or higher." Major Gruesome was relieved from command for poor judgment in ordering the mission. A message was sent to the Department of the Army, requesting that Gruesome be removed from the Lieutenant Colonel promotion list. He was transferred to USARV Headquarters in Bien Hoa and assigned a desk job, USARV Cost Reduction Officer.

Gruesome was mad as hell over the whole affair. He told Col. Caster that he was made the scapegoat. He said, "My career has been ruined due to the incompetence of a helicopter pilot!" His words fell on deaf ears and the next day he was on a chopper en route to Saigon. His normal arrogance was now tempered with a bad attitude. It wasn't long before he was known around headquarters as an obnoxious SOB!

He did work hard at his new duty. He was authorized to order up helicopter transport in the performance of his mission and had his own jeep and driver. He seldom used his driver and he disregarded the idea that there was any danger driving between Saigon and Bien Hoa. Consequently, he made the trip two or three times a week, without even a weapon. In less than a month, his mind was changed. One day, half way to Bien Hoa, he slowed down to pass an old Vietnamese truck stopped in the middle of the road. There were several Vietnamese standing around the vehicle. He started to accelerate as he got by them. He heard a thump and looked in the back of the jeep. A package, a third the size of a brief case, was lying on the floor. Apparently, it had been tossed in by one of the men on the road.

Less than a second from the time he saw the package, he let go of the steering wheel and rolled out of the jeep to the ground. As he rolled into the ditch, he heard a deafening explosion. The jeep was blown to bits! Gruesome crawled into the brush and lay still with his ears ring-ing. The Vietnamese piled into the old truck and drove off, laughing. He stayed hidden until a machine-gun mounted Military Police vehicle came along. He hitched a ride to Bien Hoa. After that day, he always used his driver. They were both heavily armed and they waited to follow an M.P. patrol vehicle on each trip.

Gruesome had two and a half years left to complete twenty years of active military service. He completed his tour in Vietnam with orders to Fort Benning, Georgia. He served out the remaining time until retirement as Officer Club Manager. He repeated the rappelling incident over and over again to anyone who would listen, hoping for sympathy.

Chapter 26

PAUL & BEVERLY MARRY IN HAWAII

*B*everly was happy for Jean's luck in finding a good man to help her raise her sons. She was also anxious for Paul to complete his tour in Vietnam. She realized the danger of being an assault helicopter flight leader. She prayed daily for his safe return and he was on her mind a great deal of the time. Each letter she received, she read several times. They took a minimum of ten days to arrive. The day a letter came asking her to meet him in Hawaii for a six-day R&R leave, she was filled with happy anticipation.

Several weeks after Walter died, she had hired Charles Clarkson as dispatcher. He had learned the job well and it had taken much of the load off her. She finally had time to stay home a couple days a week and work in her flowerbeds. Walter's dad was in poor health and he had lost touch with running the trucking business. It seemed to set him back considerably when Walt died. She was so thankful that she had learned the business. It would have been a disaster otherwise when Walt got too sick to work.

She wrote a letter right back to Paul telling him she would meet him for the R&R. The letter included this paragraph:

Forgive me for this, but could we get married in Hawaii? Walter's parents are near and dear to me. It would be appalling to them for me to meet you other than as man and wife. They would look at it as you and I shacking up. It would be a bad influence for my children too. They are aware of how much I care for you and I believe they would accept our getting married. Of course, I want your honest answer as to whether you want me as your wife. If you do not like the idea, I don't feel, in good conscience, that I can meet you. Believe me, I want to very much.

Her letter was in the mail before the day was out and her hand trembled when she slid it through the mail slot. She couldn't help remembering when he rejected her many years back. At the time, her feelings were deeply hurt. She had never lost her love for him. Even during the many happy years with Walter, she often thought of Paul. She still felt guilty for their secret meeting in New York. She was now glad that Paul had returned to duty three weeks early. She would have gone right on meeting him and the truth would have inevitably come out.

It was twenty-three days before she received an answer from Paul. During that time, she kept herself busy in an attempt to get her mind off wondering what he would say. She gave Charles a week's paid vacation so she would have to run the business without his help. She was still filled with anxiety and anticipation. She would toss and turn in bed at night even though she was tired. It was usually after one a.m. before she went to sleep. She made several calls to Hawaii to find out the requirements for a couple to marry. The only thing she had a problem with was the ten-day waiting period after a license was issued. She got an exception approved by the mayor of Honolulu. Everything was arranged.

Finally, there were two letters from Paul the same day. She opened one and quickly scanned it. It was obvious; he had not received her proposal of marriage at that time. The other letter was dated a day later.

December 1, 1966

My Dear Future Wife,

I am thrilled at the thought of us getting hitched in Hawaii next month. I had planned to ask you to marry me after I completed this tour. I understand your feelings completely. I am looking forward to our R&R together with my favorite girl friend and wife.

I plan to resign from active duty as soon as possible, once I complete this tour. I am not sure what I will do as a civilian, but it will probably have something to do with helicopters.

I just wrote to you yesterday, so I will get this in the mail right away. We will celebrate Christmas and New Years a little late in Hawaii.

>*All my love,*
>*Paul*

Beverly was overjoyed and she drove to her in-laws to tell them. They seemed pleased, especially when she told them that Paul planned to leave the military service. Her mother-in-law said, "That's wonderful, Bev. Children need a full time father." That night after dinner, she broke the news to her children. They were less than enthused. Her oldest son, Philip said, "Does this mean that he will be trying to tell us what we can or can't do?"

"He will be your stepfather and legal guardian. Yes, he will have the authority of a father. I'm sure it will work out for the good of everyone." The two boys headed for the stairs and went to their rooms. Tears started down her cheeks. Luanne, her ten-year-old daughter, went to her mother and hugged her. She said, "It's okay, Mom. I know you have been lonely since Dad died. We will all get used to it."

For the rest of the vacation holidays, the boys never brought up the subject of a stepdad in front of Beverly. She knew it was on their minds because they were quiet and subdued. She overheard Luanne tell them one morning, "You two ought to be ashamed of yourselves. You're both selfish and uncaring. Mom needs someone in her life, too." They were attending Mount Hermon School, on Route 10 beside the Connecticut River. Philip was a junior and Steve was a freshman. Both boys were consistently on the honor roll. Phil played first string on the varsity football and basketball teams. Steve was on the junior varsity wrestling team and he loved the sport. The school, founded by D.L. Moody, was proud to have young men from countries around the world in attendance each year. Bible classes were a mandatory part of the curriculum. A diploma from Mount Hermon was almost a guarantee of being accepted into any college in the United States.

The 5th of January 1967, Paul caught a ride on the battalion commander's helicopter, which was making a run to An Khe. He got a seat on an Air Force C-123 enroute to Cam Ranh Bay, where he was scheduled to depart for Hawaii the morning of the 6th. The chartered United Airlines, DC-8, left at 0800 sharp with every seat occupied. There were six beautiful stewardesses aboard and they had a great time serving the GIs who had not seen an American woman for months. They were constantly being told they were pretty or beautiful and each one received several offers of marriage. United had gone all out to serve excellent in-flight meals. There was a never ending patter of loud, joyful talk for several hours followed by only the sound of the jet engines when most of the men had fallen asleep.

After arriving in Hawaii, military buses transported the men to Fort DeRussy where they were herded into a large room for a briefing. It seemed like forever before they were finally turned loose to find their loved ones. Paul and Beverly ran into each other's arms, kissed, and held each other for several minutes before they could talk. Tears streamed down her cheeks and he had a lump in his throat. They had a room at the Ilikai Hotel and they never let go of each other until the cab pulled up to the front door.

They entered their room on the eighth floor just before noon, dropped their bags, and fell into each other's arms. They couldn't get enough of each other for a full hour and a half, and then they fell asleep. It was well after three p.m. before Paul woke up. He had been dreaming that he was in the jungle of Vietnam smelling the aroma of a beautiful flower. When he woke up, it took him a couple of seconds to realize that he was in bed with Bev. It was wonderful. He kissed her and they made love again. Then Paul said, "I'm starving. Let's call room service."

"Great idea. I'm famished too."

Paul ordered a bottle of Rhine wine, bacon, eggs, country fried potatoes for two, and a quart of milk. He had not had a glass of real milk for months. They took a shower together and finished dressing just before their breakfast arrived. Half way through the meal, Paul asked, "When do we tie the knot, Honey?"

"Tomorrow at 2:00 p.m. Are you getting cold feet?" She raised her eyebrows with a slight smile.

He thought, she looks even more beautiful when she does that. He said, "Are you kidding? Do you think I am going to let you get away again?" After they ate, Paul walked out on the balcony to absorb the view and sweet smell of Honolulu. He turned to Bev and said, "Tell me it is not a dream. I am so happy."

At 5 p.m., they heard a loud low-pitched sound that seemed to have no end. They rushed out on the balcony and looked down at the patio. A large Hawaiian man was blowing on an enormous seashell, making the strange noise. He was dressed like the ancient King, Kamehameha. Once he put down the shell, twelve Hawaiian girls, dressed in ti leaf grass skirts and floral leis, danced the hula. Five Hawaiian men provided the music by singing and playing ukuleles and guitars. The hula dance told a story through the swinging and swaying of the girl's hips, arms, and fingers. The show lasted thirty minutes and it was beautiful. The girls rotated their hips faster then it seemed humanly possible for the finale. This was a daily event at the hotel.

Paul and Bev went for a walk and window-shopped. They went in a store that specialized in Hawaiian apparel and purchased two sets of matching, brilliantly colored shirts. Paul also, bought a white, haband type dress shirt for the wedding ceremony. When they got back to their room, both were hungry again. They changed into one set of their shirts and took a cab to the Wharf Restaurant. They enjoyed an elegant meal with premium service. Their dinner included red wine, turtle soup, fresh fruit salad, broiled mahi mahi fish, and dessert. Paul drank two large glasses of milk. They stuffed themselves.

Paul said, "Would you believe me if I said I'm tired?"

"I'd believe you if you said that you wanted to go to bed." They both laughed.

On their second day together, they were at Walgreen's Drug Store for breakfast. They both were having difficulty convincing themselves that it was real. Beverly was living the long awaited dream of having Paul as her mate and husband. Paul was still trying to believe that he was actually in this paradise called Hawaii and a few hours from marrying the woman he had loved most of his adult life. Just two days ago, he was in the jungles of Vietnam. He thought, she is still a beautiful woman. I have never felt so content with life. She was thinking, we really are made for each other. The only way I can be happier is when he is home with me to stay. Please, God, make that time come soon.

At 12:30 noon, they were at the Fort DeRussy Officers' Club drinking a Mai Tai. The club was built before World War II. There was an outside patio with a stage, tables and chairs. The area was fringed with coconut palm trees and decorated with a Hawaiian theme. They finished their drinks and took a taxi to the Fort Shafter Chapel. Paul was not aware that it was the same chapel that Lester had attended to meet

Lilanii. Chaplain James LaRose, a US Navy Commander, conducted the marriage ceremony. Beverly wore a light blue dress, white-flowered lei, an orchid corsage and a veil. Paul wore the white shirt he bought for the occasion, dark blue trousers, and a blue-flowered lei. For the rest of his life, he would remember the fragrance of the flowers during the ceremony.

They went to the *Honolulu Advertiser* to drop off the marriage notice with a nice write-up. Beverly arranged to have a copy of the paper mailed to Walter's parents. They would also pick up a paper for themselves the next day. Paul could see that she was extremely happy and he felt a sense of satisfaction too. They returned to the officers' club to celebrate the occasion. Their happiness must have radiated from their faces because it wasn't long before all the people in the club knew they had just been married. They couldn't pay for their drinks due to the generosity of those present. They were invited to join one table with four couples and a gala time was had by all of them. A small Hawaiian dance band started playing easy listening music mixed in with native island songs at nine p.m. During the last dance, Paul said, "Honey, I have never enjoyed a day more than this one." They looked into each other's eyes and Beverly tried to speak, but couldn't. Tears of joy rolled down her cheeks. They kissed until the music stopped. Everyone on the dance floor was looking at them. They all applauded.

It seemed like only a moment had passed when they awoke the next morning. While Paul was shaving, he felt a flash of pensiveness. He thought, "The time is passing so fast." After breakfast, they put on swimsuits and took a long walk on the beach. It was mid morning when they got to the Royal Hawaiian Hotel. There were beach chairs provided by the hotel. They hung their shirts on one of the chairs and went swimming. The water was just cool enough to be exhilarating. It was a gorgeous day. The ocean view and Diamond Head in the distance looked beautiful. After the swim, they sat in the beach chairs to dry off. Then they went into the hotel and ordered Bloody Marys. Paul had noticed a strange looking tree near the hotel. It had limbs running almost horizontally with vertical limbs reaching the ground. They had rooted and provided support. One of the hotel waiters told him they were Eucalyptus trees, better known as "government trees" (you clipped us). The bartender placed a dish of macadamia nuts and a bowl of freshly cut pineapple in front of them. Both items were a delicacy in the islands.

Buses provided public transportation and Paul and Bev paid a quarter to ride to Paradise Park. It was nothing short of exquisite with dozens of exotic birds and boardwalks through a large area of rain forest. Included was a thirty-minute show with birds doing a variety of tricks or talking. Paul looked at Beverly during the show and thought, I love her so much. I can't believe that nearly half of our time has gone on this R&R. That evening after dinner, they went to the movie, the Blue Max. Beverly fell asleep a couple of times. Neither one had gotten adjusted to jetlag.

All too soon, it was day four. They both realized that more than half of their time in the Hawaiian paradise had gone by. After breakfast at Walgreen's, they rented a car for the day and started driving the road that circled Oahu. They came to an area of the beach with huge waves rolling in. Numerous surfers were riding the forward crests of the waves. Some lost their balance and disappeared under water for several seconds. They continued on their drive and the road became hazardous and dangerous due to solid slanted rock. Paul stopped the car and looked at the map he had been given. He said, "Uh oh, we are on a piece of the road that is off limits to these rental cars. We were supposed to turn off the beach road a quarter mile back and by-pass this part." With difficulty, he got the car turned around. They both felt relieved when they got back to the recommended route. On the trip, they visited a pineapple farm, a Japanese temple, and ate a nice lunch in a small village. They returned the car close to 4:00 p.m. and took a taxi to the officers' club. They had signed up for a traditional native luau sponsored by the club. They went back to their room, stuffed and tired, about mid-night.

On the fifth day, they rode the shuttle boat to the Arizona Memorial. More than 1,000 sailors were still entombed in the sunken ship, since December 7, 1941. They walked through the Ala Moana Shopping Center. It was huge and had a built-in pool, loaded with colorful fish, running through the main walkway. They were back in their room at two p.m. to take a nap.

They had tickets for a dinner cruise on a large catamaran boat at six p.m. The boat sailed off shore just before dusk to enjoy the beauty of the Hawaiian sunset. They were served mai tais and an excellent meal. There was also a dance band. Paul and Beverly thoroughly enjoyed themselves. The setting sun reflected off the water and scattered cirrus clouds while the lights of Honolulu blinked on. It was a breath taking experience. They were back at the hotel near nine p.m. and went to the lounge. There was an underlying thought in both of their minds. It was their last night together in Hawaii. The band played slow dance music most of the evening. Paul and Beverly stayed until the lounge closed at one a.m.

They got up at seven, showered, dressed, packed, and left for breakfast at Walgreen's. They both put on a front of cheerfulness while they actually felt a crushing emptiness. They each wished they could stop the passing of time and be allowed to stay in this beautiful part of the world. Paul thought, I wish we had not wasted our time going to that movie. The only other time he had such a terrible feeling was when it looked like he had to leave Les in Russia. Beverly had been on the verge of crying since she awoke that morning. Several times she wiped tears from her eyes hoping that Paul did not notice. It was the most heart wrenching feeling of her life. She thought, I may not ever see my wonderful man again.

Paul's plane left at 2:00 p.m. During their last kiss, Beverly did break down and sobbed heavily in his arms. They held tightly to each other and neither could speak. Paul felt the tears flooding his eyes and he kept wiping them away. He finally had to let go and board the plane. All the men kept looking back and waving with solemn faces. Paul looked out the window and watched her crying, holding a hankie to her face, until the plane taxied away towards the runway. The laughter and happiness expressed by those same men en route to Hawaii, was totally gone on the return trip.

Chapter 27

PAUL IS CAPTURED NEAR BONG SON

The battalion commander's helicopter was at An Khe when Paul arrived from Hawaii. He caught a ride back to the jungle location. His unit was at LZ English near Bong Son and they experienced a rough week while he was on R&R. The NVA had units scattered all through the Bong Son area. They were fighting viciously to hold their positions. Every one of his four helicopters had taken hits and one door gunner had been killed. His first day back, he led six combat assaults. When he had time to think about Beverly and Hawaii, it already seemed like a dream. That night their location came under a mortar attack between two and three in the morning. Shrapnel hit several troops as they ran for previously dug foxholes. Those who lay down on the ground as soon as the explosions were heard, seldom got hit.

It was another five days before the moderate to heavy hostile fire started to abate. Each night when the crews finally had a chance to sleep, Paul found himself wondering whether or not he would live through another day. He was convinced that he would have already been killed if the division did not apply the heavy artillery fire on each LZ just prior to the arrival of the assault helicopters. He gave credit to his supporting gunships as well. Invariably they effectively attacked enemy positions, which took the attention away from the lift choppers.

On the eighth day since his return to duty, it appeared the enemy had withdrawn from the area around LZ English. C Company was co-located with Battalion Headquarters. Major Milton told Paul to report to Lt. Col. Packwood, the battalion commander, at the operations tent. The first thing Packwood said was, "Paul, who is the senior man under you in your flight platoon?"

"1st Lieutenant Jack Seymore."

"Is he qualified to lead the platoon on combat assaults?"

"Yes, sir. I believe he is."

"Good. As of this minute you are the battalion flight operations officer and Seymore has your flight platoon." Paul was taken by surprise. He was looking at another five months as flight leader one minute and the next minute he had a staff job.

The new job included nearly as much flying time as before. Lt. Col. Packwood wanted to be in the air during every combat assault and he wanted Paul to fly with him. It was considerably less dangerous than leading flights, but they always flew without a wingman. If they got shot down, no one would know exactly where they were. It would especially be true at night and they flew two or three nights a week. Paul was usually busy in operations from 2200 to 0200 hours at night receiving missions from the infantry battalions. He then scheduled times for each request and assigned the mission to a particular lift company. More times than not, the infantry asked for more helicopter support than was available. He had to make decisions as to what mission to give higher priority. Occasionally, one of the infantry commanders bitched to Packwood and Paul got overruled, but most of the time his decision was law. Packwood was a good man and Paul liked his new job. He was so busy, there were precious few hours off each day.

At 2115, February 28th, 1967, Packwood said, "Paul, grab your helmet. We're going to LZ Uplift to plan an assault with Joe Wiggins" (Joe commanded the 1st of the 5th Infantry Battalion). The flight to LZ Uplift was less than fifteen minutes, but it wasn't wise to fly direct routes. Snipers would set up along the route and shoot at single helicopters, especially at night. They decided to fly east about five miles, then south, and approach the LZ on a westerly course. They had been on the southerly leg about two minutes when they heard a loud snap, followed by the panel lights going dark and a total loss of engine power. There was a full moon so Paul could see what he thought was a clear place to make an auto-rotation. Due to his reduced visibility, he flared late, hit the tail boom, and then landed hard enough to spread the skids. All four crewmembers were badly shaken but not seriously hurt.

Whatever caused the accident took out the electrical system. It had disabled the radios as well. Packwood ordered, "Get the weapons and ammo. Move into the woods in case NVA troops saw us land. Be quick about it!" The two officers helped the door gunners get the machine guns and ammunition. They headed westerly and forced their way into the thick jungle growth. Sergeant Miller, door gunner and crew chief said, "Sir, I want to return to the chopper to get some C rations and smoke grenades."

Packwood answered, "Good idea."

Paul said, "I'll go with him, Sir." They started back at a fast pace. They had a box of rations, six smoke grenades, more ammunition, and a machete when they got back.

Packwood said, "Where did you get the machete, Sergeant Miller?"

"Sir, I had it stashed in the chopper."

"Good man."

The officers agreed to stay put while it was dark. They all took turns pulling guard duty while the others tried to sleep. They heard nothing other than normal jungle sounds throughout the night. Packwood had wrenched his ankle when they had left the chopper. It swelled to twice the normal size by morning and he couldn't walk on it. At daylight, Paul and Sergeant Miller started through the jungle towards LZ English. They took two of the smoke grenades, the handguns, machete, and some rations. They figured they were ten miles at most from LZ English. Packwood and the other door gunner set the machine guns pointing towards the clearing and the downed chopper. They were prepared to pop smoke if a helicopter flew over.

It was tough going through the jungle. Without the machete, it would have been nearly impossible. It was more than an hour before the two who stayed behind could no longer hear them. Paul and Miller stopped to listen every few minutes in case some NVA troops might have heard them. A little less than four hours had passed when they did hear human sounds ahead. They had not been detected so they moved further ahead being as quiet as possible. Finally, they saw NVA troops eating a meal. They estimated their numbers at twelve to fifteen. After a few minutes, they started off going almost in the same direction as Paul and Miller. It was obvious that they were following a trail.

Paul reasoned that if they followed the NVA troops and stayed just out of sight, it would probably be safe. He said, "I will move up the trail alone a hundred yards or so. Then I will motion for you to come. We will keep doing that and we should make good time. If I am caught, stay hidden and maybe you will be able to get through for help." Paul ran in a crouch until he either caught a glimpse of the NVA troops or started to lose sight of where Sergeant Miller was waiting. He and Miller moved along in this manner for about an hour. Paul was making another run when suddenly, NVA troops were all around him. They had their weapons trained on him and a couple of them looked like they were about to shoot. He felt the muzzle of a gun pressing against his back and he dropped his handgun. Suddenly he was pushed into the woods surrounded by the NVA.

A few moments later, a flight of two choppers flew directly overhead. They were in view for about two seconds. The troops pulled Paul back in the open and tied his hands behind his back. They all started back down the trail from where they had come at a trot with Paul in the middle of the line. It seemed like an hour before they stopped for a short break. One of them opened a can of C rations that they had taken from Paul. Two of them tasted the food and made faces of distaste. The can was offered to Paul and he finished the pork and beans. He was hungry and it tasted good. He could see that they were discussing how bad the food had tasted to them. Near dark, they turned off the trail to a much less obvious trail. In a few minutes, they came to an NVA camp. Paul estimated that there were eighty to a hundred troops there.

He was amazed to see so many enemy troops camping so close to LZ English. He figured they were about five miles away or less. The jungle thickness was the reason they could safely be there. Paul's hands and feet were tied tightly. His feet were pulled up behind him, and then a rope was looped around his neck and tied to his ankles. If he tried to straighten his feet, the rope choked him. The position the ropes forced him to stay in grew more painful as time went on. It seemed like the night would never end. He found himself praying for a miracle, which he felt was his only salvation at this point.

After several hours, he still had not slept. He wondered if he would be able to walk when and if they untied him. Thoughts of Beverly and their short stay in Hawaii occupied his mind. He thought he heard a noise behind him, he felt someone grab the rope around his neck and then the rope was being cut. He was able to straighten out his feet. He felt the rope around his wrists being cut and then the ones around his ankles. The feelings were gone from his arms and legs. Someone whispered in his ear. It was Sergeant Miller. He rubbed his lower legs and ankles for several minutes. Finally, with Miller's help they moved quietly into the jungle thicket. Paul ached all over, but Sergeant Miller kept urging him on.

They were finding it more and more difficult to travel due to the thick underbrush. As soon as dawn started to break, Miller suggested they lay still and wait. Paul was in favor of that. They heard yelling back at the NVA camp. Apparently, Paul's escape had been discovered. Within a few minutes, Paul was sleeping from exhaustion and relief of being free. The need to relieve himself woke Paul after about four hours. He and Miller shared a can of C rations together and Paul thanked him for rescuing him. He said, "I had no thought that you would follow me and my captors. Thanks a million and one times!"

"Sir, there is no way I would leave you with those monkeys if there was any possible alternative. I thought I would have a good chance of getting you back after dark! It worked out that way, too." He laughed.

"Miller, when we get back to the battalion, I'm putting you in for the Silver Star. You have probably saved my life!" They did get back to base camp late that afternoon, tired hot, sweaty, and covered with insect bites.

Sergeant First Class John Miller was born and raised in Waukesha, Wisconsin. He graduated from high school with honors and went to work at the local firehouse. In less than a year, he and a friend decided to join the army. Due to his high aptitude score, he was selected to attend the aircraft maintenance school at Fort Rucker, Alabama. He graduated in the upper third of his class with a promotion to PFC. He was assigned as a maintenance trainee on the flight school helicopters. He had an excellent attitude with a good work ethic. In six months, he was promoted to specialist fourth class and he made Post Soldier of the Month six weeks later. He was transferred to duty as assistant crew chief on the commanding general's helicopter. Two years later when he received orders to Vietnam, he was a staff sergeant. The commanding general liked Miller's job performance so much he got him a special promotion to sergeant first class and he awarded him the Army Commendation Medal. When he arrived in Vietnam, his record got him the job of crew chief on the 227th Assault Helicopter Battalion's command and control helicopter.

Chapter 28

ARA GUNSHIP AND C-47 COLLIDE

One evening the week following the forced landing, Paul and Packwood were in the air to observe a ten ship combat assault by 227th AHB helicopters. The destination of the assault was a valley northwest of Bong Son. An Air Force C-47 would be dropping flares to illuminate the landing zone. Night assaults had additional hazards to concern the pilots. The chances of a mid-air collision were many times greater. Careful planning by the flight leader was imperative to avoid flying into a mountain. He had to time each leg of the flight route to know when it was safe to start descending towards the LZ. One mistake in this planning could result in flying into a mountain and the loss of several aircraft.

Once the flight came under the canopy of light provided by the flares, it was as bright as day. There would be two or three flares floating down under small parachutes. Occasionally the flares had a short burn time or didn't work at all. If the sky went suddenly dark, it would be several seconds before the pilots could see anything. It further increased the chance of a mid-air collision. Once the choppers left the light of the flare on take-off, the same problem occurred adjusting their night vision.

Paul and the battalion commander were orbiting overhead waiting for the troops to load at LZ Uplift. They were monitoring Yellow One's radio net and heard White Three report that his transmission warning light was on. That chopper could not be flown until it was checked by maintenance. Paul said to Packwood over the intercom, "Sir, I recommend that we fill in for White Three rather than let the assault go with one less load of troops."

Packwood answered, "Let's do it."

Paul transmitted, "Yellow One, this is Tiger Tail Three, we will fill in for White Three."

Yellow One answered, "Roger and thanks."

Minutes after the troops were loaded on Packwood's command & control aircraft, the gaggle took off on the mission. They headed west, climbed to 1500 feet, and maintained that heading for twelve minutes. Yellow One then turned north to a heading of 350 degrees. In less than ten minutes they could see the artillery rounds exploding at their destination LZ. When they were five minutes from touch down, flares started illuminating the area.

Yellow One received last round confirmation from the artillery unit two and a half minutes from touchdown. He immediately switched to ARA and told them to make their run. The assault was going exactly according to procedure when they heard on the radio, "Oh God, no...Turn right...TURN RIGHT!!.... It's too late...." There was an explosion high over the LZ. One of the ARA choppers had collided with the C-47 that was dropping flares. Both aircraft were going nearly straight down in flames and neither one made a radio transmission after the collision. They hit the ground about a quarter of a mile apart and burst into bright orange flames. The investigation later revealed that they hit nearly head-on.

Packwood got on the radio and said, "Yellow One, this is Tiger Tail Six, take the flight back to LZ Uplift."

"Roger." He applied climb power and turned southeast once he was above 1500 feet.

During the return flight, Packwood instructed Yellow One, "As soon as we land at Uplift, I will off-load the troops on my aircraft. I will then return to the crash site with your gunships and see what we find. You monitor your radio for further instructions. Keep the infantry troops close by, just in case."

"Roger, sir."

It was more than forty minutes before Packwood's Charlie Charlie and the gunships were back. The two aircraft were still burning. Packwood transmitted, "Devil One, Tiger Tail Six, I will be making a slow low pass over the two burning aircraft. There may be someone alive. Orbit five hundred feet above and report anything unusual like hostile fire."

"Roger, sir."

They passed over at about fifty feet with their landing light on and saw no one at either location. They made a second pass perpendicular to the first with the same results. Packwood said to Paul, "Let's head back to Uplift."

Just then, one of the door gunners said, "Sir, I see a light flashing off to our right."

Paul looked down and said, "I see it too."

Packwood got on the radio, "Devil One, we have a light in sight on the ground. We will check it out. Keep us covered."

"Roger, sir."

They made a low pass and a GI was seen illuminated by their landing light. Paul said, "I think we can pick him up, Sir."

"I think you're right. Door gunners, keep your eyes peeled for any obstructions. One of you may have to help him." The man kept flashing his light as they came around again and descended to a two-foot hover. Sergeant Miller jumped off the chopper and helped the man aboard. Packwood transmitted, "Devil One, we have our man and we are coming out."

"Roger, sir. We have you in sight."

Air Force Staff Sergeant Peter Smith from Sacramento was the man they picked up. He said that he was sure no one else on the C-47 got out. He was the only one who had a parachute on when the chopper hit them. He said he always wore one and he received a lot of ribbing for it. He further stated that the plane was spinning so fast that he almost couldn't get out. He knew without having the chute already on, he would not have made it.

Troops were put on the ground at daybreak the next morning. It took several hours to get the remains picked up at each site. It would be weeks before positive identification could be made of all the bodies. A definite cause for the accident could not be determined. Each had been assigned altitudes, which were 1000 feet apart. The crew of the other ARA chopper swore that they were at 4,000 feet, their assigned altitude. Smith couldn't say at what altitude the C-47 was. He was in the back involved with dropping flares. He said he heard one of the pilots yell over the intercom, "Pull up. Pull UP!" There was a bright flash and it felt like the plane jolted to a stop. He and two other crewmembers were thrown against a forward bulkhead. He bailed out the door where they were dropping the flares. It was difficult due to his arm being broken when the two aircraft collided.

There was some good fortune in the tragic ordeal. Intelligence reports had indicated an NVA unit in that area and it apparently was false information. They would've had a perfect opportunity to attack while the recovery of bodies took place.

Beverly's flight departed Hawaii nearly two hours after Paul left. She had never felt so distraught during that time. She sat in the terminal staring at the spot where Paul's plane had been parked. After she boarded her plane, a handsome young sailor sat next to her and immediately attempted to talk with her. She tried to ignore him by looking out the window.

Finally, he said, "Ma'am, you are very beautiful but you look sad. If I am being a pain, just say so and I will shut up."

She said, "A couple of hours ago, I said good-bye to my husband on his return to Vietnam."

"Oh. I understand completely. I'm sorry. Do you mind telling me what he will be doing over there?"

She explained Paul's duties and then the sailor told her all about his girl friend he would be seeing soon. He did help to get her mind off Paul's departure and she felt better.

Once she got home, she went to work every day and stayed immersed in her job. Her sons stayed on campus at Mount Hermon. Luanne was in the seventh grade at Greenfield Middle School. As young as she was, she seemed to understand her mother's grief and tried to be helpful. She didn't ask about the trip to Hawaii. The first Sunday morning after Beverly returned, she asked Luanne if she would like to hear about the trip. They had a fine time discussing it most of the morning. On the way to church, Luanne said, "Mom, it sounds like you had a wonderful time and I am happy for you. It's nice that Paul is going to get out of the service, too. You won't have to keep saying good-bye all the time."

The following weekend, Beverly picked up her sons at Mount Hermon. They all sat down to the evening meal on Friday night.

Steve said, "Mom, did you have a nice time in Hawaii and do we now have a stepdad?"

"The answer to both questions is yes. Thank you for asking."

Phil said, "Mom, Steve and I have talked it over and we will try to accept Paul into the family. I guess it must be tough to lose a husband, but it's tough for us to get used to the idea of someone replacing dad.

"Oh, Phil." She got up from the table and rushed over to hug both boys. Tears were streaming down her cheeks. Tears came to both boys' eyes and Luanne left the table crying. It was several minutes before anyone could eat. It turned out to be an upbeat weekend. They all went to the Garden Theater Saturday night and saw the movie, *No Time For Sergeants*.

Beverly felt so much better now that her sons had accepted her marriage to Paul. She wrote a long letter to him Sunday night after she took the boys back to school. She also prayed for his safe return and it took awhile for her to go to sleep.

Paul was so busy that it was the middle of May before he knew it. He received orders to the U.S. Army Aviation Test Board at Fort Rucker, Alabama. Lt. Col. Packwood had written to the Department of the Army recommending him for the assignment. His orders arrived May 18th directing his departure from Vietnam on or before June 10, 1966. It authorized a 30 day leave prior to reporting to Fort Rucker. He departed Saigon on June 7th aboard an Eastern Airlines DC-8. He looked out the window and watched the coast of Vietnam pass out of sight. He looked up and thought, thank you, Lord for letting me live through this ordeal.

It was a long flight but the thoughts of going home to be with Beverly occupied his mind. He called her from San Francisco and gave her his arrival time at Bradley Field near Hartford, Connecticut. En route across the country, he wondered how soon he would be able to leave the service. He had written DA but received no answer. He planned to stop there on the way to Rucker after his leave. Perhaps he would be able to get out without reporting in to the Test Board. He was going to look into the possibility of opening a helicopter operation based at the Turners Falls Airport. It was certainly feasible with the money Les had given him.

Beverly and Luanne met him at the airport. Tears of joy flowed freely and Luanne even called him daddy. Bev handed him the keys to her 1966 bright-red Cadillac. It was easy getting on I-91 North and in a little over an hour they were driving up the steep driveway to the mansion on the north side of Greenfield. Walter and Beverly had bought the house when they first got married. Paul was overwhelmed with the ornate beauty of the buildings and the manicured landscaping. He said, "Bev, I had no idea how nice your home would be. It is nothing less than luxurious."

"It has been a lonesome place for me for a long time. I think that is about to change."

"Does it bother you having me in here?", he asked.

"Absolutely not. Does it bother you?"

"No, but if you want to buy another place, we will."

That was the only time the subject came up. There was no uneasiness by all three and Luanne seemed to like calling Paul "Daddy". The boys were in Malone, New York, at a summer camp. They called their mom each Sunday night and never asked about Paul. They were apparently having a great time.

The second day after getting home, Paul went to see his parents and Les. His folks were in their late sixties, and in good health. Matt was still selling used cars and having a great time doing it. Primarily, his inventory consisted of fancy or limited edition automobiles like convertibles, 1956/57 Thunderbirds, Edsels, etc. Les had built a beautiful home on Fox Hill. He also bought the Perry Farm in north Bernardston and the Henry Root Farm on the south side of town. He hired Louis Parks, his uncle, to manage both farms. He owned one of the finest dairy herds, registered Holsteins, in New England and produced record quantities of milk per cow. Ernest Parker of Northfield hauled his milk to Springfield seven days a week. All the buildings and equipment were kept in top notch condition. They raised corn and hay each summer to feed the cattle during the winter months.

Les also ran the auto restoration shop on Hoe Shop Road. He added three more stalls and employed eleven men, including the manager, to restore classic cars. He and Dorothy traveled much of the time, buying vehicles for the business. "Baker's Classic Cars" was the title of a full-page advertisement he ran in *Hemming's Motor News*, published in Bennington, Vermont. He had established such an excellent reputation; it took a man full time to answer phone calls from all over the country. A restored vehicle was usually sold within three weeks after completion of the work. One 1941 Ford four-door convertible was purchased by a Sheik in Saudi Arabia. It was loaded on a jet cargo plane at Bradley Field. It was not unusual for a vehicle to be sold before work was complete. Every car produced a fine profit.

The brothers went to the garage on Hoe Shop Road and Paul was amazed at how much larger the operation had become. The men were working diligently and with determination at their respective locations. When they were in Les' office, Paul remarked, "Les, every one of your employees seem to have an excellent attitude. Are they really as good as they look?"

"Yes. I run my shop using a method developed by Lincoln Electric of Cleveland, Ohio. Mr. James F. Lincoln, founder of the company, named it *Incentive Management*. Each man is paid a base hourly rate, which, by the way, is darn good. At the end of the year, they receive a bonus, which can be as high as 80% of their gross pay for the year. The foreman runs a grading document on each individual. Any mistakes or faulty work can be traced back to the person who did it. Each fault found takes a large bite out of their bonus. It pays them to do their work with perfection. It's a great system."

Les said, "Paul, I sold one of my more expensive cars to one of your wife's truck drivers. I am still wondering how he could afford it?"

"What's his name, Les?"

"Sherman Summers from Millers Falls and he paid me in cash. He brought the money in a tackle box and it took more than an hour to count it. The bills were of all denominations from five to a hundred and the condition ranged from nearly worn out to new. They were all mixed up in the tackle box. The price of the car was $18,000.00. He seemed nervous while we were counting out the money. I guess he still had a couple of thousand left. I delivered the car to his house and we put it in a shed there."

Paul said, "That is peculiar. I'll ask Beverly about the guy."

Les restored a 1932 Stutz Bearcat, which he kept in his garage on

Fox Hill. He and Dorothy used it for Sunday drives during the warm months. They also took it to antique automobile shows in the New England area. One or more people at these shows always tried to buy the car, but Les would not part with it. The owner of an automobile museum in Daytona Beach, Florida, offered him $50,000.00 at a show in Roxbury. Les took his name and address and said, "If I find another one to restore, I'll call you."

During Paul's leave, he and Les took their wives on a ten-day Caribbean cruise. They flew to Miami and boarded the ship there. All four enjoyed the trip immensely and they hit it off well together. One evening at a beautiful restaurant and lounge in Nassau, Paul thought, Les looks twenty years younger right now than he did when we met in the Russian prison. The four of them discussed how long it took both couples to finally be together.

Les said, "Paul do you realize that if you and Bev had married when she finished nurse's training, I would have been in a Russian prison for life."

Paul said, "Look at the bright side. I'd have twice as much money as I have now." They all laughed.

Paul left for Washington on his twenty-fifth day of leave. He drove Beverly's red Cadillac and he thought he would be able to resign his commission and be home in a week to ten days. He was at the Signal Branch in the Department of the Army offices the next morning. He was sitting at the desk of Major Thomas Dudley waiting for an answer to his request to resign. Dudley was going through his records, jotting down numbers every so often. When he finished, he took a calendar and did some more calculating. Finally, he said, "Major Baker, you owe the Army twenty-two more months of active service before you can resign. You accrued the time by attending the Signal Officers' Advanced Course and the helicopter transition course."

Paul was stunned and said, "It never crossed my mind that I owed additional time for those courses. By the way Major Dudley, I am a Captain."

"Major Baker, you were promoted this past June 7th to major." Paul called Beverly and told her the bad news. He said, "Honey, I have to continue on to Rucker and sign in at the Test Board. You and Luanne can join me when I get a place for us to live."

Chapter 29

SHERMAN SUMMERS

Sherman Summers from Millers Falls, Massachusetts, dropped out of school after the eighth grade. He had repeated both the seventh and eighth grades and quit the day he turned sixteen. He got a job pumping gas for thirty-five dollars a week at the ESSO station in town. After six months, he had saved fifty dollars. He also met a girl, Sheila Tidwell, at the Friday night square dance in Turners Falls. She was about his age, extremely well built for her age, and had come to the dance with her folks. They lived on Western Avenue in Brattleboro, Vermont. Sherman danced every slow dance with her throughout the evening. Bill Shattuck's Band played round dance music after each set of three squares. By the time the last dance was in progress, the young couple moved their feet very little. Their arms were wrapped around each other holding their bodies tightly together. They were definitely in love.

Every day that Sherman had off, he hitchhiked to Brattleboro to see Sheila. One day he had been at the junction of US Routes, 5 & 10 in Bernardston for more than an hour trying to get a ride. He had been looking over at the cars for sale at the Baker Mansion and he knew they were much too expensive for him. He noticed a 1937 Ford V-8 pickup truck parked back near the garage. He decided to walk over and look at it.

Matt came out of the house. "Can I help you, young man?"

"Yes, sir. I was wondering if that Ford pickup is for sale?"

"Every vehicle I own is for sale, but let me tell you about that truck. It has to be held in second gear and it needs a ring job. It smokes all the while it is driven."

"If it can be driven on the road, I am interested. How much would you have to get for it, Mr. Baker?"

Matt guessed that the boy probably had no money. He answered, "I will sell the truck, as is, for $150.00."

"Sir, could I pay you $50.00 down and $20.00 each month until it is paid off?"

"You will have to leave the truck here until it's paid off."

Sherman worked at saving his money. He wanted that truck more than anything. He actually paid between thirty and forty dollars each month. In less than three months, he was driving between Millers Falls and Brattleboro. He and Sheila started going to the drive-in movie at Hinsdale a couple of nights a week. The seat in the truck was small, but he managed to get her pregnant. They got married when she was two months along and his folks let them stay at their house. Sherman was a good worker. The owner of the ESSO station sold heating oil and had a sizable delivery route. The driver got another job driving a trailer truck for Raymond Puffer, so Sherman was offered the oil delivery job. It paid $60.00 a week and he jumped at it. He had favorably impressed Matt Baker too.

Matt had taken, in trade, a 1941 Chevrolet Coupe, which was in fair condition. He had a price of $300.00 on it. He allowed Sherman $100.00 on his truck and let him pay $40.00 a month on the car. He let him take the car when they made the deal and Sherman made the payments on time every month.

As time went on, Sherman managed to buy a small house in Millers Falls. He and Sheila had two kids and his folks were glad to get them out of their house. His dad co-signed the loan with him. The grandchildren nearly drove him nuts and he was willing to do almost anything to get his privacy back. Sherman and Sheila were much happier too. He continued to maintain a good work ethic and paid all his bills on time. He was now driving the fourth vehicle that he had bought from Baker Motors. He applied for a job with Barnes Trucking in Turners Falls and listed Matt Baker as a reference. Matt's dealings with the young man had always been excellent and that is what Matt told Walter Barnes when he called. Sherman got the job.

The policy at Barnes Trucking with a new driver was to schedule him on local area trips towing a thirty foot box. Local meant the New England states and Sherman did a good job for Barnes. He was never late for work and business people who used their trucking service made good comments about him. Walter Barnes took a liking to him. Sherman dressed neatly, was reliable, and he had an excellent attitude. After about six months, Walt asked him if he was ready to start hauling a forty-foot box and drive long hauls. His pay would go up a hundred a week and he would have a travel allowance. Sherman said, "Yes, sir. That sounds wonderful to me."

Deliveries to the northwestern states always included a stop in Chicago. Deliveries to the southwestern states always included a stop in Atlanta. If there was any space left in the box, it was usually filled in those cities. The dispatcher at the home base in Turners Falls always had all the arrangements made for those pickups. The first time Sherman made a run to Los Angeles, everything went without a hitch. He off-loaded and reloaded at the same terminal. When he left the terminal, he did make a wrong turn. He drove nearly twenty miles before he corrected his route from that mistake. Once he was clear of the heavy city traffic he took an exit to refuel and get a bite to eat.

As he went into the truck-stop restaurant, a young man with a ponytail and beard was walking close behind. He said, "Sir, just a moment. Would you sit at a booth with me? I have something to ask you."

Sherman didn't like the look of the guy, but he said, "Yes. I guess so."

After they sat down, the man said, "You are the driver of the Barnes Motor Express truck, aren't you?"

"Yes. I am,"

"Do you drive through Atlanta on your return trip to Massachusetts?"

"Yes."

"Would you drop off a box for me? I will make it worth your while and it is small, about the size of a shoe box."

Sherman said, "What's in the box? Why don't you mail it?" The waitress stopped at their table and they both ordered lunch.

After she left, the young man said, "Sir, I can't tell you anything except where to drop it off. I won't tell you my name and I don't want to know yours. If you do it, I have an envelope in my pocket with five hundred dollars in it for you."

Sherman asked, "This is something illegal, isn't it?"

"The less you know about this the better. All you will know, if someone asks, is a person asked you to drop off a small box."

Sherman said, "Let me think about it while I finish my hamburger." He thought to himself, it seems like an easy way to make five hundred dollars. He is right. The only thing I will know is that I have a box to drop off. Finally, he said, "Tell me exactly what is involved."

"Take the exit Six Flags Over Georgia just west of Atlanta off I-20, turn right to the Texaco Truck Stop. Pull to the back part of the parking lot and leave the box on the passenger seat with the door unlocked. Call this phone number. He handed him a small piece of paper with a phone number written on it. When you hear the phone start to ring the second time, hang up. Don't go back to your truck for at least forty-five minutes. That's it."

Sherman said, "I get five hundred dollars from you now, before I leave?"

"Yes."

"Okay, I'll do it."

"A couple more things. Don't tell one person what you did. No one. The next time you are in this area, if you want to make another delivery, dial that same number. When the phone starts to ring the second time, hang up. Don't forget to leave the passenger door of your truck unlocked and stay away from it for at least forty-five minutes. You deliver it the same way as this one. By the way, memorize that number."

Sherman asked, "How do I get paid the second time?"

"There will be an envelope with the box," he answered.

Sherman got the package and his five hundred dollars and headed east. At first, he considered hiding the package. Then he thought, I'll just leave it sitting here in the cab with me. All I know is I am doing a guy a favor and dropping the package off. He had never been stopped on the road, even for speeding. He figured that it was an easy way to make five hundred and there was little or no risk. The drop-off went according to plan. When he got home, he put the money in his tackle box in the shed and placed it on a high shelf. Walter Barnes asked him how he liked the long haul. He said, "I liked it and I'll make that trip anytime. On that southern trip, there is less risk of bad driving conditions."

Sherman found himself making that trip three or four times a month. Each time, he delivered a box at the Six Flags exit. They had more than doubled the size of the box, but they had also put a thousand dollars in the envelope. Sometimes the bills were shabby and other times they were new in all denominations from five to one hundred dollars. When he got home, he always put the money into the tackle box. He didn't dare put it in the bank.

He made the Los Angeles run so much, the other drivers kidded him about having a girl friend there. Sheila didn't like him gone so much and she didn't know that he volunteered for the trip. The other drivers hated to drive in that city.

He kept a mental tally of the approximate amount of money in the tackle box. He knew there was close to $20,000.00 and he became concerned as to what he should do with it. He was afraid to take it to the bank. They would be suspicious and they might report it to the police. Then he got a bright idea. He could buy one of Les Baker's restored antique cars. It would be as good as putting it in the bank. He would tell his wife that he was storing it for Baker. The following Saturday night after supper, he said, "Sheila, Les Baker wants to store a car in my shed. He will pay me $50.00 a month rent."

She said, "That's nice. Why does he want to do that?"

"It is sold to a customer out west. They want it stored until he comes to pick it up. Please don't talk to anyone about it. I don't want someone trying to steal it."

When he made the deal with Les, he felt extremely nervous. He could tell that Les thought it strange that he had all that cash in a tackle box. While they were counting the money, Sherman said, "Please don't mention this to anyone. I've been gambling on my California trips and doing quite well at it."

"I guess you have."

Sherman received a "Paid in Full" bill of sale. He rented a safe deposit box at the Franklin Savings Bank in Greenfield to store it. He put the balance of the money in a cloth sack and put it in the box too. He wasn't too sure how he would eventually be able to use the money, but he felt it would require a major move several miles away. He would probably sell the car back to Les, which would provide him with a legitimate check to deposit when they moved.

A week after Sherman bought the car, Walter Barnes died from advanced cancer. His death caused a shake-up in the trucking operations. Beverly became much more involved and she made some policy changes. One affected Sherman directly. All long hauls would be on a rotation basis among the drivers. She felt that it was not fair to any one driver to be gone so much. Sherman thought about going to her directly, but he thought it could make her suspicious. He had become paranoid during the months of delivering those damn packages. Every time he saw a police cruiser, he got a strange feeling in his stomach. One day a Georgia State Trooper followed him into a diner. He almost panicked and ran. His hands trembled all the while he ate his lunch.

He made the Los Angeles trip once every seven or eight weeks. He couldn't resist making the phone call and there was always a package when he returned to the truck. The money in his tackle box accumulated at a greatly reduced rate.

About a year after the operational change for the drivers was in effect, Sherman's dad stopped at his house. He asked Sheila if he could borrow his son's tackle box to go fishing. She said, "Help yourself, Dad. He hasn't gone fishing since we moved here." George Summers was shocked when he opened the box. He went immediately to the house and asked Sheila if she knew what was in it. He could tell by her response that she had no knowledge of the money. George put the box on the kitchen table and opened it. Sheila said, "My God. Where did all that money come from?" They counted it and it came to $5,230.00. There would have been more, but Sherman had been dipping into it. There was the $50.00 each month he was supposed to be receiving from Les Baker and he took an additional $50.00 for spending money.

The next day, Sherman returned from a trip to Trenton, New Jersey. When he got to his house, his folks were there and his tackle box was sitting in the middle of the table. Sheila and his folk's faces all had the same expression. His dad said, "Son, I found the money and I want to know where it came from? I also want to know where you got the money to buy the 1922 Franklin Touring Car. I called Les Baker and he said you bought the car with cash." Sherman told the whole story in detail. They talked way past midnight and George convinced him to call the state police the next day.

The first thing the police did was to arrest Sherman for suspicion of delivering drugs. Then they impounded the money and antique car and filed a report with the FBI. An agent was at the county jail interviewing Sherman the next morning. He made a complete confession and promised to co-operate fully. Agent Thompson got him released on his own recognizance and told him not to leave his house. The FBI moved quickly. They put the two contact points under surveillance and had Sherman make a trip to Los Angeles. He made the normal pickup and delivery and never heard what happened after that. He was given two years' probation. The FBI sold the Franklin back to Les.

Sherman was glad it was over and he felt himself lucky receiving only probation. He told the whole story to Beverly, who by then was married to Paul. She kept him on the job and he was thankful. Sherman told his dad, "I wish you had found that money a lot sooner. Thanks."

Chapter 30

US ARMY AVIATION TEST BOARD

M ajor Paul A. Baker signed in at the United States Army Aviation Test Board on July 10th, 1967. Ten days later he was attending the OV-1 Mohawk transition course. The Mohawk is a twin-engine, turbo-prop, 18,000lb, surveillance aircraft manufactured by Grumman. It has two seats, side by side, for the pilot and equipment operator and is capable of three primary missions, infrared, photo, and radar mapping. With a pair of 150 gallon drop tanks, it has a flight endurance time of 4.5 hours. Equipment included an FD-105 integrated flight control system and Martin Baker ejection seats.

Landing and take-off training was conducted at Malone, Florida. During this phase of the transition course, an unexpected and startling incident occurred. Paul and his instructor pilot were on downwind at Malone. The IP was explaining a portion of the pre-landing check. Paul glanced at him just as he heard a loud noise along with the IP leaving the aircraft through the top of the cockpit. His ejection seat had apparently malfunctioned and fired accidentally. As Paul turned on the base leg of the approach, he glanced back and saw the IP descending attached to his parachute a few feet above the ground.

Paul landed and parked the Mohawk. By the time he got to the IP, he had his chute rolled up. Paul said, "What were you saying?" The IP looked at Paul and laughed. He wasn't hurt and it now seemed funny.

The balance of the course went without incident. Paul liked flying the Mohawk and he was detailed to work on a new transponder under test. His first mission on the test was to fly to Providence, Rhode Island. He contacted the air defense office in that area to start the project. An armed technician met him at the aircraft each morning to install the new transponder. The unit was classified secret. Then Paul took off and made radio contact with the radar personnel. He flew specific courses until he was out of range, then reversed course. Once he was back in range, he climbed one thousand feet and reversed course again. This procedure was repeated throughout the day.

Normally, the tests were started at five thousand feet. At Providence, they started much higher due to a solid overcast, which reached eleven thousand feet. Paul had to file an instrument flight plan to get above the clouds before the flight legs were flown. The northeast is a high-density air-traffic area. As he flew the assigned courses, he saw two or three commercial jets each hour. The third day of the flight test, as he was climbing up through the overcast, an Aero Commander suddenly appeared out of the clouds. They were on a collision course and both pilots took evasive action. They were too close and hit right wings at approximately 7,000 feet above the ground. Paul felt a tremendous jolt. In seconds, he realized that his starboard engine was stopped. The wing had sheared off just beyond the engine nacelle. He was in a tight flat spin and the aircraft would not respond to his attempt to control the plane. He glanced at his altimeter and saw his descent passing through five thousand feet. He mashed on the radio transmit button and said, "May day. May day. Army 14247 has sustained a mid-air collision. I'm out of control and I will eject. "

He repeated this the second time and pulled the ejection handle. The next thing he became aware of was the opening of his parachute and the lack of noise. He could not see a thing and he prayed that the Mohawk would not crash on people or buildings. It seemed like forever before he started hearing automotive traffic and then a baseball field appeared below him. He landed with a jolt and the chute snatched him against the backstop behind the batter's box. His left arm was wrenched against the wire and he felt a sharp pain in his shoulder. He pulled the parachute's quick release straps and dropped safely to the ground.

Paul had landed at Norfolk Downs, south of Boston. The Mohawk had crashed into Quincy Bay and sunk. A pilot and co-pilot were in the Aero Commander and neither man got out. It crashed on Thompson Island just east of the University of Massachusetts, Boston Campus.

Both men were killed and burned beyond recognition. The following investigation revealed that the Aero Commander had turned left when the pilot had been told to turn right, which resulted in the mid-air collision. Paul was taken by ambulance to Chelsea Naval Hospital. After a complete physical, he was given two weeks convalescent leave. He rented a car and drove to Greenfield. Beverly was still living at the mansion on the Bernardston Road. She had enrolled Luanne in Stoneleigh Prospect School and she planned to fly to Dothan, near Fort Rucker, as soon as school started.

They took advantage of the unexpected two weeks together. Paul's sore shoulder put a damper on some activities they might have done, but they had an enjoyable time. Phil and Steve showed no animosity towards him during the four days before they returned to Mount Hermon. They recognized how much happier their Mother had become since she married Paul. Both boys agreed. They were a family again and a happy one. When they were alone together, they often talked about their dad. They did have one regret. They wished they had had more time with him before he died. It seemed like they were away at school, camp, or he was too busy and they vowed that it would be different when they had families of their own.

During the second week of leave, Paul and Beverly vacationed in the White Mountains and the scenery was magnificent. They drove to Maine and took the coastal route south to Portsmouth, New Hampshire. The fishing villages looked like something out of a travel guide. They rented a cottage for two days, which overlooked a bay full of boats with the ocean in full view beyond the highway. The second morning in the cottage, before they got out of bed, Paul said, "I will always regret not marrying you when you finished nurse's training. Because of me, we lost a lot of years together."

"Things usually happen for a reason. Lester was probably right. If you had not gone in the army, he would have died in a Russian prison."

The day after they returned to Greenfield, they both flew to Dothan, Alabama. They moved into post quarters which had been reserved for them.

During the first week back at the Test Board, Beverly ran into Jean Walker at the commissary. They were both glad to see each other. They visited several minutes in one of the aisles, then finished up shopping. Beverly drove over to Jean's house after she put her groceries away. They planned to get together on the weekend being sure their two men would like each other.

Claude Hargott checked Paul out in the U-8, a twin-engine Beach aircraft. It was used by pilots who took turns flying the transponder test around the country. He had been back at the board one week when he was flying to Providence in the U-8. The first morning he flew the Mohawk again, he was apprehensive but it didn't last long. The weather was beautiful and seeing the New England States from the air was fascinating. One day he was released from missions over Portsmouth. He descended to 2,000 feet and picked out the motel where he and Bev had stayed less than two weeks before. He turned west and in twenty minutes he was flying over Greenfield and Bernardston. He made two low passes over Les' garage. On the second pass the men were outside waving. He couldn't tell whether or not Les was one of them.

He had a room at the Diplomat Motel and he had a rental car, authorized and paid for by test board funds. He was off duty Saturday and Sunday so he drove to Bernardston, just over a hundred miles. He stayed at his folk's house, but spent most of the time with Les. He took Les and Dorothy out for dinner at Bill's Restaurant in Greenfield. Mike was still tending bar or hosting the restaurant there. The restaurant was kept in excellent condition and the food was always superb. He went by Stoneleigh Prospect School to see how Luanne was doing. She cried with tears of joy when she saw him and he had lunch with her in the school cafeteria. Luanne was enthused with the school, especially the horseback riding classes.

Paul was back in his motel late Sunday afternoon after a relaxing weekend with his relatives. He flew missions for the air defense personnel all week and the weather had been beautiful. After the last flight on Friday, he saw the test board U-8 parked on the ramp. Bill Grady had flown in to take over the mission for the next ten days. Paul decided to get an early start back to Fort Rucker the next morning. Friday evening during dinner, Bill said, "Rumor has it that you are off this project. I got it from a good source that you are now on the AH-1G Cobra test."

Paul said, "Really."

Bill continued, "While you were in the Mohawk transition course, Colonel Amode reviewed your records. When he saw how much helicopter time you have, he wanted you right away. He is the chief test pilot on the Cobra project. The board president, Colonel Kyle, wouldn't let him have you until you logged a hundred hours in the Mohawk."

"Wow! What a great surprise. I am thrilled with the idea!"

"Don't quote me and it is not official, but I'm sure it's the straight skinny."

By 1000 hours Monday morning, Paul was officially assigned to the Cobra project. By noon, he had a new desk in that department, and he was scheduled to start his Cobra checkout the next morning. He considered the turn of events a wonderful opportunity. He would be a test pilot in the world's first attack helicopter.

It took Paul a couple of hours to get used to the flight controls of the Cobra. They were very sensitive, especially the rudder pedals. He was surprised to find that it handled more like an airplane than a helicopter. By the time the IP signed his qualification sheet, he had fallen in love with the Cobra. He said to Beverly, "I am now glad that I couldn't get out of the army last summer. The Cobra is another landmark in the refinement of rotary wing development. I never thought a helicopter would be flown with techniques similar to fighter aircraft. It is a joy to fly."

She said, "I'm happy for you, Paul. I like the idea that you are home with me every night too."

The crew of the Cobra consists of two pilots seated in tandem. The aircraft can be flown from both positions; however, flying from the front seat is primarily for emergency situations. The flight controls are very short and flying with finesse is not possible. The main mission of the pilot in the front seat is to aim and fire the weapons turret. The pilot in the rear seat has a dual mission of flying the helicopter and firing the weapons attached to the stub wings. The old B model Huey Gunships were cumbersome and strained to become airborne. The Cobra contrasted all those characteristics with half the crew, higher cruise speed, and was more difficult to hit by enemy fire.

The test board maintained and operated an auxiliary facility at the Apalachicola Airport in Florida. Test aircraft departed Fort Rucker's

The Mohawk
Surveillance Aircraft

US Army U-8

AH-1G Cobra, World's First Attack Helicopter

Cairnes Army Airfield early each morning and flew to Apalachicola for the day. This provided necessary separation from the student flight training, which was conducted for many miles radiating out from Fort Rucker. A major segment of the Cobra test was firing the weapon systems to determine accuracy, reliability, and endurance. There was an offshore range marked by buoys where the firing took place.

Paul thoroughly enjoyed the days he was involved in firing the weapons systems. The Cobra was rigged with four folded fin aerial rocket pods. Each pod held twenty-four rockets for a total of ninety-six. The mini-gun ammunition tray held four thousand rounds of .30 caliber belt mounted bullets. A round trip to the firing range and back took approximately thirty minutes plus another thirty minutes to reload. There were few problems with the new systems and it was easy to hit targets with high accuracy. Accurate records were also kept to determine the type and number of repair parts that would be required once the Cobra was deployed to Vietnam. It was obvious to Paul that the Cobra would be a great improvement for the gunship pilots.

On test firing days, Paul usually flew with Major Allen Whitney of the Canadian Air Force. The United States and Canada had an agreement allowing for officers to be exchanged for two-year assignments. This policy developed good relations and both countries benefited from the shared knowledge of officers on these assignments. On alternate trips to the over-water range, Paul and Al switched off between the front and back seats. It was amazing to Paul how quickly one became proficient firing the weapons systems. Every seventh round fired by the minigun was a tracer, so it was easy to put the impact point on the target. Firing the rockets from the back seat was just a matter of adjusting the attitude of the aircraft. The second or third pair of rockets fired would be on target. An additional benefit was the high maneuverability of the Cobra.

On the days Paul didn't make firing runs, he flew profiles (putting flight time on the test aircraft and logging instrument readings every fifteen minutes). Data from profiles provided information to establish operational performance charts. When an engine, transmission, or other sub-components failed, unusual variation from normal instrument standards might predict failures. Compiling the data was boring but important and could save lives and equipment in the future. Paul flew a round robin flight to Port Saint Joe, Blountstown, Dog Island, and back to Apalachicola.

He made a pit stop each time at the auxiliary field. He was intrigued with a test that was in progress on the northeast side of the airfield. A rescue device was being tested that was dropped from a hovering helicopter. A man rode the device to the ground to retrieve a wounded person. Both were winched back aboard the hovering chopper. A wire mesh stretcher could be used to strap wounded personnel on and it was lifted vertically. A tandem chair was used to retrieve those stranded who were not hurt. They also tested the device making pickups from the water. The Bell UH-1D Helicopter was the test-bed for the lift test.

While flying profiles, Paul tuned his AM radio to local radio stations. He enjoyed listening to big band era music and both Panama City and Blountstown each had dedicated stations. One morning on the ten o'clock news, he heard that a man was near the top of a twelve hundred-foot communication tower. He had climbed the tower to work on it and became scared. His co-worker had tried to get him to climb down but the man just held on with his eyes closed. He had never climbed a tower higher than 300 feet. When he had gotten nearly to the top of the tower he was now stranded on, his foot slipped and he almost fell. The news reporter on the radio stated, "It is a real dilemma and they are not sure what the outcome will be." The tower was located five miles north of Blountstown.

Paul turned the helicopter directly towards Apalachicola and applied maximum power. He landed at the airfield, shut down, and went to the men testing the rescue device. He told Captain Ken Hill, the testing officer, about the man at the top of the communication tower. Hill said, "We are not authorized to use a piece of test equipment for an actual mission. But I guess it won't hurt to fly up and take a look." Staff Sergeant Black was the man who rode the winch hook.

Captain Hill looked at him and said, "What do you think, Sergeant Black?"

He answered, "Maybe we can save him, let's give it a shot."

In five minutes they were en route towards Blountstown. Paul refueled the Cobra and took off in the same direction. He caught up with the rescue helicopter before they reached the tower. The man was still perched near the top of the tower when they arrived.

Paul called Captain Hill on the radio, "What do you think, Ken?"

He answered, "There's about fifteen feet of tower higher than where the man is. Sergeant Black will ride the tandem seat down thirty feet below the chopper. I'll ease over towards the tower and see what happens. We have never tried to make a rescue twelve hundred feet in the air." Paul circled, keeping well clear, and watched as Black was winched below the helicopter. The helicopter started moving closer to the tower. Finally, Sgt. Black was right beside the man on the tower. A few minutes went by and it was obvious the man would not release his grip on the tower.

Captain Hill transmitted to Paul, "He has his eyes closed and a death grip on the tower. Black is trying to get him to mount the seat and he won't do it. Oh,...wait.,...my winch operator said that the man opened his eyes. He's climbing onto the seat..... We're pulling him up." Paul saw the chopper move away from the tower as the two men were pulled up closer. Finally, Captain Hill said, "We got him aboard. We'll drop him off at the foot of the tower." When they were back on the ground at Apalachicola, everyone was pleased with the successful rescue.

Chapter 31

TOWER RESCUE / PAUL WOUNDED

Ronald Jones was born April 5th, 1949, in Chipley, Florida. He was a happy child and had a natural love of music. Even before he could walk, he swayed his little body in time with music when he heard it. His dad, Henry Jones, adored his son and liked taking him on the job. People who had TV or communication towers knew Henry from Tallahassee to Pensacola. There were very few towers in that area which he had not climbed at one time or another. He was as much at home at the top of a fifteen hundred foot tower as he was sitting in his living room.

He assumed that his son would be helping him in a few years. Ronald was a good student, and as soon as he was old enough, he was in the school band. He made remarkable progress playing the trumpet. Half way through his second year, the band teacher moved him to the high school band. In a couple of months, he was playing fourth chair. He brought his instrument home nearly every day and played at least an hour each night after he completed his homework.

After he turned twelve, his dad had him work at the tower sites with him. Initially, he helped with attaching and snubbing up the guy wires. During this time, he never thought about the possibility of climbing a mast or tower himself. He learned the work easily and Henry was proud of him. The summer of his fifteenth year was the first time his dad asked him to climb. Radio Station WZEP in DeFuniak Springs, Florida, hired Henry to remove the existing antenna and transmission cable to install new equipment. The mast was only 175 feet high and Henry thought it would be a chance for Ronald to get his feet wet as a climber.

Henry said, "Ron, you are the boss and I'm your helper. You tell me what you want me to do." Ronald started up the mast, disconnecting the transmission cable as he went. When he was about fifty feet in the air, he looked down to speak to Henry. He got butterflies in his stomach and it was the first time he realized how high he was off the ground.

His dad saw his face turn white and he yelled, "Don't look down, son. Keep your eyes focused on the mast right in front of you. After awhile, it won't bother you at all and you will be able to look down." Ronald had to force himself to keep going higher as he disconnected the attachments holding the transmission cable. The higher he went, the more he noticed the slight sway of the antenna mast and he felt unsafe. He completed the job, taking much longer than his dad would have. When the job was finally done, his face was still white and he looked as if he would be sick.

On the way home he said, "Dad, I don't think I'm cut out to be a climber like you."

Henry said, "Oh, you'll get used to it. It's really easy."

Ronald continued to work for his dad when he was not in school. He dreaded each workday because his dad asked him to climb the masts and towers. He knew he was not getting used to it but he didn't want to disappoint his dad. He told his mother he hated climbing and he was scared every minute. Frequently, he had dreams of falling from a tower.

His mother said to Henry, "Maybe Ronald won't become a climber."

He answered, "He'll get used to it."

On a Saturday in late November 1966, Henry and Ronald arrived at the tower north of Blountstown, at daybreak. Henry had been hired to install a power amplifier for the top antenna system on the 1200 foot tower. The amplifier had to be attached close to the top of the tower. It was a day without the slightest breath of wind.

Henry said as they drove onto the antenna field, "Ron, today is perfect for your first high climb. There is no wind and after this job all the climbing you have done in the past will seem easy."

Ronald was immediately gripped with fear and he got a case of butterflies in his stomach. He had left the house this morning feeling good because his dad always made the high climbs. He looked at his father with a startled expression.

"Son, it's no different than a 300 foot climb, just higher. Concentrate on what you're doing and don't look down."

While Ronald buckled on his work belt and attached the amplifier he wanted to refuse to make the climb. He knew that his dad wanted him to do it, so he reluctantly started up the tower. When he got above five hundred feet, it took all the willpower he could muster to keep going. A stiff breeze had started blowing at that altitude and he got the sensation of sailing through the air. He thought, why am I doing this?

He finally got to the point where the amplifier would be installed. He attached the safety belt and started to pull on the rope that was hooked to the amplifier. It had hung about the level of his knees as he climbed up. He made the mistake of looking down and his right foot slipped off the ladder. He fell about a foot and a half when the safety belt stopped his fall. Fear gripped him like it never had before. He thought, if I ever get down from this damn tower, I'll never climb another. He re-established his footing, held on for dear life, and closed his eyes. Each time he tried to open them, he felt like the tower was falling.

Henry knew his son was in serious trouble. He could see that he wasn't moving at all. He had heard about people freezing on a tower, but this was the first time he had seen it happen. He went to the tower base and started to climb the ladder to help his son down. He was climbing too fast and in his haste, at no more then ten feet as he was reaching for another rung, his foot slipped. He fell to the base of the tower and broke his left arm. He tried to climb again but it was impossible. He drove to the nearest house and called the fire station. He thought that one of the firemen could make the climb. The dispatcher at the firehouse called the police and the local radio station.

Ron continued to hold on with his eyes closed. He was in such a panic, installing the amplifier didn't enter his mind. He kept thinking, oh God. Please get me out of this mess. He lost track of time and felt dazed. Suddenly, he heard the helicopter coming, but he still couldn't open his eyes. He did realize that the chopper was directly overhead, then there was a man right beside him.

To keep Sergeant Black suspended beside Jones required maximum concentration by Captain Hill. He could not see the two men. He had to rely on the winch operator's notification of any drift, reported over the intercom. There was a real danger of getting the winch cable tangled with the tower or moving Black away from the tower just as Ronald was trying to get onto the chair. Black and Ronald were also affected by the helicopter rotor wash. It was in excess of forty miles per hour and made the transfer of Jones to the seat much more precarious.

Sergeant Black told Ronald several times to open his eyes and climb onto the rescue chair. He didn't budge. Black lost his patience and said, "Look, you stupid jerk, open your damned eyes and help me save you. If you don't, I'm going to punch you unconscious. Do you hear me, dummy?"

Ronald opened his eyes. Black said, "That's better. Now, unhook your safety belt and ease over onto this seat." As soon as Ronald unhooked the safety belt, Black grabbed it and attached it to the rescue seat. He knew he had him. Ronald ever so slowly moved onto the seat.

As soon as he was aboard, Black signaled the winch operator. Six minutes from the time Ronald was on the rescue seat, he was climbing out of the chopper at the foot of the tower. Henry waved at the pilot and mouthed a "thank you". He rushed to his son and hugged him with tears rolling down his cheeks. "Son, you will never have to climb another tower. Thank God you are safe!"

The rescue of Ronald Jones from the tower made all the local papers, radio, and TV stations. Channel 6 in Tallahassee had footage of the total rescue operation. One of their television teams was passing through Bristol on Highway 20, east of the Apalachicola River. A town resident heard the story on the radio and waved them down. They were on site and filming before the helicopter arrived. They zoomed in and the close-ups were vivid of Black and Ronald at the top of the mast. The television footage also showed the men being winched up to the Huey with the Cobra orbiting.

As soon as Colonel Kyle, the test board president, became aware of all the facts, he had Captain Ken Hill and Sergeant Black report to him. He said, "Captain Hill, I have grounds for court-martialing you. You are well aware that it is against standard procedure to use equipment under test for an actual mission."

"Yes sir."

Kyle continued, "You are lucky it worked favorably because you and Sergeant Black are heroes. You might thank God and Bell Helicopter as well. I am awarding both of you Army Commendation Medals. Sergeant Black, you are promoted to sergeant first class effective today. It was a hazardous job well done."

Both men left Kyle's office pleased. Outside the building, Hill said, "Sergeant Black, if we had screwed up and someone got killed, we would have been thrown out of the service."

"Yes sir, and if we go into combat some day, we may get killed." They both laughed.

Paul and Al Whitney, the Canadian, hit it off well together. Both men had outgoing personalities and they thoroughly enjoyed flying the Cobra. Al and his wife, Earla, lived in post quarters on Red Cloud Road. The two couples plus Clark and Jean Walker socialized together every weekend. Some weekends, all six were in Destin, Florida, fishing offshore from Clark's boat if the weather was good. Paul and Beverly purchased a cottage on Pompano Street, which was a five-minute walk to the snow-white beach on the Gulf of Mexico. Clark left his boat at the cottage under the carport. It was just a short drive from there to the boat ramp at the East Pass Marina. They enjoyed eating at the Blue Room on the main drag in Destin followed by an evening of dancing at the Green Knight. The manager and staff of the Green Knight always welcomed the three couples with enthusiasm. They danced nearly every number and their laughter and fun-loving attitudes energized the other customers at the club. When the manager saw them walk through the door, he knew he would have a full house until he closed. No group could pack more fun into a weekend than those three couples.

Sometimes they cooked freshly caught fish or inch-thick T-bone steaks over charcoal behind the cottage. Some evenings were spent on the beach if the moon was out or they were inside playing cards.

One Monday morning in mid-January, 1968, Paul and Al were scheduled to put on a Cobra firing demonstration for VIPs at Matson

Range. They would be flying Bearcat 14 beginning the program at 0900 hours. The range had WW II tanks spaced out for targets to add realism to the firing runs. The procedure for making each run called for a starting altitude of 1500 feet, descending to a minimum of 500 feet at the end. That altitude was considered high enough to keep the aircraft from running into ricochets off the targets. For demonstrations, the rocket heads were solid lead rather than explosive rounds.

Al flew in the main pilot's seat and Paul was in the front to fire the mini-gun. The first run went according to procedure with better than eighty percent of the rounds hitting the targets. Just as Al started to pull up at the end of the second run, the two pilots heard a loud thump. An instant later, Paul came on the intercom and said, "Al, I've been hit in the leg. It looks pretty bad. You better head for the hospital." They had flown into one of the lead heads of a rocket that apparently ricocheted into their flight path. It penetrated the airframe of the Cobra and hit Paul in the right leg, below the knee, severing the main artery. He was bleeding profusely and feeling faint. Al immediately banked sharply to head for Lyster Army Hospital on the main post at Fort Rucker.

He got on the radio and called, "May day! May day! This is Bearcat 14 en route from Matson Range to the hospital with a seriously wounded man on board. I say again. I have a seriously wounded man on board."

A voice answered his call, "Roger Bearcat 14, this is Specialist Carey at the hospital. We will have personnel at the helicopter pad. Over."

Al answered, "Roger out."

Al had pulled in maximum power and the Cobra was making better than 170 knots. In minutes, he was flaring to decelerate and land at the hospital pad. Medical personnel were nearby with a white Chevrolet Suburban. The moment Al set the chopper down, they were at the gunner's door. Paul was conscious and able to help get himself out of the cockpit. Al got a glimpse of Paul's wounded leg. Blood was dripping off his pant leg and boot.

Paul might have bled to death. He had twisted his pilot's clipboard, attached to his leg with an elastic strap, round and round which reduced the flow of blood considerably. He was in the emergency room for nearly two hours. The projectile had taken a large chunk of meat and muscle out of his leg. It took half the time in emergency to reconnect the severed artery. More than an inch of that was gone. He was moved to intensive care for the rest of the day. Beverly was allowed to see him; however, he was heavily sedated and unconscious. Two days later, he was allowed to go home after learning how to use crutches. He was not supposed to put any weight on that leg. One week after the accident, he was at his desk and still on crutches. He used them for three weeks and it was another five weeks before he was allowed to fly.

During that time, Lieutenant Colonel Amode sent him on liaison trips to the Bell Helicopter factory at Arlington, Texas. Bell personnel were working on several modification improvements for the Cobra. Jack Byers was the Bell representative Paul worked with and the two got along fine. Jack took him through the factory and Paul liked the look of the new Bell Jet Ranger, 206. The Army would be getting a half dozen to test, designated the OH-58.

Paul asked Jack, "What would a civilian version cost?"

"Are you actually interested or just curious?"

Paul smiled and said, "There is a chance I can afford one."

Paul's stock had increased in value to three-quarters of a million dollars. He put $10,000.00 down on a new Jet Ranger. Bell Helicopter had to fill the military orders first, so it would be at least six months before Paul's came off the production line. He ordered it equipped with the latest communication and navigation equipment. The total price to be paid the day he picked it up was $103,210.00. They had given him all the aircraft manuals and Paul read and re-read them. He knew as much about that helicopter as any Bell engineer. Beverly was apprehensive about the whole idea but that didn't dampen Paul's enthusiasm.

Jack Byers called Paul at the test board to tell him his Jet Ranger was ready for pickup. He had already arranged for two weeks leave. He and Beverly flew to Love Field in Dallas to get it. The aircraft was painted blue and white. One of the Bell test pilots checked him out. Paul couldn't believe how easy it was to make auto-rotations. The flight characteristics pleased him as well and two days later they were headed for Rucker. Each time they stopped to refuel or eat, people came out of the terminal buildings to look at the sleek new helicopter. The aircraft cruised at 120 mph and burned 27.2 gallons per hour. Paul received permission to park it on the test board ramp.

Paul never made a lot of his and Beverly's wealth, so the Jet Ranger was a big surprise to most of their associates. The day after they returned from Texas, they were in Enterprise looking for land. They found a twenty-acre parcel on Highway 134 between Daleville and Enterprise. Paul planned to build a house and a hanger for the 206. He wanted enough land to be able to operate the chopper without disturbing neighbors. The land he purchased gave him nearly twenty-five hundred feet of highway frontage and it was four hundred feet deep.

Before Paul wrote the check for the land, he contacted personnel at the Fort Rucker air space authority. They mapped out a corridor and altitude for Paul's use to enter and depart Rucker's control zone. He had to call departure or approach control each time to inform them of his intentions. By the time he returned to work from his two weeks' leave, he had signed a contract with Evans & Mitchell builders in Atlanta. The house would have over five thousand feet of living space. The hanger would measure 80 by 100 feet with roll doors at both ends. A total area of one acre would be hard surfaced around the hangar and up to the house. It would include a lighted helicopter pad on the northeast corner. The price was a staggering $178,000.00.

Word of Paul's project and purchase of the Jet Ranger spread throughout the Fort Rucker and surrounding communities. He was elevated to celebrity status almost overnight. A news reporter from the Dothan Eagle wrote a comprehensive article about Paul's life. It included the story about him and Les being in the same Russian prison. Television Channels 7, Panama City, and 4, Dothan, had him on their morning shows. Ann Varnum of Channel 4 called CBS-TV in New York City. When Paul was interviewed on CBS, they devoted an entire 15 minute segment. He and Beverly had been home from the New York trip less than a week when ABC and NBC scheduled him for appearances.

The reaction did not stop there. Les became swamped with orders for restored antique automobiles. Without cancellations, if he could find the vehicles, he had five years of work ahead. Barnes Trucking of Turners Falls, MA, was overwhelmed with new business. They hired more drivers to keep their trucks running twenty-four hours a day, seven days a week. The first six months of new business for Barnes Trucking, generated by Paul's newfound fame, more than paid the cost of the Jet Ranger. Beverly's general manager, Charles Clarkson, was doing a good job running the business for her.

On the flight home from Arlington, Texas, Paul's leg started aching within an hour after departure. He tried to keep it from Beverly, but she noticed the change in him. Each time they stopped, he took a couple of aspirin, which gave some relief. When they got home, he went to see the flight surgeon. He prescribed Darvon to relieve the pain, but Paul was not supposed to drive or fly while using it. He hired Clark Walker at $10.00 an hour to teach Beverly to fly their helicopter. After a slow start and a lot of tears, Beverly showed real progress.

One morning, after a couple of months, she said, "Paul, I do like flying the Ranger. At first, I hated it and I didn't think I could do it. I'm glad you wouldn't let me quit."

Two months later, she passed her check ride with a civilian IP at the Dothan Airport. She was now a licensed helicopter pilot and proud of it.

Bell Model 206 Army versions/OH-58 Kiowa

Bell OH-58A Kiowa of the 25th Aviation US Army based in Germany.

Chapter 32

PAUL QUITS THE ARMY

*P*aul's leg continued to give him trouble. Most nights, he was awake two to three hours due to the pain. The Darvon relieved most of it, but he hated being on pain pills. When he returned to the flight surgeon for the third time, he said, "Major Baker, I am medically grounding you until further notice. I am sending official notice to the test board through distribution. I am also putting you on limited duty to keep you off that leg."

Paul said, "What does that mean?"

"You can sit at a desk, but no prolonged standing or walking. If there is no improvement in the next few weeks, you will be medically retired."

Without the Darvon, Paul walked with a noticeable limp.

His social life with Beverly was adversely affected too. Paul just didn't feel in the mood for taking part in all the activities that had been so much fun. Beverly noticed a huge change in him. He had gone from being fun to be with much of the time to moody. She tried to be understanding of the change, but it was difficult to be around a person who talked in clipped sarcastic sentences. He had been restricted to desk duty about a month, when Beverly had had enough of his sour attitude. One morning at breakfast, she said, "Paul, I need to go to New England for awhile. It's time I paid some personal attention to my trucking business. I haven't looked at the books for months. I also want to spend some time with the children. Phil will be graduating from Mount Hermon in June."

"Sure. Sure. That's fine. You have been away for a long time."

Beverly flew from Dothan two days later on Southern Airways to

Atlanta, then on Delta to Bradley Field in Hartford. When Paul dropped her off at the Dothan Airport, he said, "Bev, I'm sorry I've been so difficult lately. You deserve a break. Maybe things will get better." It was the first time he had talked with any compassion in his voice for weeks.

"I pray that it will, Paul."

She had notified the couple who looked after the mansion of her arrival date. She found the place in immaculate condition and well stocked with groceries. Charles Clarkson had rented her a new red Cadillac DeVille from Don Lorenz Cadillac-Olds-Buick for her personal use. She had been in the house for less than an hour when the phone rang. It was Paul, "I wanted to make sure you got there okay. I love you and I miss you already."

She said, "Thanks for the call. I love you, too." Tears came to her eyes and she couldn't say anything more.

"I'm sorry, Honey." He hung up the phone.

She drove the short distance to Stoneleigh Prospect School. Luanne had no idea that her mom was home and she was thrilled to see her. The dean of students authorized Luanne to live at home while her mom was in town. Beverly noticed that Luanne had matured considerably since she had started school last fall. She was taller and starting to physically develop. She had lovely facial features, natural blonde hair, blue eyes, and a gregarious personality. Beverly thought, "She is a gorgeous young lady and when she smiles, a spontaneous explosion of natural beauty appears. The really nice part is she doesn't seem to be aware of it."

Luanne talked about school with great enthusiasm. Her marks were excellent and she stayed on the dean's list. She especially enjoyed the equine riding classes. One mare, Athena, she liked the best. She didn't seem to wonder why her mom was at home without Paul. She asked how he was since the accident. Beverly said, "Honey, he is still having considerable pain in that leg." She didn't mention how miserable he was to be around. They drove to Mount Hermon on Friday afternoon and picked up Phil and Steve. All three seemed glad to have their Mom to themselves again. Phil brought up the subject of having his own car. Beverly said, "We have discussed this subject before, Phil. You couldn't take it on campus, and having it here would just be a temptation to leave school to drive it. Wait until you are in college and we will see."

"Mom, that always seems to be the answer around here. Wait and we'll see! I'm not sure I want to go to college. I thought I'd spend the summer learning the trucking business. Mr. Clarkson said he would be happy to teach me all about it. He suggested I ride with some of the truck drivers this summer to learn what their problems are. He said it would make me a better manager. Are you going to be here for the summer?"

Beverly said, "Phil, I thought you were interested in a football scholarship."

Steve spoke up; "He's in love with a girl from Northfield and doesn't want to leave." Phil headed for Steve as he ran towards the door laughing. Phil caught Steve with a flying tackle half way down the driveway. They wrestled on the front lawn for nearly thirty minutes even though Beverly kept yelling at them to quit.

Luanne told her Mom that Phil had met Bonnie Hall at school functions when Mount Hermon and Northfield School for Girls co-mingled. She lived in Northfield and attended school as a day student. Her folks owned a dairy farm near the Connecticut River, off highway 63, south of town. Luanne added, "Bonnie is considered the prettiest girl in school and she is well developed for her age."

"How have you found all that out?"

"Steve and I talk on the phone about once a week and he told me. He said she has a big set of boobs." Beverly looked shocked to hear her fifteen-year-old daughter talk like that.

Luanne said, "Come on, Mom. We aren't little kids anymore."

Beverly told Paul about her weekend when he called Sunday night. When she repeated what Luanne said about Bonnie Hall, Paul burst out laughing. It was the first time she had heard him laugh in weeks.

He seemed in better spirits and talked with less confrontation in his voice. He told her that he missed her very much and he was sorry for being such a pain since the accident. He seemed to think that Phil's idea of working for the trucking business was good. He said, "Forcing a person to attend college isn't really good. They often lack motivation which is the most important ingredient attending any school. Let's encourage him to go and leave the final decision up to him. When he's ready, he will go and do well." Beverly felt better after their talk. He sounded like he had improved in the short time since she left. Just before he hung up the phone, he said, "I really miss my personal helicopter pilot." She slept well for the first night since she got home. Leaving Paul alone for a while was apparently the right thing to do.

He called her the following Wednesday night. He was upbeat and said, "I had a long talk with Colonel Kyle. I told him that I would like to resign my commission. I explained what the flight surgeon had said about medically retiring me if the intense pain in my leg didn't let up. He indicated that I would be paid eighty percent of my base pay forever. I told him I didn't need the money so if they let me resign, it would be best all around. I don't like sitting at that desk every day and I'm not earning my pay. Kyle seemed to favor the idea and he said he would get back with me in a couple of days."

She said, "Have you made plans if they let you out?"

"Yes, I have a young warrant officer and his wife willing to take care of our place here. They will move in and pay me what they draw for quarter's allowance. They are both thrilled with the idea. Clark has agreed to fly with me in the Ranger to Turners Falls. I'll fly him back commercially. Then I'm going to have my favorite helicopter pilot take me to Mary Hitchcock Hospital in New Hampshire and have them take a look at my leg. If anyone can fix it, they can."

Ten days later, Paul and Clark landed at the Turners Falls Airport. They had flown the entire trip on instrument flight plans until they reached the Hartford VOR. Paul cancelled his flight plan and continued on following the Connecticut River. The view over Washington, DC, and New York City was marvelous. When they stopped for fuel at Teterboro in New Jersey, there was a Learjet refueling. Painted on the side of the aircraft was "The Golden Nugget Casino, Las Vegas". A well-dressed middle-aged man walked over to Paul from the Learjet. He said, "Are you the owner of that helicopter?"

"Yes, sir."

"I want to buy it and I'll give you $25,000.00 more than you paid."

"Sorry sir. It's not for sale. Contact Bell Helicopter. They will sell you one just like it."

It took three days before Paul was admitted into Mary Hitchcock Hospital. Two days later, Doctor Lavine told him they would attempt to correct two problems in his leg. One was muscle and the other tendon. They would take some muscle out of his left thigh and re-construct it in his lower right leg. They would lengthen one tendon with a fraction of an inch of synthetic material. He said, "We believe those two areas are the source of your pain. You will be on crutches a couple of weeks after the operation. In about six months, you should be as good as new."

After Paul was released to convalesce at home, the pain had diminished considerably. When he started walking on the leg, though, it was painful by the end of each day. It took a Darvon to get to sleep, but he slept all night. He hadn't felt so good since the accident. As Doctor Lavine predicted, in six months he had no pain, no limp, and he felt great. His old personality had returned and Beverly enjoyed his company again. The $8,000.00 expenditure in medical bills was worth every penny. It was nice to enjoy life once more and it was more fun flying the 206 than when he first bought it.

One day, he flew to White River Junction to give Doctor Lavine a ride in the Ranger. The view flying over the Connecticut River valley was beautiful. Doctor Lavine had a nice home on twenty acres northwest of Norwich on Route 135. They made a couple of low passes and returned back to the airport. The Doctor treated Paul to lunch at The Coach's Restaurant in White River. It's a basement establishment with a bar and fine dining and located across the road from the train station.

When he got back, he said to Beverly, "Honey, I have realized that all the wealth in the world is useless without good health. Most people go through life without knowing how fortunate they have been. I plan to treasure every day from now on."

One Thursday, Paul and Beverly were shopping at Foster's Super Market on Silver Street. He noticed a large refrigerated truck turn into the store yard. It had the store's name in large letters on the side and a gigantic red lobster painted there as well. He asked Frank "Bud" Foster, the storeowner, what he did with the truck. Bud explained that the truck made a couple of trips to the Boston markets each week. It was the only way he could be sure that his fish and produce were really fresh. Bud added, "I often make the trip myself. Would you like to ride along some time?"

Paul said, "I'd like to go the next time it is convenient for you."

"Be here at 1:00 a.m. next Thursday. I can't wait for you if you're late."

Paul was on time and at 1:05 a.m., they left the store yard. It was a fascinating trip. Bud was an interesting person and they talked all the way to the first stop in Boston. It was just over a hundred miles from Greenfield on Route 2. They stopped at a diner in Ayer for coffee and a jelly donut. As Bud backed up to the first loading dock, Paul was intrigued to see the large number of trucks and all the activity.

He went along as Bud made the individual purchases in case lots of fresh fruit and vegetables. All of the venders knew Bud and they called him, "Mr. Foster". Paul helped load the purchases on the truck as they were bought. They had three quarters of a truckload when they stopped at the fish market. It was quite a sight for Paul to see large fish being dressed by men in rubber boots, pants, and aprons. No time was lost as they sliced up each fish with razor sharp knives. Bud made his selections, which were boxed in ice and put on the truck. The last stop was for $2,200.00 worth of lobsters.

Paul said, "That seems like a lot of lobsters."

Bud replied, "It is not unusual to sell twice that amount in our store each week."

Bud explained to Paul on the way back to Greenfield the importance of being at the market when it opened. The prices were at their lowest at that time. Over the next two to three hours, as the venders sold their product, the prices went up. If a buyer arrived a couple of hours late, the cost of his truckload would be several hundred dollars higher. That would mean higher prices in the store. One of the keys to his success was providing his customers with really fresh fruit, vegetables, and fish at competitive prices.

Paul asked, "Would it be feasible to fly lobsters to Florida?"

"It would depend on a couple of things that I can think of right now. How many hours it would take and the expenses involved. I imagine the price would be pretty high once they were in the store tank for sale."

Paul thoroughly enjoyed the trip and he was enthused about the possibility of transporting live Maine lobsters to Florida. The next day, he flew the Jet Ranger to Bradley Field and located Pace Transport, which flew charters of airfreight to any destination in the country. He asked the owner, Lance Humphrey, if he would fly lobsters to Florida.

"As long as they don't stink up my airplanes."

Paul got a price for a round trip to Tallahassee in a DC-3. When he got home, he spent a couple of hours on the phone to locate a fish market in Florida interested in the idea. He found "Joe Patty's Fish Market" in Pensacola. Joe was not only interested, he was all for it. After Paul explained that he could deliver five thousand live lobsters to the Pensacola Air Terminal at $6.00 a pound on each flight, Joe Patty said, "I'll call you back." He hung up the phone without waiting for an answer.

A week went by and Paul heard nothing from him. At six a.m. on the eighth day, Joe called. "Bring me a load of lobsters. Give me the arrival time at Pensacola and the price. I'll meet you with a check." Paul had one of Barnes refrigerated trailer trucks pick up the lobsters in Boston at dawn. They were being loaded into Joe Patty's delivery trucks that afternoon. Paul netted a little over $1,100.00. He thought, if I can find something worthwhile to bring back, it will improve my profit margin. He discussed the idea with Charles Clarkson. On future trips, there was usually a load of cargo to be picked up in Atlanta. This increased the profit for a trip four to six hundred dollars.

Before the year was out, he was shipping lobsters to Tampa and Miami. With each place wanting a shipment every week to ten days, his supplier in Boston said they were at their limit. Paul enjoyed co-ordinating the shipments. He usually flew to Bradley Field in the 206 and supervised the loading of the lobsters. He would write Lance Humphrey a check for the trip as the plane taxied for take-off. Lance said, "I like dealing with a man who pays the way you do." The price Paul paid for lobsters averaged a little less then $3.00 a pound at the wholesale market. He added $3.00 to cover transportation and his profit. Florida super markets sold live Maine lobsters for about $9.00 a pound. Restaurants priced a Maine lobster dinner at $14.95 and up. The idea had gone over well and Florida seafood establishments advertised "Live Maine Lobsters" in neon lights.

Phil started work at Barnes Trucking Company the Monday follow-

Frank & June Foster, Founders of Foster's Super Market

ing graduation. He told Charles Clarkson to assign him to trips where he could be helpful to the driver. Charles said, "How would you like to attend truck driver's school in West Springfield? In four weeks, you will have a license to drive any rig we own. You will be able to switch off with the driver on long trips." Phil agreed as long as he could commute in his car. His mother had given him a new 1970 Mustang Convertible for a graduation present. Phil was also pleased when his mom told him what Paul said about going to college, leave it up to him.

He found himself liking Paul better all the time, but he couldn't bring himself to call him "Dad". They had spent several hours in the Jet Ranger on weekends and Phil was doing better then average at learning to fly it. He asked Paul for the operator's manual and made a concerted effort to learn more about the 206.

Beverly was as happy as she had ever been. Her children had accepted Paul into their lives and he had fully recovered from his leg injury. Steve and Luanne were doing well in school and Phil demonstrated an excellent attitude on his job. Charles told Beverly, "Phil handles a big rig real well. He just lacks experience."

Phil was dating Bonnie Hall most Friday and Saturday nights. The first time he brought her home, Beverly couldn't help noticing that she did have large breasts. Bonnie was wearing a T-shirt and with each step she took, they bounced. She had a small waist and a big butt with long legs. Her red shorts couldn't have been shorter. Beverly thought she looked thirty years old. When Phil introduced the two women, it was difficult for Beverly to be cordial.

Phil and Bonnie were going to play tennis. She sat down on the couch to wait for Phil to change and get his racket. Beverly sat across from her and thought, my God, she is all bust and legs. I wonder if Phil has ever looked at her face. Beverly said, "Do you mind telling me how old you are?"

"I'm twenty one. Most people say I look old for my age," and she laughed. "I have bought beer since I was seventeen," she laughed again.

Beverly said, "Do you drink a lot of beer?"

"Sometimes when I'm at a party and we're having a good time," and she giggled.

"Do you have a driver's license?"

"Oh sure and I've had my own car since I was sixteen. I don't make a habit of driving when I've had a couple of beers, though. Since I've been dating Phil, he always drives. You know how men are about women drivers," and she laughed louder then ever.

Phil came bounding down the stairs and said, "Let's go, Bonnie. Bye Mom." Beverly stood at the living room window and watched them drive out of the yard. The convertible top was down and Bonnie was against Phil in the seat. It looked like she was kissing his cheek.

Phil drove back in the yard late that afternoon. When he came in the house, Beverly said, "Where's Bonnie?"

"I dropped her off at her house. We're going to a movie later. How do you like her?"

Beverly looked at her son several seconds before she answered. "Phil, she isn't the type of girl that I would pick out for you."

"Mom is it because she has big boobs or what is it about her you don't like?" Phil could tell by his mom's expression that she did not like Bonnie.

"She seems so mature and experienced for her age, Phil. She told me she has been drinking beer since she was seventeen."

"She started drinking beer long before that. Everyone in her family drinks beer except her dad. He drinks scotch and water. I'm disappointed that you don't like her, Mom."

"Phil, she just doesn't seem your type. How serious are you about her, Dear?"

"We don't have any plans to get married right away. Her parents want her to go to college before she gets married. To be totally honest, she isn't that interested in going."

"Phil, I want to be frank with you and I hope I don't hurt your feelings."

"Go ahead, Mom. I can handle it."

"A female as well developed as Bonnie at twenty one will more than likely put on fifty or more pounds by the time she is thirty. She is also brash, loud, and outspoken. Are you sure you want to marry a girl like that?"

"Wow! She made that bad of an impression on you in those few minutes. I was going to invite her for dinner. I guess I better forget that idea!"

Beverly then said, "Phil, I love you and want only the best for you."

That was the end of the conversation about Bonnie on that day.

Three days later, Phil received a letter from the department of defense. It was his draft notice. The United States was still involved in the Vietnam War. Beverly felt intense mental anguish because of that notice. She had been watching the evening news for years depicting the war in Vietnam. She had felt sorry for all those young men who had lost their lives over there. The possibility of having her son in that war was a devastating thought.

The night Phil received the notice, he took Bonnie to a drive-in movie. A few minutes after the movie started, she said, "Phil, you seem unusually quiet tonight. Is there anything wrong?"

"I received my draft notice today. It looks like I'll be going in the army soon."

"Oh no! They can't take you away from me! I love you, Honey!" She started to cry. He had never seen her cry before.

"Please don't cry, Bonnie. I don't want to leave you either but I can't see anyway to avoid it. We have to make the best of it."

She wiped her eyes and said, "What if we get married? Would that make a difference?"

"No. We would have to have had at least one kid to qualify for an exemption. If I had enrolled in college and attended ROTC, I would have qualified for a deferment but it is too late for that too."

She burst into tears again. "I'll write to you every day!" When they got to her house after the movie, they sat in the car and talked until nearly three the next morning. They talked about getting married and decided to wait and see where he got assigned after basic training.

Paul had been away on an overnight trip with Matt and Les to northern Maine. They went to pick up two antique cars Les had bought. Matt always enjoyed going with his sons on those trips. Beverly hoped Paul would have a solution to the draft notice problem. She also hoped and prayed that Phil did not get Bonnie pregnant. She did not like that girl. She was in bed and still awake when she heard Phil come home. She finally dozed off a few minutes later.

Chapter 33

PHILIP BARNES GOES TO VIETNAM

When Phil received his draft notice, Paul suggested that he enlist in the army right away for helicopter flight training. He pointed out the fact that as a draftee, he would probably be an infantry soldier on orders to Vietnam in a few weeks. Flight school would keep him in the States an additional nine months and perhaps the war would be over by then. Phil took his advice and received a reporting date for induction thirty days later. During that time, he and Paul were in the Jet Ranger two or three hours a day. Paul spent most of those hours teaching Phil to fly instruments. The Warrant Officer Flight Training Program consisted of the most basic instrument training. Paul knew that a proficient instrument rated pilot had a huge advantage during the monsoons in Vietnam.

Phil graduated from basic training third from the top. After the first two to three weeks, he found himself enjoying the training. He carried the company flag when they marched to and from the training activities. He had two weeks leave at home before reporting to Fort Rucker for flight training. He and Paul logged about twelve hours in the Jet Ranger while he was home. He had retained most of his previous instruction, which pleased Paul. He also became proficient at making successful auto-rotations (landing a helicopter without engine power). They made one round-robin flight to New Haven, Providence, Boston, and Keene in actual instrument conditions. Paul rode as a passenger and he didn't have to make one correction.

During in processing at flight school, Phil received a promotion to specialist E-5. It was a policy for all cadets starting school ranked E-4 or below. The first time he climbed into the TH-55 helicopter to start military flight training, the instructor was surprised that Phil could hover with no problem. The first time a student tried to hover, he unknowingly changed the position of the cyclic slightly and the aircraft started moving rapidly in one direction or another. Phil took the controls and held the hover as the instructor had been doing. The rest of the training in the TH-55 was just a matter of him becoming a better pilot. The instruction from Paul had made it easy. Learning to fly the UH-1 was something else. It took nearly ten hours before Phil started feeling at home at the controls. When he reached the instrument training phase, Phil found it a breeze again. He completed flight training first in his class with a promotion to warrant officer W-1 and orders to the 28th Assault Helicopter Company, Phu Loi, Republic of Vietnam.

Less than forty hours from his departure from the Dothan Air Terminal, he was walking across the tarmac at Cam Ranh Bay, Vietnam. Two 28th Assault Helicopter Company Hueys flew in from Phu Loi to pick him up. En route to Phu Loi, the choppers flew at treetop level in tight formation. Phil thought the pilots were showing off for his benefit. He found out later it was normal procedure and logical. When they flew over enemy troops at treetop level, there was little time for the enemy to get an accurate shot at the aircraft. Flying in close formation got all choppers out of enemy sight quickly.

Captain James Hodges, flight operations officer, briefed Phil on the primary mission of the 28th Company. Their helicopters carried assault troops on search and destroy missions within a twenty-five mile radius of Saigon (Phu Loi was ten miles north of Saigon). Captain Hodges mentioned the new policy of Vietnamization of the war and ultimate departure of US troops. The 28th had not received a projected date to leave but some of the units had. AVEL Central, an avionics maintenance unit located at Phu Loi, would be gone in sixty days. The 28th planned to take over its buildings and bunker. After Phil left the briefing, Hodges thought, my God, that kid looks like he should be a freshman in high school.

Phil flew with the 28th AHC instructor pilot the first ten hours of flying in Vietnam. This was standard policy and he received a lot of valuable information, which increased a pilot's chances of living to complete his tour. Two months later, the 28th started receiving Vietnamese helicopter pilots who had been trained in the States. As more and more of these men arrived, each was assigned to fly with an American pilot. Eventually, those with the most experience flew together as a Vietnamese flight crew, including door gunners. During this time they were carrying mostly native assault troops. Phil had been in the country nearly three months when he realized that the 28th was being turned over gradually to the Vietnamese Army. Vietnamese were replacing American GIs who completed their tours.

Phil had been in the country about six months, when Captain Hodges spoke to him about becoming a gunship pilot. He said, "Barnes, I need an experienced pilot to transition into gunships. You have been doing a good job flying lift ships. How would you like to fly Cobras?"

"Sir, I would like that. Are you serious?"

"Yes and flying gunships is serious business. It takes a cool head with nerves of steel to do the job effectively. You have probably noticed the gunship pilots strafe the hedgerows and tree lines during combat assaults and troop extractions. They draw enemy fire away from the lift helicopters."

"Yes, sir. They do a fine job of protecting those of us flying the lift choppers."

Hodges continued, "You will be flying with a hunter killer team consisting of an OH-6 scout and two Cobras. We have intelligence reports that the NVA is using the many branches of the Mekong River in the delta area to move men and equipment. We are going to attempt to stop them."

"Sir, it sounds interesting to me and I want the job."

"Good. Report to Major Royce in the gunship platoon today. He will tell you where to move your personal gear. Good luck." Phil was thrilled. Paul had told him how much he enjoyed flying the Cobra at Fort Rucker. Now he would be flying it in combat.

The following morning, Phil was in the pilot's seat of a Cobra receiving flight instruction from Major Royce. They flew to the Vung Tau airfield to practice takeoffs and landings. Phil noticed that the controls were more sensitive to the touch than the UH-1. It took about an hour before he started to feel at home at the controls. By the time they broke for lunch, he felt at ease and even the auto-rotations had not been a problem.

After lunch, it was a different story. Royce said, "Barnes climb in the front seat. We'll see how you do there." The front seat of the Cobra is primarily for the turret gunner; however, the helicopter can be flown from there. The flight controls are short which make it difficult to fly with any finesse. It is for an emergency in case the pilot becomes disabled. Phil felt embarrassed with his poor performance. He managed to take off and land after a fashion with jerks and bumps. Royce said, "Mr. Barnes, your performance is satisfactory. No one flies this bird well from the front seat. I have the controls."

"Yes, sir." They left Vung Tau and headed north along the coast. Royce explained the function of the turret gun controls and the sighting device. He turned the chopper out to sea and had Phil fire the turret for familiarization. He said, "As you can see, the tracers make it easy to see where your rounds are going. Just make sure you have the turret pointing in the general direction of your target before you squeeze the trigger. You make the necessary adjustments once the gun begins to fire."

"Yes, sir."

"That completes your checkout. When we get back to Pho Loi, I'll get you an operator's manual. Make sure you learn the emergency procedures in chapter seven. All future flights will be on assigned missions. For the first couple of weeks, you will fly with me. Do you have any questions?"

"Not at this time, sir."

The next day they began scouting the Mekong River. The cobras stayed at five hundred feet and about a quarter of a mile behind the OH-6. The OH-6 flew just a few feet above the water. The first suspicious boat they found was about fifty feet in length and sat quite low in the water. The pilot's call sign in the scout was Snoopy. He transmitted, "Viper, this is Snoopy, I'm going to check this one out. He looks heavy."

Royce answered, "Roger, Snoopy. We have you in sight." They watched as the OH-6 circled the boat at a slow speed.

"Viper, this guy is carrying something in the boat covered with palm leaves. Make a low pass and shoot a short burst just in front of the bow."

"Roger. We are on the way." Royce and Phil were in the lead Cobra. Royce said, "Barnes, fire a two second burst a few feet in front of the boat as we go by."

"Roger, sir." They completed the pass.

"Viper, that did it! All three men on the boat dove into the water. They're swimming towards the east bank!"

"Snoopy, stay clear. We'll come around and shoot some rounds into the boat and see what happens." Royce made a climbing left turn and lined up on the boat at five hundred feet. "Barnes, squeeze off a couple of short burst right in the middle of the boat."

"Roger, sir." The first burst was long and missed. The second one hit the center of the boat and it blew up. Royce and Phil felt the concussion of the explosion. Snoopy transmitted, "Bingo! I'll bet that was a load of mortars. Viper, see if you can knock off the boat crew."

"Roger. We're coming in now. I don't have them in sight."

"I don't either, Viper. They are probably hiding in the foliage hanging from the riverbank. We got rid of their load anyhow. Good work." There was no other action that day or the next.

On the third day, Royce said, "Barnes, take the pilot's seat and I'll operate the turret. Captain McAda will fly lead in the other Cobra. Keep at least two rotor widths away as you fly formation on him. If we get into enemy action, space out even more. We don't want a mid-air collision."

"Roger, sir." Phil felt a nervous twinge in his stomach. He'd be flying in actual combat for the first time as a Cobra pilot. The day was uneventful until just before dusk when Snoopy came on the radio, "A couple of boats just came out of an inlet up ahead. I think they spotted me because they are turning around." Then he shouted, "I'm taking fire from both boats! They have machine guns mounted on the bows."

Viper answered, "Roger, Snoopy. We're coming in. We have them in sight." Both Cobras were firing their mini-guns and rockets at the boats. A pair of rockets hit one boat and it broke in half and started to sink. As they passed over the boats, Phil heard snapping noises. He felt the aircraft jolt to the left and he saw his engine instruments dropping towards zero. He snapped the collective down to unload the main rotor and pulled the cyclic to flare back and slow his forward speed. He knew he was going in and he decided the best place was the river.

Royce was slumped over in the gunner's seat and made no movement at all. Phil was going to hit the water near the bank across and up river from the gunboat. He managed to stop forward speed and level the skids about five feet above the water. Then he went hard left with the cyclic, which turned the helicopter on its side as it hit the water. He opened the canopy hatch just as the Cobra was sinking. He tried to get out and he realized that he had his safety harness still on. He released that as the chopper went under water but he got out and came to the top.

His next thought was Major Royce. He swam under water attempting to save Royce but it was muddy and he couldn't see anything. He came to the top gasping for air and noticed the current was bringing him down towards the gunboat. It was still exchanging fire with the remaining Cobra.

Then he heard engine noise and looked to his left. The OH-6 was hovering towards him just above the water. They positioned the chopper right over him and inches off the water. Phil grabbed the skid and the door gunner helped him into the aircraft. As they climbed to a higher altitude, he saw the front of the gunboat blown off by a rocket. When the two helicopters landed back at the company location, it was dark. Phil was grateful to be alive but felt remorse for the loss of Major Royce.

Captain Mike McAda replaced Royce as gunship platoon leader. He said to Phil two days after the tragic loss of Royce, "Mr. Barnes, get your flight gear, we're going to Saigon to pick up a new Cobra."

"Roger, sir."

McAda added, "Meet me at the flight line in twenty minutes." It was after lunch and they flew to "Hotel 3". The 34th Group had a maintenance facility there. Their mission was to assemble new helicopters, which had arrived from the States by ship. Trailer trucks brought them from the boat docks. Major components were disassembled in the States and strapped together to make a smaller package for shipment. Each one was covered with heavy gauge plastic for protection against the salt air on the trip. The main rotor assembly was shipped in a special airtight container.

Mike and Phil went to the administrative office to arrange the release of their new cobra. At the office, Specialist-5 Wyatt said, "Sir, sign this transfer document, please. It is then your responsibility to test fly the new chopper. Once you complete the test flight, return here and initial this paper to indicate the test flight was satisfactory. It is a policy of the 34th Group Commander that you do the test flight solo. Do you have any questions, sir?"

Mike said, "I see no problem, specialist." He signed the paper and they left. After making a thorough preflight, Mike climbed into the pilot's seat and cranked up the new cobra. All the instruments were reading normal. He rolled on the throttle until the main rotor was turning at operating rpm. He looked over at Phil, who was standing well clear and watching. He gave Phil a thumb up, then pulled in collective to come to a hover.

The moment he raised to a hover, the flight controls became extremely stiff and difficult to move. Each movement caused the chopper to jerk or jump and he nearly lost control. It took him two to three minutes before he got the machine sitting safely on the ground. A couple of times he thought it was going to turn over. He shut the engine down and said to Phil, "I think the SAS malfunctioned." He was right, the Stability Augmentation System had blown a fuse. It took the mechanics nearly two hours to find the cause of the problem.

Captain McAda made a second attempt to test fly the aircraft. When he got airborne, the airspeed indicator stayed on zero. While the mechanics worked on that, he said to Phil, "How are you at flying instruments? It looks like fog is forming. I hope we can make it back to Pho Loi before it gets too bad."

"Flying IFR is no problem for me, sir."

Mike said, "When we depart, keep in tight formation on me. If you do lose sight of me, immediately climb a thousand feet and tell me on the radio. We don't want a mid-air!"

"Roger, sir." When they finally headed for Pho Loi, it was dark and the fog had thickened. Mike called on the company frequency, "Viper three, Viper six, how's your weather. Over."

"Viper six, Viper three, we are fogged in, sir. Estimated visibility is zero."

"Roger. I'll call Hotel-3 and see if we can get back in there." He switched frequencies. "Hotel-3, Viper six, how's your weather."

"Viper six, Hotel-3, we are socked in with fog. Visibility is near zero. Contact Corpus Christi radar at 119.2 and their ADF frequency is 540. Good luck."

Mike switched frequencies and transmitted, "Corpus Christi, Viper six, a flight of two choppers ten miles north of Saigon. Potential landing pads are obscured in fog, please advise." The ship was permanently anchored five miles off Vung Tau with an aircraft maintenance mission. They had excellent search radar aboard and a reliable ADF beacon.

A deep southern voice answered, "This is Corpus Christi radar. Proceed direct to Corpus Christi ADF. Your altimeter setting is 2996. One of you hold at three thousand feet and the other at four thousand. Report when you are in the holding pattern. Over."

"Roger, sir. We are en route. Out." He switched to the company FM frequency, "Viper four one, continue to fly formation on me until we reach the beacon. After we pass the beacon, I will climb to four thousand feet. You hold at three thousand. Over."

Phil answered, "Roger, sir." Phil thought of all those hours of instrument instruction Paul had given him in the 206. It appeared that it would prove to be well spent.

As soon as they passed over the ADF, Mike proceeded to climb to four thousand feet. He transmitted, "Corpus Christi, Viper four one is holding at three thousand. Viper six is climbing to four thousand. Over."

"Roger. Viper four one depart the ADF on a heading of 090. Descend to one thousand feet. Report level at one thousand. Over."

"Roger. Viper four one is leaving three thousand feet at this time." Four minutes later, Phil transmitted, "Viper four one, level at one thousand. Over."

"Viper four one, turn left to 260 degrees and maintain ninety knots. Over." Several minutes went by. "Viper four one, you are two miles from touch down, start your descent at five hundred feet per minute, now. Turn on your landing light. Over." Phil answered and commenced to descend. He concentrated strictly on his instruments.

"This is Corpus Christi, you are a quarter mile from touch down. Slow to thirty knots. Report the ship in sight."

Phil glanced out the window and saw nothing. He looked back at his instruments and he was passing through 200 feet. He looked out again and saw a faint light. He started to flare to slow the chopper more and the ship came into full view. "This is Viper four one. I have the ship in sight."

"Roger. You are cleared to land." There was a large H painted on the fantail of the ship. As Phil came to a hover, he saw a deck hand directing him to a parking spot, forward of the H. A few minutes later, he heard and then saw Captain McAda's Cobra approaching the landing pad. A sailor led them to the officers' mess. Mike looked at Phil and smiled. He said, "Mr. Barnes, I have never tasted a better cup of coffee." They both laughed.

For the next nine months, Phil flew with the hunter/killer team patrolling the river. The number of NVA boats they located became scarce. They felt their patrols were effective. During one confrontation, an enemy bullet hit the dash panel in the Cobra. Fragments from the ashtray were blown into his left leg and he was awarded the Purple Heart. Phil experienced several exciting engagements with enemy boats and his chopper took occasional non-disabling hits during those operations.

Phil completed his tour with more than 500 combat hours logged. He had become a proficient gunship pilot. The day he left Pho Loi for his flight to the States, he took a long look at the parked helicopters on the airfield. He had no way of knowing that those aircraft would be used during the last days of the war as escape vehicles. The Vietnamese crews would fly them to American aircraft carriers rather than be captured by the North Vietnamese Army. Many of those escape helicopters would be pushed over the side into the South China Sea.

Most of his thoughts on the long flight were about home. It would be great to see his family again. He wondered what Bonnie was doing. She had written him regularly for a couple of months and then the letters stopped coming. In one of his mom's letters, she said she had seen Bonnie on Federal Street in Greenfield arm in arm with a man. She said she looked happy.

The San Francisco air terminal was a welcome sight. He had orders assigning him to Fort Rucker with a thirty-day leave en route. He felt anxious to get home but the first flight available to Hartford was the next morning at seven twenty.

Paul, Beverly, Steve, and Luanne met him at Bradley Field. It was a happy reunion. When they arrived home, Paul poured wine to toast his homecoming. Later in the evening, Beverly said, "Phil, take a look at this article. It was in last Sunday's paper."

After he read it, he said, "Mom, it's probably for the best. She stopped writing to me after a couple of months." It was Bonnie's wedding announcement to a man in Hinsdale, New Hampshire.

Phil had a great time on his thirty-day leave. It was a pleasure to drive his Mustang again. He surprised Paul by giving him a hug. "Thanks for all the instrument training. You may be responsible for saving my life."

Beverly was thankful he was safely home and relieved that Bonnie Hall had married another man while Phil was gone. She shuddered to imagine having Bonnie as her daughter-in-law.

Matt and Julie had become involved with Beverly's three children and had come to love them. Matt threw a big celebration at the mansion for Phil's safe return. The whole family was in attendance including Sam, Nora, and their two sons. All the men played horseshoes and Matt was the champ in spite of his years. That evening, Sam played the Steinway grand piano with about half the family members singing along. Julie said to Matt, "Wouldn't it be wonderful if Charlie was here with us." Matt looked at her with tears in his eyes and said, "Honey, he is."

Three Cobras & Six UH - 1D Troop Lift Helicopters
Vietnam

Epilogue

*I*nterstate 91 now passes through the town of Bernardston just east of Fall River and Streeter's Store. The construction of the exit, the last in Massachusetts going north, filled in the Mill Pond. As a teenage boy, this writer spread cow manure on fields where I-91 is now located. The town-hall clock purchased by Mrs. Coy more than ninety years ago still strikes on the hour and half hour.

Powers Institute looks the same and is a museum. The Cushman Library is still in operation. The Cushman Mansion was burned to the ground several years ago. The people living there at the time attempted to use the fireplace with the broken chimney.

Harold Streeter's descendants still run the country store. For many years, the town fire truck was parked in the basement of the store. During the years Harold Streeter was in charge of the successful operation, new cars and trucks were sold at the store. After World War II, several young men in town purchased their first new vehicle from the Bernardston Auto Exchange. My dad, Myron E. Barber, bought a new 1949 Ford Station wagon from Harold. Part of the deal probably included a used car, a farm implement, a cow or two, and money. H. S. Streeter did whatever it took to close a deal. New farm equipment is still sold and a major maintenance operation continues in the store basement today.

River Maple Farm is still operated by the sons and grandsons of Howard and Evelyn Grover. A tractor pulls the vat to collect the sap each spring. It is not unusual for River Maple Farm to mail maple syrup to individuals all over the country. The farm still produces a large volume of milk and it is never exposed to the air from the time it leaves the cow. Milking machines extract the milk from the cow and it is piped directly to a large stainless steel container. A tank truck pumps the milk out of the container and it is on the way to the milk processing plant. The cows are milked twice a day, seven days a week. They know when it is milking time and they line up at the entrance door. They enter in the same order and walk into the same stall in the milking parlor. This phenomena occurs without any control by a human. The cows do it naturally. The Grovers harvest hundreds of acres of hay and corn each year to feed their cattle along with store bought grain. Through artificial insemination, the volume of milk produced by each cow has increased drastically over the years. Computerized information is kept on the cows indicating the volume of milk produced by each.

Foster's Super Market is now a large store at the corner of Conway and Allen Streets in Greenfield, Massachusetts. It is independent and a strong competitor to the local chain stores. The owners continue to make frequent trips to Boston to provide their customers with fresh produce and fish. Frank and June Foster's eldest daughter, Janice and her husband, Sam Deane, operate the business; however, Frank is still actively involved.

Lou Barber—Arabian Horse Show, Garrett Coliseum, Montgomery, Alabama.